MISSION
DISTRICT
MURDERS

by

Michael D. Kelleher

Christine Mrazovich & John P. Rutledge, Editors

ISBN 1-929429-97-5

November 5
20044 Hill Street
7:30 A.M.

Lieutenant Chris Spell leaned forward and to his right, bending stiffly at the waist to look directly into the face of the body on the landing. Her skin was ashen — almost gray. Her jaw was unnaturally extended and her mouth hung slightly open, forming a bizarre, gruesome scowl. Thankfully, her eyelids were tightly closed, as they probably had been at the moment of her death. Two thick rivulets of blood, which hours earlier had run bright red from her nostrils, were now blackened from the morning air and caked to the pale skin on her upper lip. It was clear this had been a very pretty woman. But that was years ago.

Spell hated tagging vics with their eyes locked open. And twenty years working Homicide hadn't changed that fact.

"Ah, Officer…" he mumbled, struggling to remember her name.

"Janus, sir," she interrupted, saving him from the obvious next question. "It's Sandra JA-NUS," she confirmed, using a phonetic overstatement that seemed very cop-like, but under the circumstances, entirely unnecessary. He grimaced a bit at her reply and nodded a perfunctory, unsmiling greeting in her direction.

"Right, Officer Janus. Sorry…"

"No problem, sir" she interrupted again, as she moved closer to the body on the landing.

"Well, Janus, they say you were first on the scene. So who was she?"

"Yes, sir. I was here first," the officer responded. "Her name was Jessica Callohan. She's a prostitute who'd been working this area for the past few years, mostly down on Mission Street. Early

1

twenties, I think, and lives, uh... lived, a few blocks down on Lexington."

The lieutenant looked up at Janus as she finished speaking. 'She has nice eyes,' he thought. His look made her uncomfortable. She turned slightly and pointed away from the body, towards the parking garage, and repeated, "south... toward the garage."

"I know where Lexington is, Janus," sarcasm in his voice.

"Of course. Sorry," returned the young officer. After seeing that her grin didn't break the Lieutenant's stare, or the uncomfortable silence between them, she added: "I've talked to her on the street a few times."

"In her twenties?" he whispered, mostly to himself. "She looks a lot older..."

He leaned over the body, meticulously examining the wounds on her chest with his eyes.

"Yeah, she's had it rough, I guess," Janus replied, mimicking his severe tone, but adding her own sorrowful expression.

Spell turned his back to the corpse and faced the young officer, his full attention captured by the noticeable change in her voice. Gone was the staccato, formalized cop-talk. In its place, he heard a softer, low delivery that seemed almost pained. He took a moment to evaluate his inexperienced colleague, to study her in that visceral way that men who spend most of their time with other men are known to do.

From his vantage point of just over six feet, Janus appeared frail. She had a small presence – petite – a doll-like woman, despite the recognizable bulk of police paraphernalia adorning her beat cop's uniform. With richly dark, short-cropped hair hanging evenly to the tips of her earlobes, Sandy Janus seemed unusually young to the man who had already celebrated his half-century mark. To Spell, she seemed conspicuously out of place in her bulky blues, especially with that teenage face and wispy build. 'There's no way she's twenty-five,' he thought.

He studied her tiny frame with little subtlety, noticing how she'd wrapped it so carefully and ostentatiously in the SFPD uniform. He criticized himself for that familiar, instinctive feeling — the well-known inner voice that told him he already knew everything he needed to know about her. It was all so obvious. She'd been cast helplessly adrift in a man's only world — copland, where masculinity is everything. Spell had seen it all before, and every bit of it was getting old, just like him.

Still, he instinctively liked her looks. Like the dead woman in the doorway, she had a dark, compelling beauty that seemed approachable yet fragile. He liked that look. And he liked the austerity of her dress and her fumbling attempts to impress him with the formality of her training. Janus had yet to lose the irreplaceable exuberance of youth — always the first victim of police work. And he liked that too. For a moment longer, he lingered with his stare, thoughtfully studying her dark eyes and searching his memory bank. Yes, now he recalled. That's why he knew her face. He'd seen her on the eastside. Unconsciously, his head bobbed up and down quickly in a ripple of recognition.

"Janus... weren't you at the Ruminez scene?"

"Yes, sir. I was working crime scene control on that one. You do mean the one across the boulevard? About three weeks ago?"

"That's the one. I saw you there."

She nodded up at him and began her own, secret investigation of the Lieutenant. Dressed in a muted beige suit, neatly offset with a white shirt and mahogany-colored tie, Chris Spell could easily have passed for one of the thousands of successful businessmen who roamed the Financial District each weekday. She worked to conjure up a meaningful description, to sum up what she saw. Pristine —

that's the only word that came to mind.

Well, she thought, good maintenance, but older than most of them. They were usually a bit younger, and with far less gray.

Indeed, Spell looked nothing like a homicide detective, much less one whose reputation was citywide and unremitting. Somehow he looked less important than that. With pale blue eyes and a shock of graying hair as thick as when he was twenty, Spell was austere in his good looks; stark, and attractive in that certain way that blesses a few lucky men in middle age. When he spoke, he had that recognizable, understated delivery of a naturally quiet guy — habitually frugal with his replies and surprisingly direct in his questions.

Most impressive to the young policewoman, though, was the way he carried himself. He wasn't stooped, like so many of the detectives she knew. His movements weren't bent or hurried. Nor did his hips swagger and arms dangle like a meandering gorilla. He didn't walk like most cops. No, this man had a posture and a style that was unmistakable, and quite compelling. He exuded an aura of grace and self-confidence as he moved around the landing. This was not a rogue, shoot-em-up cop, who'd made his way to the top by crushing a path through tough cases. This was a man who finessed his way across the complex pattern of an investigation, weaving each step and every action into a quilt of knowledge and understanding that gave him the highest closure rate in the Homicide Division. It was clear that he was a man who believed in detail, hard work, and intelligence. Brute force wasn't even an option.

Janus decided that he even looked sexy in his well-pressed suit. 'Still,' she thought, 'he seems a bit too old' in the bright morning sun.

Officer Janus slid her eyes away from his as casually as she dared, aware that he'd been watching her as she studied him. She moved still closer to the corpse in the doorway and made a dancing, up-and-down gesture with her head, trying to move on to a more familiar line of communication.

"This is the work of the same guy, isn't it, Lieutenant? The same freak who murdered Alvina Ruminez."

"That's guesswork and nothing else, Janus! And guesswork doesn't solve cases, it makes them harder. It clouds things. It's what the press does, not what we do." He finished his pronouncement with a second, more intense stare — a look that made his pale blue eyes seem especially cold and foreboding as she turned to face him.

Her face was crimson. She felt the full flush of a potent cocktail of anger and embarrassment rise from her stomach to her chest. So what if this guy was a legend in the Homicide Division. That didn't give him the right to snap her head off. 'Fucking men,' she thought. 'Fucking old men! They're the worst.'

She looked away, not wanting him to read the anger on her face. His jaw relaxed a bit as he waited for some kind of reaction.

Janus quickly reconsidered her position, searching for a recovery. Maybe he was right. Maybe it was a stupid statement, or at least a premature one. A few minutes at the crime scene and she was already making noises like she knew what had happened.

She realized it was time for a tactical retreat.

"Sorry, sir," she replied plaintively, but still gritting her teeth. "It's just the pattern of the chest wounds and the marks, uh, abrasions on her neck, they look the same to me — the same as Ruminez."

She pointed to the corpse with her left hand, watching Spell's eyes as he followed her gesture to the area of the victim's chest. The dead woman was propped against the frame of a peeling Victorian door with her legs outstretched and spread unnaturally far apart. Dark and small, looking much like an older Officer Janus, her clothes were completely soaked in blood from her neck to her waist. There was very little remaining of the original soft blue hue of her sheer blouse.

And across her chest was a dark, nearly black, sickening mass of red. Through the tattered blouse, Spell could easily see a series of clustered wounds that were deep and lethal. No medical examiner pronouncement was necessary. The woman had been stabbed repeatedly with a large weapon.

Encircling her blood-spattered neck, Spell saw a bruising pattern that he instantly recognized as evidence of strangulation — deep marks near the victim's thorax, but fading as they passed beneath her ears and vanished into her hairline. It looked to Spell like she'd been attacked from behind by a considerably taller, stronger person. She'd been strangled with something fairly thick, perhaps a stout piece of rope or multiple thin pieces bound together to strengthen the weapon.

For Chris Spell, the most disturbing element at the dumpsite was the mutilation of Jessica Callohan's body. The victim's right hand had been cleanly severed at the wrist and removed from the scene. The lack of blood around the area told Spell that the mutilation had occurred after death — just as in the case of Alvina Ruminez three weeks earlier. Whoever did this had considerable strength and skill.

He was sure that Janus was right, even though he'd just pedantically labeled his young colleague's idea "guesswork." This was the work of the same man who'd murdered Alvina Ruminez.

"Yeah, the pattern of the wounds is similar," Spell conceded in a dry voice, still looking at the victim.

"And the missing hand, sir? What about that?"

"That too, Officer Janus," his voice trailing off as he moved carefully around the body, trying to take in everything he could while keeping his fastidiously clean jacket from brushing against the victim.

As he studied the wounds closely, Spell heard voices coming from the sidewalk below the landing and instinctively turned to face them. Two of the Midtown Station's forensics personnel were working their way up the steps to the landing, chatting excitedly with each other. Their arrival meant the medical examiner was close behind and the Lieutenant would soon have to turn the crime scene over to the specialists.

Dressed in their predictable, cheap, black sport jackets, the criminalists approached the body. Spell stepped back without speaking, motioning for Sandy Janus to follow him. He walked her to the edge of the old wooden landing, just at the top of the stairs that led to the sidewalk below, and spoke in a hushed but unhurried tone.

"Officer Janus, can you tell…"

"Sandy," she said with a smile, mistakenly assuming his quiet tone for an invitation to familiarity.

"Officer Janus," he repeated in an official voice, again shooting a cold stare into her smile. "Can you give me any history on the victim's whereabouts last night?"

"No," she replied, once again feeling the flush that seemed to ride with this man's every comment.

"Well, you said she lived on Lexington, right?"

"Right."

"What was she doing here? Do you know?"

"No, sir. I have no idea."

"Have you talked to the occupants?" motioning beyond the closed door that separated the victim from the residents of the flat in front of which she was found.

"Yes, sir. They're next door now… at the neighbor's house. They're an older couple… Mr. and Mrs. Simonez. They found the body and called the station. They were leaving to walk their dog a little before seven this morning, and found the victim where she is now. I was dispatched from my beat and arrived here about five minutes later. I checked the victim and saw that she'd been dead for some time. I called you guys about quarter after seven. They didn't want to go back into their own flat, so I took them next door."

"Did you get a statement from them?"

"Yes, sir. It's right here." Janus pulled the draft of her Witness Statement from behind a stack of papers on her metal clipboard and offered it to Spell. He waved at it with the back of his hand, silently telling her that he didn't really need to see it. She seemed a bit disappointed.

"How old did you say they were, Officer?"

"They must be in their late sixties, early seventies, I'd guess."

"You guess?" he shot back.

"Well, wait a minute..." She fumbled around once more in the stack of papers, nodding her head from side to side as if she was a bird watching for a hungry cat on the fence. Finally, she found what she was looking for.

"Mr. Simonez said he was seventy-one, but she wouldn't tell me how old she was. She told me it was none of my damn business."

Spell chuckled and gave her a rare smile. Officer Janus looked apprehensive, he thought. She was pleasant, though, and he was being more of a jerk than usual — even by his own standards. Maybe he should back off a bit. After all, she had controlled the scene, took the initial statement, and did it all by the book. She'd done everything she was supposed to do and her only reward so far was his grumbling. He decided to apologize, but only in his mind.

"How long have you been on the force?" he asked in a casual tone. The signal was clear enough to Janus. She took his question as an apology and accepted it in silence.

"Almost three years now, sir — all that time out of Midtown Station."

"Good. Well, you did a good job here, Janus."

"Thanks. Do you think it's the same guy who did Ruminez, sir?" she pressed.

"That's guesswork," he answered. But this time there was no

snap in his voice, no harshness at all. "You know, guesswork is a real problem, isn't it?" he said softly.

She instinctively nodded, but remained quiet.

"Still," he continued, "if I *had* to guess, I'd say that your observation was a pretty good one. I'd guess it was the same freak too."

Sandy Janus beamed at the tall man and swayed her head, her dark hair spinning at the sides of her face. "Can I do anything else to help out here, sir?"

"Yeah, actually, you can. It would be a big help if you could talk to the neighbors around here and see if they saw or heard anything last night. Maybe someone caught a peek of this guy dumping the body here. Would you mind doing that?"

"Not at all, sir. That's fine with me." In fact, it was just what she was hoping for — a break in her endless routine of rousting drunks and trying, usually unsuccessfully, to mediate family disputes. For the young officer, this was a rare and welcome opportunity — a chance to work a small piece of a real homicide investigation. She was more than happy to do the legwork, even though she understood that what he had given her was not much more than a scrap from the Homicide Division's plentiful table of eye-catching, career-making crimes. After all, Sandy Janus didn't want to be a beat cop forever. Like the man who'd just thrown her an interesting bone, she had visions of a career that would take her out of the blues and into something far more meaningful and rewarding — the Homicide Division.

"Good, Officer. I appreciate that. Will you stop by my office tomorrow before you begin your shift and let me know what you found?"

"Well, sir, I begin my shift at seven. Isn't that a bit early for a Sunday?"

MISSION DISTRICT MURDERS • Michael D. Kelleher

"No!" he shot back. "I wish it was."

With a curt nod of his head and a painfully frugal smile, Chris Spell brushed passed the officer on the landing and carefully stepped down the steeply angled stairs to the sidewalk. Janus watched him go, assuming he would jump into his unmarked, white Ford sedan and leave her alone to begin her inquiries. Instead, he passed by his car and walked down the hill, heading east toward Mission Street. She watched him as he strolled quickly away, wondering why he'd left his car. Wondering a lot of things. But she didn't know Chris Spell. She didn't know that he was a man of habits, detail, and experience. Absolved of the emotions of his twenties and thirties, he'd become a bit more hardened than he'd planned. He liked to work his way through an investigation using only the facts of the case. This morning, both the facts and his experience told him there was a reason why the body of Jessica Callohan had been dumped on this particular block of Hill Street, maybe even a reason the murderer had selected this particular flat. Now he wanted to get a feel for the neighborhood. He wanted to see what the murderer had seen. He wanted to understand why this site was so special. But, most of all, he wanted to be alone — to have a few moments to think things through without distractions.

November 6
Midtown Station
7:10 A.M.

The Midtown Station sits stoically at the corner of Capp and Twentieth, strategically positioned in the heart of the chaotic, multicultural Mission District. Pristine and impressive in 1930, the edifice is now a weathered and undernourished faded salmon color that looks more like it belongs in a Beirut ghetto than in this bustling area of San Francisco. Still, it remains a hub of incessant activity throughout the day and night, a perpetual stream of patrol cars, unmarked vehicles, and foot traffic constantly surrounding its perimeter and assaulting its main entrance.

There's an adjoining parking area with access to the station through a side door, but it's reserved for those with the rank of detective or higher, and the status that comes with rank. All the others, the unrecognized masses of beat cops and desk jockeys, are left to fight over the sparse commodity of parking spaces along crowded South Van Ness Avenue, a long city block from the Station.

It was already ten past seven when Janus jammed her decade old Corolla into a parking space at the corner of Twenty-first and Van Ness. 'Hell of a thing,' she thought — late for a meeting for which she'd tried so hard to be on time. She bolted her way through the main entrance, badge in raised hand to avoid being tackled by the unlucky uniformed cops assigned to front door security. As she climbed the staircase up to the Homicide Division, she felt the sweat gather at the base of her neck and along her temples, and she cursed the excess baggage of her beat cop uniform. Silently she prayed that he wouldn't be too angry.

Chris Spell sat casually behind an enormous oak desk that was as old as the station itself, chatting with two other men as she approached the open door to his office. He briefly looked up from his conversation and waved her inside. She stared intently at him, looking for an indication of his mood, searching for a warning of the reception she feared. His expression was blank and distant.

She quietly slid beyond the office door and stood stiffly in the corner opposite the two unknown men. They both turned slightly in her direction, each with a blank expression that mirrored Spell's. Neither smiled or even acknowledged her presence. She nervously tugged at a wayward strand of hair that had drifted across her left cheek, and fought to brush it smooth, finally tucking it harshly behind her ear with a frustrated jerk of her hand.

"Good morning, Janus," the Lieutenant said without looking up, obviously preoccupied with the papers on the desk in front of him.

"Sorry I'm late."

"Parking, right?" the short man with red hair announced from across the room.

She smiled and nodded in his direction, tilting her head to take him in more completely. He was an odd one, she thought. Didn't look like a cop at all.

"Officer Janus, this is Sam McCannell," the Lieutenant mumbled, nodding in the direction of the man with red hair. "He's our forensic psychologist and he'll be working the case with us. Over there," he continued, this time pointing at the taller man with brown, short-cropped hair, "is Sergeant Joe Mendoza. He's the primary on the Ruminez murder." Then, looking directly at Janus, he told the others, "This is Officer Janus… Sandra Janus. She's agreed to help us out with some legwork on the Callohan case."

McCannell broke into a broad, toothy smile and stepped from the corner where he had been standing, extending his hand to the visitor. "Hi. Call me Sam."

"Sandy," she replied, noticing that his grip was strong and warm. "Call me Sandy."

She glanced in Mendoza's direction and began to move toward him, extending her hand, but he turned his head away from her, staring down at the papers in front of him, ignoring her completely.

"Hello," she said in his direction, expecting her salutation to get some kind of response. He said nothing, although she thought she might have seen a slight bobbing of his head. She hunched up her shoulders at the little red man and got a wisp of a smile in return.

"Well, don't worry about him," McCannell said apologetically, gesturing with his head in Mendoza's direction. "He isn't much of a morning person. But by happy hour you won't be able to shut him up."

Sandy giggled politely, a light laugh that was immediately interrupted by Mendoza's hog-like snort from the corner of the office. She decided that the red man with the warm hands was a real charmer – not at all like a cop. She quickly scanned him from top to bottom and noticed that he wasn't armed with the usual belt holster common to most detectives. In its place, he had clipped his badge onto the belt, partially covered by the ragged tip of a light green shirt that he'd failed to coerce completely into his trousers. By contrast, Mendoza looked like he had just walked out of a tailor's shop on Harrison Street. Everything was in its place — everything was coordinated. Sandy glanced down at her uniform shirt to make sure that she looked as good as Mendoza. She didn't.

"All right, people, now that the introductions are over, let's get on with it," Spell announced. "Janus, what did you find out?"

"I have a few things for you," she said proudly, not bothering to look at the notes in her hand. She thought it would make a better impression that way.

"Callohan lived alone on Lexington Street... in the back two rooms of a flat that belongs to a woman named Elizia Fernandez... an old lady who has owned the building since the fifties. Fernandez was apparently fond of Callohan and pretty lax about collecting the rent. Callohan had lived there for about three years. No problems to speak of. The landlady doesn't think she had any family, and says she never had any visitors."

For a brief second, Sandy glanced across the room. Were they listening? She continued.

"Callohan worked the streets at night, usually on Mission between Eighteenth and Twenty-first. She was a dime hooker and had a real problem with booze. I have her arrest record here, but I guess you guys have already seen it, right?"

Spell nodded. Mendoza looked comatose. The red man had his eyes closed.

"Ok, well, on Friday night, around ten o'clock, she stopped by Dougall's Bar on Lexington and Mission. Apparently, Dougall's was her hangout and she'd stop by there almost every night. Sam Dougall, the owner, said he'd give her a little credit now and then when she needed a drink but forgot the cash. And he said she always paid her bill.

"Anyway, she was in the bar drinking and talking to Dougall from about ten to ten-thirty that Friday night. She paid her tab – about thirty bucks – and had a couple more drinks. When she left, Callohan told Dougall that she was off to pick up a trick on the boulevard and would be back before he closed. Dougall never saw her again.

"I talked to a few of the bar's regulars who were around on Saturday morning. Then I went back there Saturday night after my shift was over to find a few more. I talked to six or seven of them in all, but none of them remembers her leaving the bar on the night in question.

"So, the bottom line is that no one seems to know what happened to Callohan after she left Dougall's. I talked to the neighbors on Hill Street and no one saw anything. The only lead from the neighborhood was two gay guys who live right across the street from the dumpsite. They say they were on their stoop around eleven that night, doing some stargazing or whatever. They said there wasn't a body in the doorway at that time and that they would have had a good view from across the street. They said they went inside about midnight. If they're reliable, and I think they are, I guess Callohan's body would have been dumped near the doorway sometime after midnight."

Suddenly she realized she'd used that word – *guess* – and shot a worried glance in Spell's direction. His head was still down, but she could tell he was listening.

"So, Lieutenant, that's all I have, for now," she finished, waiting for someone to break the silence.

Chris Spell pulled his head away from the papers in front of him and looked directly at her. "Good work, Janus. That's helpful. Did I hear you say that you went back to the bar after your shift ended?"

"Yes."

Now she was worried. Sandy had thrown that comment into her story to convince him that she was serious about helping out with the case, even if it was on her own time. Now, his stare told her that something was wrong. She probably should have kept her mouth shut.

"Listen, Janus, I appreciate your enthusiasm. Your instincts were good — to go back that night and look for the regulars. But don't be a cowboy, ok? Next time get back-up."

She nodded apologetically, but thought to herself, 'next time?'

"Ok, listen up," Spell said in his best lieutenant's voice. "I've asked the Captain to assign Officer Janus to us temporarily to help out with these two murders. We have a hell of a staff problem here and you all know that we've probably got a serial whacko working the District. I think Officer Janus can be of some help to us, don't you?"

Sandy felt a bolt of surprise jet its way from her stomach to her throat. McCannell suddenly opened his eyes, reinstated his beaming smile, and began nodding his head up and down, obviously pleased with the announcement. Mendoza never moved a muscle and remained transfixed on the papers in his hand.

"Well, Joe, are you with me on this, or what?" Spell demanded. Mendoza slowly raised his head and stared at Spell sitting behind the desk. He said nothing, but he snapped a quick glance in Sandy's direction and made another guttural sound that either meant "pleased to meet you" or "fuck off." Whichever, Spell seemed content with the result.

"Good. Then it's set. We'll work these two cases as a unit. Joe will stay as the primary on Ruminez and I'll take Callohan. I'll try to get one more person on the team, if I can squeeze the Captain a little more. But don't get your hopes up. Janus, is this all right with you?"

"Yes!" she yelped, trying unsuccessfully to throttle back her excitement.

"Well, I won't be seen with her dressed like *that*," interrupted a husky voice from the corner of the room. It was Mendoza.

Sandy quickly examined her uniform and tried to tuck in a small wedge of blue that had crept out from underneath the heavy, black leather belt weighted down with cop trinkets that a detective wouldn't be caught dead with.

"I mean, Chris, can't we send her home to put on some *real* clothes? Try and make her look like a woman?" Mendoza complained. "You are a woman, aren't you?"

"Hey, fuck you!" Sandy shouted back at him without thinking. "You know where you can stuff that macho shit, don't you?"

It wasn't a question.

Spell and McCannell roared in unison. Even Mendoza couldn't help but crack the tiniest of smiles. For her part, Sandy was rocket red across her cheeks and leaning forward like a boxer. It took her a moment to spear the thick cloud of humor in the room and make it her own. Then, she realized that *this* was the inner sanctum. This was the traditional domain of men — and only men. She leaned back on her heels and relaxed her arms slightly, trying to understand what had just happened.

From behind his desk, Spell was still gurgling with laughter. He moved his hand across his face to wipe a tear from the corner of his eye. Sandy whipped around to fully face Mendoza, once again feeling the anger in her chest. But now, he, too, was laughing and moving toward her, his hand outstretched.

"Well, Sandy, you've got some big brass cajones," he announced in his own private language. "It's a pleasure, partner."

"Partner?" Instinctively, she reached out to grab his extended hand, not sure if she wanted to shake it or bite it. Like McCannell's, it was warm, firm and sincere, or so she thought. She studied her new partner carefully and figured his age at thirty-five, or perhaps a bit more. With straight, thick brown hair and eyes colored to match, he had the look of Hispanic extraction and a sir name to go with it. She supposed that "Joe" was really "Jose," and pictured him growing up in the very neighborhood where they both now worked. He was lean and fit, with smooth skin and a robust glow that told her he was anything but a desk jockey. Like his boss, Chris Spell, he was perfectly groomed, unwrinkled, and gave the impression of something other than a cop.

"Ok, enough of this hippie, free-love shit," Spell interrupted in a playful, singsong voice. "Now that you two have learned to adore each other, can we get down to work?"

McCannell gave another huge roar, his face turning as red as his hair, his protrusive belly jiggling up and down. He'd obviously enjoyed the show. Mendoza nodded to the beaten, black leather couch across from Spell's desk and nudged Sandy in that direction. She sat down, facing the Lieutenant, with Mendoza next to her. McCannell propped himself on the ripped arm of the couch and reached around her shoulder, giving her an arm hug.

"Listen, Sandy, when we're done here, go home and get changed, ok?" the red man advised in a stern tone. "That'll keep Joe off your back for a while, right?"

She nodded and smiled back at him, leaning a bit harder into his arm.

November 6
Midtown Station
7:35 A.M.

"All right," the Lieutenant said, "let's go around the room on these two cases. Joe... start with the hard stuff. Sam, you take a shot at the soft, right? Sandy, you need to catch up, so pay close attention."

Janus nodded, pulled a pen from her pocket, and arranged the clipboard across her knees to take notes. Mendoza slid to the edge of the couch and began his report, looking directly at the Lieutenant. His expression was impassive and businesslike, as if a switch had been thrown somewhere in the back of his head.

"Alvina Ruminez was a married woman, twenty-six years old, and the mother of a six-year-old girl. She lived on Twenty-first Street, in a flat the family rented. She worked at the Munoz Grill six days a week, from three in the afternoon 'til the dinner crowd left, usually around nine o'clock. She had Sundays off.

"Her husband had been out of work for about a year at the time of her murder, so the family was struggling financially. Both of them had clean records and were well regarded in the neighborhood. Neither had family in the area or close friends. Mr. Ruminez did handiwork in the neighborhood for extra cash and was considered a reliable guy. We checked him out completely after his wife's murder. He's clean."

Spell pushed his chair away from the desk and cocked his head, obviously intent on hearing the rest of Mendoza's story.

"Alvina was a creature of habit; a hard-working gal; walked to work everyday... down the hill to Mission Street, then down to Eighteenth, where the Grill is located. She'd always get there on time; just in time for her shift. She'd work until the place was ready to close, then she'd walk back home the same way she got to work. Same routine, rain or shine. Never late and never missed a day in the four years she was there.

"On Friday night, September fifteenth, Ruminez left the Grill at 2135. The owner is sure about this because he was balancing the cash register when she left and he noted the time on her timecard. Plus she called her husband right before she left… said she was running a little late and didn't want him to worry about her.

"So, at 2135, Alvina left the Grill and began her walk down Mission Street, about five blocks from her flat. Now, it was a Friday night, the boulevard was crowded with people and there were cars cruising up and down the street. Somewhere between the restaurant and Twenty-second, she disappeared. By midnight, Mr. Ruminez was at the Midtown Station to file a report. The desk sergeant said Ruminez was visibly shaken. Actually, he said he looked 'worried and agitated.'

"The desk sergeant took the Incident Report and told him to come back that afternoon to file a Missing Person's Report. The sergeant also put out a Watch Notice to the patrol cars in the district. But nothing came of it.

"Sometime after midnight, her body was dumped in the doorway of a private residence on Valencia Street, near Twenty-first but it wasn't found until the next morning. The M.E. says she was stabbed eleven times in the chest with a large, single-edged knife. Or rather, 'a large, *sharp*, single-edged knife.' At least three of the wounds were fatal. After she was stabbed, the victim was strangled with a piece of heavy rope; probably seaman's rope or something similar, a half-inch or so in diameter. After that, the perpetrator severed her right hand at the wrist, probably before he transported her body to the dumpsite. He sat her upright next to the doorway, leaving her purse by her side. There was no indication of sexual assault or robbery. She had thirty dollars in tips in her purse. And the purse was on her right side… where her hand should have been."

"Ok, Joe, good," Spell mumbled. "We have any leads so far?"

"Not really. There's nothing from forensics that could do us any good, nothing from the victim's neighbors or coworkers, and nothing from the regular patrons at the Grill. There were no disturbance reports on the boulevard at the time the victim disappeared and no one has reported anything on the tip line. Nothing from our regulars on the street either. There was a small piece about the murder in the *Chronicle* the next morning, but no TV coverage. When it comes down to it, we ain't got squat."

"Ok, Joe, thanks," Spell said. He pulled himself close to the desk and rummaged through a stack of papers directly in front of him. "I have a few preliminary reports on the Callohan murder to share with you. The M.E. did his thing last night and the similarities between the Ruminez murder and this one are striking. Other than the multiple stab wounds to the chest, both women were strangled with a heavy rope after they were dead. And both had their right hands severed. Like I said before, let's keep that out of the press. That'll be our holdback on this sick bastard.

"Anyway, there was no indication of sexual activity with either victim. And both women had their purses next to their bodies, on the right side. Both purses had identification and a few dollars.

"The hooker disappeared along the boulevard after leaving the bar, just like Sandy said. The body was probably dumped around midnight. And I'm willing to bet the forensic evidence won't be worth shit with this one either. Since we didn't have any witnesses in the Ruminez case, we've got to hope for better luck on this one, right?"

They all nodded.

"Ok, Sandy, I want you to work with Joe. Start pounding the streets for witnesses. Also, Joe's going to have you do some background research, right?"

"Sure," she replied, looking at her new partner. Mendoza wasn't smiling — it was obvious that he was troubled by the case.

"So, Sam, tell me what you make of all this?" Spell asked, slightly turning in his chair to face the psychologist.

The red man stood up from the arm of the couch and began to pace across the room with his head bowed. For a few moments, he said nothing — he just paced. McCannell seemed to have his eyes closed as he shuffled his way back and forth across the office floor. Then, without warning, he was ready.

"Well, there's not a lot of hard stuff to go on here, but let's give it a try. It seems like this guy prefers female victims of a certain type. Ruminez and Callohan were quite similar physically. I believe these are both sexual homicides, regardless of whether there's hard evidence of it. We can definitely rule out robbery, and I don't think we're dealing with an ordinary hate or lust crime. Neither of them was targeted by anyone we know of. In both cases, the occupants of the house where the bodies were found weren't involved, right?"

Spell nodded and followed McCannell with his eyes as he continued to pace back and forth at the far end of the office.

"For Callohan, the risks were high by virtue of her profession. She knew and accepted this. But the same wasn't true for Ruminez. And that bothers me." For a moment, the psychologist was quiet and stopped his pacing. The others in the room waited, almost able to sense McCannell trying to get inside the head of the man who'd murdered two women in little more than a month. Then, he began to move again, his eyes still closed, somehow feeling his way across the office.

"Both victims were murdered and dumped elsewhere. According

to the medical examiner, both of them died within an hour or two of midnight, either way. That tells me the killer didn't spend much time with them. He murdered them quickly and dumped their bodies right away. He probably had the dumpsites picked out before hand. These weren't random spots. He staged their bodies for our benefit."

On the couch, Sandy sucked in an audible breath and stopped taking notes, fixing her stare on McCannell.

"He has a location... a specific place, where he feels safe, a place he knows like the back of his hand, a place where he won't be interrupted and the screams won't be heard. Now, we can be pretty sure that there wasn't a struggle in either case... too many people around. So his attack must have been rapid and lethal. Given the close proximity of the abductions, and the dumpsites, and the short time that he was with the women, the guy's got a good knowledge of the District.

"These were murders of control, domination, and anger. To him, that's what sex is... control, domination, brutality. This guy is angry as hell, and something set him off. Maybe it was a break-up, maybe not. But I'll tell you one thing, it's a psychosexual problem that goes back a long way... adolescence, or maybe before that. He's pissed off, and his rage targets a particular kind of woman. This guy's fucked up, Chris. For him, it's not enough to murder his victims... he's got to strangle and mutilate their bodies. He doesn't want to communicate with them. He doesn't want any interaction at all. He wants to brutalize them. So, he kills them as quickly as he can, then he goes about the part of the crime that really feeds his need to dominate and brutalize. That's why he strangles and mutilates them *after* they're dead. This guy's got a real problem relating to others, particularly women, and it's gonna get worse."

Spell made a rumbling noise as if he was about to speak, but the red man waved him off with a swing of his stubby right arm. He had more to say.

"This guy is very unsure around women, probably not very articulate, and a real social loser. Judging by the sophistication and organization of the crimes, he's probably between twenty-five and forty-five. And he's a Monday through Friday, nine-to-five kind of guy. But, boy, does he let lose on the weekends!

"And one more thing, Chris. The problem with this kind of assessment is that it runs counter to how the murderer manages to abduct these women in the first place. I mean, there's no evidence of a forced abduction or struggle in either case. It was as if these women voluntarily went with him. Since both Ruminez and Callohan vanished from a crowded street on busy nights – Friday and Saturday – he must have taken them inconspicuously. That's a real problem for us. If this guy's a social misfit, how'd he do that?

"Then, there are the dumpsites and the condition of the bodies. These were well-organized murders. He didn't just grab the victims off the street, beat them into submission, throw them into a vehicle, and take them off somewhere indefinite to finish them. Somehow, he managed to get control of them quietly, transport them to where he'd already planned to kill them, and then dump the bodies in specific locations. And nobody saw anything? I find that hard to believe. But you can see we've got a contradiction here... I mean, he's intelligent, he's organized, and he's psychotic. That's a dangerous mix."

McCannell swung his stout frame away from where the Lieutenant was seated and faced the wall.

"The medical examiner's report tells me that this guy is strong, medium height or better, and easily able to physically dominate his victims. It seems to me that his physical strength was a big asset, once he had the women under his control. But, that still leaves us with the issue of how he abducted them in the first place. My guess is that he used a vehicle. He may have pulled up alongside the women and somehow induced them into his vehicle. Now, that means a couple of things. First of all, Callohan would have gotten into an unknown vehicle with a strange driver because... well, that's what she did. But, Ruminez would never have done that. So, either Ruminez knew the vehicle and the driver or she thought it would be safe to go with him. That may have been the case with Callohan, too. Both women probably thought it was safe to get into that vehicle... if that's how it went down. But why put themselves at so much risk?"

He didn't wait for an answer.

"Maybe it wasn't a risk. What if it was an authority figure? They *might* get into his car, right? I mean, suppose a black and white pulled up while they were walking down the boulevard... and the driver told them to get into the car? They might go. Now, I'm not saying that we're looking for a cop. In fact, I don't think we are. But it is a possibility."

He was pacing faster now, skirting the office with his eyes half-open and his arms swinging. "Here's another. Suppose it was a taxi or a boulevard shuttle? More likely a cab... 'cause there'd be other people in the shuttle, right? But, what if there weren't any other riders? We should look into that. Bottom line? There *are* reasons a careful woman like Alvina Ruminez might get into a stranger's vehicle."

After a brief pause, the red man continued.

"Once they were in, the killer must have struck quickly. There's no way he could drive around the Mission District on a crowded night and fight off a frantic woman at the same time. That would be far too dangerous, and this guy's not into risk. He had to strike quickly, and he had to convince the women, at least Ruminez, to go with him quietly."

"Chris, I'd be looking for a vehicle that wouldn't stand out on the boulevard; one that would blend in; something no one would notice.

Now, the killer is a strong guy, maybe even imposing. He's probably got some kind of physical impairment... a speech problem or something similar. He doesn't interact well with other people, especially women."

"Our guy probably lives alone. If not, he's definitely got a place to take his victims... a secure location... somewhere fairly close to the dumpsites. It's even possible that everything takes place in his vehicle. But that's a bit too risky with all the people around on a weekend night in the Mission District."

Once again, the red man paused and scrunched up his face into a round ball, his mind drifting. In a moment, he was back.

"I'm worried about this one, Chris. Why'd he dump the women in the doorways of these private residences? In one way, it doesn't really matter; in another, it's vital. I think he did it to send us a message. And you can bet that he expects us to figure it out. On the other hand, it doesn't help us right now, does it? I mean, once the bodies are dumped, he has the upper hand, so long as he's been careful in committing the murder. And he knows that."

"What really bothers me is that we don't know what the message means. And he's going to keep sending it till we get it. Each time, he'll draw us deeper into the game. He'll become frustrated with us... with our inability to figure it out. And the message will become clearer and more blatant. We've got a real problem on our hands. This guy's got a lot more to say before he's through. We've got to find a witness... or some forensic evidence. Otherwise, we may never catch him. He's bright enough, careful enough, and just sane enough to keep killing for a very long time.

"Jesus..." Sandy whispered from the couch, her eyes large and glassy.

The men remained quiet, contemplating McCannell's verbal epiphany. It was true — there wasn't much to go on. Spell and

Mendoza knew that the red man had given them the best he had to offer. Sam McCannell was not the kind of guy to hold anything back, even if it was pure guesswork. He had a good track record with the SFPD. He'd helped break some difficult cases. But those cases had an evidentiary foundation, something to push the investigation in a particular direction. With these murders, there was almost nothing, and the four of them knew it.

"Thanks, Sam," the Lieutenant mumbled. "We're eyeball deep in shit in this one."

McCannell nodded from across the room and bowed his head, his concern and uncertainty obvious.

"Ok, we just need to rustle the bushes as much as we can, right?" Spell said to the group.

"Yeah, we need to stir up something new on this, boss," Mendoza offered. "Have the press been on you about the Callohan murder? Is that an angle we can work with?"

"No, not yet," Chris replied. "I expect it to happen soon, though... like today." He swung the chair around again to face McCannell. "Listen, Sam, if the press starts speculating about a serial killer... do I confirm or deny?"

McCannell began to pace again as he considered the question. "Well, it's going to be hard to *deny*."

"Yeah... but I don't want to feed this freak anymore than I have to."

"I'm not so sure about that, Chris. It's a two-edged sword. This guy will want to read about himself. He'll want to know that he has your complete attention. He may even want to interject himself into our investigation. Part of the control trip here is the game he's playing with us. That's why he's been staging the bodies. Let the press speculate. I'd tell them that we've got some good leads and maybe even a witness or two. I'd confirm the method of death, but keep the mutilation stuff in your back pocket. If possible, I'd try to get the folks around here interested enough to use the tip line... but not worried enough to be panicky. I know that's a tough road, though. So, you'll just have to be careful about what you say."

Spell nodded grimly from behind his desk.

"Listen, Chris, I'm sure this guy's gonna wanna dance. He'll want to play, no doubt about that. We've got to give him a reason to be more brazen... got to get him communicating directly with us. If he thinks you *have* something... if he thinks you're getting warm, he may try to find out what you *really* know. On the other hand, if he reads or hears that you've got something *wrong* he may try to correct it. The obvious danger, though, is that he'll escalate his murders... that he'll step up the pace as he gains confidence. We're on a fine line, here. And that's a tough call."

"Ok, Sam, I understand," Spell said. "I have to talk to the press anyway. I'll try to keep it balanced. What do you two think?" he asked Mendoza and Janus.

"I think Sam's right, " Mendoza replied. "But I wouldn't give the press too much. It could get folks really freaked out... and we don't have anything good to say about the investigation. I guess I'd keep it close to the vest, if I could."

Mendoza turned his head toward his new partner, silently letting her know it was her turn. She had a different subject in mind; something from much earlier in the conversation.

"Jesus..." she mumbled in a worried tone. "This is a bad situation, for sure. What bothers me the most is why he would hack off their hands. And why the right ones? Coincidence? That's pretty weird... and symbolic, not to mention disgusting. What's the deal with that, Sam?"

"Your right, Sandy," the red man snapped from across the office. "It has a great deal of significance. We just don't know what it means… yet. I think he'll tell us though… eventually."

For a moment, the room was silent, each of them staring away from the others, lost in the possibilities. It was Sandy who spoke first.

"Ok, well, I'll work with Joe here and do whatever it takes," she said softly. "I guess the best way to start is just what you guys said… beat the streets and look for some new leads."

"Listen, Sandy," the Lieutenant said, now looking directly at her. "What would it take for *you* to get into a vehicle with someone you didn't know. How would *you* react?"

She thought for a moment, dropping her eyes to her lap and playing with her hands. "Well, it depends… if it was a cop or some other authority figure that I thought I could trust, I'd probably just get in. But it would depend on *why* he wants me to get in. If it was late, and he was offering me a ride… yeah, I'd get in."

"Anything else? Any other reason?" Spell pushed.

"Well, maybe… if it was an emergency or something like that. If, say, the guy in the car said my mother just had a stroke or my best friend was just hit by a car, and he knew my name… I guess I'd go with him. But it depends upon the circumstances… and how he looked… and how he acted."

Sam shot a look at the Lieutenant, then quickly back at Sandy. It was an excellent point.

"Sure enough, Sandy. That might work, if the story was good enough," McCannell said, once again closing his eyes and imagining the possibilities. "Sure, that would work. But for a victim to fall for it, the guy in the car would have to know something about his target, wouldn't he? I mean, he'd have to know enough to make the story believable. Some personal information, yeah?"

"Yeah," she echoed in a thoughtful tone. "It would have to be *very* convincing. It would be more believable if the guy was a priest or something like that, I suppose."

Sam offered her a huge smile and moved back to the side of the couch, once again putting his arm around her shoulders. His mood was suddenly lighter and less restrained.

"Say, Sandy, if you ever get tired of beating the streets in that silly uniform, I could use a smart, good-looking assistant," he mumbled to the top of her ear. Sandy shook her head hard from side to side and whacked his arm with the back of her left hand.

"Let's check these ideas out," Spell ordered. "They're all possibilities… and that's all we've got right now. Let's find out if anyone has been snooping around and asking questions. Let's check it out."

The Lieutenant abruptly pushed himself away from the desk and headed for the door without a word.

Officer Janus noticed that, today, his posture was not what it was yesterday. Today, he looked decidedly bent at the hips; looking more like a frustrated, angry cop than he did yesterday.

Today, Spell looked his age.

November 12
Bernal Heights District
9:15 A.M.

It was an unusually bright, still, and warm Sunday morning in Bernal Heights — the area of the city just south of the Mission District. A crowded, hilly menagerie of muted, stucco homes and post-Victorian flats, this District had once been an impenetrable stronghold of tightly knit, Italian-American immigrants and their extended families. But that was decades ago. Now, like the Mission District itself, this part of the city had been transformed into a heterogeneous conglomeration of singles, couples, and families of every describable color, persuasion, and complexity. In its diversity, it had obvious strength and better economic clout than its neighboring Districts. In some ways, it had grown up — it had come full cycle and been transformed into a melting pot of its own, with a cornucopia of cultural experiences and traditions. In this way, it was an exciting and interesting stopover. But, like much of San Francisco, its soul stuttered when it tried to speak. It was often an intensely dark and unhealthy place to live. This part of the city no longer *felt* like a neighborhood. It had become a caldron of incessant, unpredictable movement and change, with no inherent stability and warmth to call its own. Now, its names were sometimes chaos, deceit, and danger — a place where few residents *knew* their neighbors, and yet *feared* them. It had become a place in which very few residents dared to care about anything beyond their doorways.

Inside the nondescript, faded, peeling gray flat on the north side of Courtland Avenue – the busy boulevard that defined and divided the Bernal Heights District – Herbert William Jamieson sat naked at his kitchen table, sipping from a stained mug of yesterday's unheated coffee. Emblazoned on both sides of the cup was an ornate, gold leaf emblem, now heavily chipped and discolored from years of use. Below the emblem, near the base of the mug, was the inscription, *San Francisco Fire Department,* in a fine, flourishing font. In front of him, nestled among the clutter of unwashed dishes and week-old newspapers randomly strewn across the table, he stared at the articles he had meticulously clipped from two editions of the San Francisco *Call.*

Gruesome Murders Concern Police
By Jane Riordan, *Call* Staff Writer
November 7, San Francisco:

The second brutal murder of a Mission District resident has the SFPD concerned, according to Lieutenant Christopher Spell, who heads the Homicide Division at the Midtown Station. On Saturday night, November 4, Jessica R. Callohan was stabbed to death, strangled, and her body dumped on the doorstep of a residence on the 20000 block of Hill Street. Six weeks earlier, on September 15, Alvina G. Ruminez was slain in a similar manner. Her body was also left in the doorway of a private residence — this one south of Mission Street. Yesterday afternoon, Spell met with reporters at the Midtown Station to discuss the cases and provide details of these gruesome murders.

The first victim, Alvina Ruminez, was a waitress at the Munoz Grill. She was a wife, and mother, who was apparently abducted from Mission Street while walking home from her job. Her body was discovered in a doorway the following morning. She had been stabbed multiple times in the chest and strangled. Ruminez was twenty-six.

Three days ago, Jessica Callohan was slain in the same way. She disappeared from Mission Street on Saturday night and was found the next morning on Hill Street. Like Ruminez, her body had been dumped in the doorway of a private residence. Callohan, also in her twenties, was also stabbed and strangled.

As far as the SFPD knows, neither victim knew the other or had any common ties.

When asked if the two murders were related, Lt. Spell said, "There is an obvious similarity in these killings. Yes, we could be dealing with the same murderer in both cases."

A tactical team has been formed to investigate the possibility that the two murders are the work of a single individual. According to Spell, "We have some promising leads in these cases and we're working them right now. I also encourage the citizens of the District, or elsewhere in the city, to call our tip line if they believe they have information that could help with the investigation. We are pursuing every lead and every tip in order to close these cases as quickly as possible."

When asked if he thought there was a serial killer loose in the Mission District, Spell answered: "It's too early to tell for sure, but we never rule out that kind of possibility when two murders share such similar characteristics. The bottom line here is that we just don't know, yet. The murders could be related, but they might not be. I can assure you that we are on these cases and following each lead. I'm confident that we will bring the perpetrator to justice."

Lieutenant Spell is personally heading the investigation into these murders. Spell was the lead investigator in the notorious Folsom Street Murders in 1991 and the Presidio Ax Murders in 1988. In those cases, a total of twenty-six individuals were slain by two serial murderers. Both were apprehended by Spell, found guilty, and eventually sentenced to the death penalty.

Stalking a Murderer
By Jane Riordan, *Call* Staff Writer

Sunday Edition – Crime Watch
November 12, San Francisco:

On September 15, a young mother and waitress at the Munoz Grill was abducted from Mission Street while walking home from her job at 9:30 in the evening. The next morning, her brutalized body was discovered in the doorway of a private residence, just a few blocks from the victim's home.

Three weeks later, the gruesome scene was repeated.

On November 4, an unemployed woman of similar age and description to the first victim disappeared from Mission Street and was found the next morning in the doorway of a flat on Hill Street. She had also been stabbed to death and strangled.

The question that now troubles the SFPD is one of serial murder.

Alvina G. Ruminez, the first victim, was in her twenties, dark, and, by all accounts, pretty. She died from a combination of multiple stab wounds to the chest and strangulation. Jessica Callohan, also in her twenties, was murdered in the same manner.

The similarities in these two cases are striking. According to Lieutenant Christopher Spell of the Midtown Homicide Division, it is possible that the same individual murdered both women.

Among the officers of the SFPD, Spell is legendary for his work on serial murder cases over the years, particularly the Folsom Street Murders in 1991 and the Presidio Ax Murders in 1988. In both cases, Spell hunted down and arrested the serial murderers, who together, had claimed more than two dozen victims. Now he is heading the investigation into the

Ruminez and Callohan slayings.

When asked how he would approach this investigation, Spell replied, "We don't work these complex cases alone. We form a team and the team works together to pursue the leads and assemble the case. These are always difficult investigations and we work them very hard."

Spell declined to provide specifics on the investigation, but did say the Homicide Division had some promising leads. His investigation team includes Dr. Samuel McCannell, who worked with Spell on previous homicides and, according to Spell, "is a master at getting into the mind and motivation of a murderer." McCannell is a forensic psychologist with the SFPD, a part-time professor at San Francisco University, and the author of The Eyes of a Serial Murderer.

Also on the team is Sergeant Jose Mendoza, a native of the Mission District and a detective with the Midtown Station for ten years. According to Spell, other officers will be assigned to the investigation as needed. He declined to say any more about the investigation, citing its preliminary nature.

When asked if there was reason for concern on the part of Mission District residents about a serial killer in their midst, Spell was noncommittal: "It's always a possibility in cases like this. We are certainly looking at that possibility. On the other hand, it's just too early in the investigation to make that kind of assumption. Until we know, for sure, we will treat it that way."

Spell was also asked if Dr. McCannell had constructed a profile of the murderer and if that would be released to the public in the near future. His answer: "Yes, Sam McCannell is making progress with that. However, until we're sure of our facts, we don't believe it would be in the best interest of the public to disclose Dr. McCannell's working profile.

We are striving for complete accuracy here, and most of all, we want to get this guy as soon as possible… and make sure that our case is air-tight."

According to Spell, residents of the Mission District should not be unnecessarily alarmed. "Just take the usual precautions if you are a woman alone at night. That just makes good, common sense these days," he said.

Unfortunately, his advice came too late for Alvina Ruminez and Jessica Callohan.

Jamieson stared at the clippings, his eyes unfocused and distant. With his left hand, he angrily brushed them to the floor, sending two food-encrusted plates with them. They crashed heavily against the stained yellow cupboard below the sink and bounced to the floor, shattering. Unseeing, unhearing, he laid his large head against his right forearm on the kitchen table and closed his eyes.

Once again, he flew away.

"I wish to call Marion Jamieson to the stand, Your Honor."

The judge nodded slightly and Marion rose from her seat near the back of the oak-paneled, ornate courtroom. She was dressed completely in black — a demure, cotton outfit, tastefully offset at the cuffs and collar by thin bands of white frill. Her extraordinarily long, ebony hair had been twisted back into a thick braid that fell to the waist of her dress. A petite, lean, attractive woman in her early thirties, Marion Jamieson moved unsteadily toward the witness stand and started to ascend the raised platform to the right of the judge.

"Mrs. Jamieson, you must take the oath," the judge ordered. Unlike the witness, the woman behind the bench was stern, aging, and overweight.

"Oh, I'm sorry," she whispered as she withdrew her foot and stood at attention in front of the witness box. The bailiff approached her and thrust a bible in her direction with his right hand. Like the judge, he was unfit, stern, and unsmiling.

Marion placed her left hand on the bible, delicately, barely touching its beaten and cracked brown leather surface. She raised her right hand, stretching the tips of her small fingers to the height of her head. She did not face the bailiff. Instead, her eyes drifted involuntarily to the right, to the defendant's table, in the direction of her husband. Instantly, her face became gray and stilted, with a threatening, demonic curl of anger embracing her red, smooth lips.

Jamieson jolted involuntarily from the heat of the morning sun, magnified and diffused on his bare back by the crusty, unclean windows over the sink. He was back.

"Bitch!" he yelled out loud as he reached down to the floor to retrieve the clippings. He carefully arranged them in the empty space in front of him, aligning them perfectly, side-to-side. Jamieson scanned the articles once again, paying special attention to the Sunday edition. Once more, he read his favorite piece — slowly, meticulously, absorbing every detail and nuance. Once again, he was drawn back to the same lines:

> Yes, Sam McCannell is making progress with that. However, until we're sure, we don't believe it would be in the best interest of the public to disclose Dr. McCannell's profile.

Jamieson roared as he read the quote. It was a fearsome sound, born of anger and disdain — a guttural, shaking, unnatural sound from deep inside his chest. Carefully, as if they were made of gossamer and gold, he lifted the clippings from the table and moved quickly to a high, open cupboard next to the undersized refrigerator near the kitchen door. Reaching to the top shelf, he withdrew a maroon, unopened scrapbook, which was still encased in its original plastic shrink-wrap. He ripped the wrapping away from the book and let the tattered plastic drift to the floor.

Jamieson slowly raised the scrapbook to his face and, closing his eyes, took in the scent of new, fresh pages. Then he gently folded back the thick cover and lovingly placed the two newspaper clippings between the first two pages of the virgin scrapbook. For a moment, Jamieson held the closed book in his hands, unconsciously stroking its smooth cover, letting his eyes drift shut and his mind flee.

The ritual was done.

There was no need to do more, right now, he decided. No need to organize the clippings or affix them permanently to the pages. That would come later. There was an order to things and this was *his* scrapbook.

There must be order.

This was *his* game and it would proceed as he'd planned.

She could go fuck herself! They could all go fuck themselves, especially *him*.

Jamieson replaced the scrapbook on the top shelf of the cupboard, carefully arranging it so that it was absolutely square to the edge of the shelfboard. He moved back to the kitchen table. Rummaging for something with which to write, Jamieson's burly hand found the stub of a pencil and a piece of torn paper napkin from a forgotten take-out meal. He inspected the scrap of paper for a clean area and teased the wrinkles from its face with his left hand. With his right hand, he wrote two lines in block script — very neat, very ordered. Each line contained a name. Each name was that of a new enemy.

He balled up the scrap of paper in his hand, crushing it so tightly that his fingers became instantly bloodless and pale, the fingernails cutting into his palm and leaving a series of semicircular wounds that immediately filled with red. When he was sure he had squeezed the life from the scrap of paper, he thrust it into his mouth, chewed it into a formless pulp, and swallowed it with an audible gurgle.

Jamieson sat back in the chair and closed his eyes once again, knowing that the ritual was complete, ecstatic at the symbolic death of his new enemies.

He was finished — for today.

November 13
Midtown Station
8:40 A.M.

"I just got finished with Marley," Spell muttered to Mendoza as he raced across the office and threw himself into the battered oak chair behind his desk. Sandy gave her partner a quick glance, wondering if what she had just heard from the Lieutenant was a good thing or a bad thing. Mendoza had his head down, shaking it from side to side. It didn't look good to Sandy.

Captain Marley was well into his third decade with the SFPD. He was the very definition of a primordial cop. He'd managed to survive his long career by being exceptionally careful, conservative, and uncontroversial. Over the years, he'd become more of a political animal than anything else. He had long ago forgotten what it was like to be a beat cop. Still, he had his role, and Chris Spell understood it well.

For Spell and the Homicide Division, the Captain's perennial love-hate relationship with the press made for a slippery ride in some investigations, while it proved to be a distinct benefit in others. If the Captain felt that a particular case was not going well in the media, he had an uncanny way of distancing himself from the investigating officers and the entire Homicide Division. On the other hand, when the SFPD was closing in on a suspect, he was always there — always ready to talk to anyone with a press badge. When he was in one of those chatty, optimistic moods, he was easy picking.

For Chris Spell, Marley was more often an asset than a liability. Spell's reputation in the Department and with the press was too solid for a man like the Captain — too strong for an aging, fearful desk jockey who disdained anything that even remotely smelled like bad news. All Spell had to do was slip a subtle threat of negative press into a conversation and Marley would inevitably give him what he needed. Still, just meeting with the Captain was never a pleasant experience.

"Marley was ranting and raving, like usual," Spell said to Mendoza's bowed head. "He was worried about the tone of Riordan's article in yesterday's *Call*. He figures that she's going to take us on with this case... that she's going to rape us all over the front page. He wanted to know what we're up to and how we're protecting our backs."

"We could use some help, for one thing," Mendoza shot back, now looking up at his boss.

Officer Janus nodded her agreement and made a light, humming sound. Mendoza glanced to his right, watching her as she moved toward the couch to sit next to him, wondering if she was about to speak. Dressed in a conservative brown business suit, which was obviously brand new, Sandy was a different woman from the beat cop who had sat next to him on the couch just a week ago. Now, he could see her taut, slim body. It was no longer hidden by the amorphous bulk of her uniform. Now, Sandy rustled when she walked. She whispered along the floor like the graceful, delicate woman she was. The stale odor of her cotton uniform shirt had been replaced by the sweet, light fragrance of lilac. Gone was the tightly collared, blue, button-up shirt that erased all hint of femininity. In its place was a thin, shapely blouse that offered a tasteful vision of her olive-hued neck and upper chest. Most appealing of all, Mendoza had discovered Sandy's legs — no longer imprisoned within the dense weave of SFPD blue. Now, they were encased in sheer, translucent beige nylon, proudly exhibiting their symmetrical beauty. Today, she was a petite, dark, perfectly formed jewel who, Mendoza thought, had been hidden away much too long in that annoying uniform.

"No problem," Spell announced in a victorious tone. "Marley agreed to give us Mary Boor from the Bayside Station. In fact, he had already arranged it before we met. She'll be here in a minute."

Mendoza perked up noticeably, an easy smile flashing across his lips. "Yeah, that's good, Chris. That's *very* good. He must have been really worried, right?"

"Who's Mary Boor?" Sandy interrupted with a hint of tension in her tone.

"She's an inspector attached to Bayside," the Lieutenant answered. "I've known Mary a long time, Sandy. So has Joe. She worked the Presidio Ax Murder case with me. I think she's one of the best we've got. One of the very best…"

Mendoza nodded his head vigorously, obviously pleased with the news. "Yeah, Sandy, she's really good. She's a bulldog. Mary gets on a case and she'll just work it to death. Very quiet, but very effective," he confirmed.

"Sounds good to me," Sandy said. Still, to Spell, she looked a bit concerned. He had been secretly studying her for any reaction to the news, watching her carefully from behind his desk. The Lieutenant couldn't help but wonder if his new recruit hadn't already been caught up in Mendoza's legendary effect on female officers. Joe never consciously intended to attract the women who worked with him — it just happened. It wasn't a simple matter of good looks. It was much more complex than that. It was his uncanny, unconscious ability to be a genuine mystery to everyone around him. He was just a hell of an intriguing guy, and he knew it. Spell couldn't help but enjoy watching Mendoza work his magic; yet, it also worried him. He was not only a terrific investigator, he was one of a kind. He was unique, and everyone who came into contact with Mendoza sensed it immediately. For someone young and unfamiliar with the ways of Sergeant Mendoza, like Sandy Janus, well, it *could* be a problem. He would keep a close eye on things, he decided.

"Listen, Sandy, maybe you'd like to work with Mary for a while, as *well* as with Joe. I mean, if we did that, it could give you some excellent experience, working with both of them. How does that sound?" Spell asked without his usual, definitive tone.

Sandy offered a quizzical look to Mendoza, searching for any reaction from her new partner. There was none. "Whatever works best," she finally answered.

"Yeah, fine with me," Joe added. "We can work that out with Mary, Chris."

"Ok, good. That's the way we'll do it."

"Do what, Chris?" came the whispered, husky voice from the office doorway.

"Hey, Mar, how are you!" the Lieutenant yelped as he jumped from his chair and headed in her direction. She stepped forward, into the office, and gave Chris a long, hard hug. From Sandy's diminutive point of view, this woman was a giant — half a head again taller than even the Lieutenant. Yet, she had an unexpected grace in her movement — a flowing, fluid presence that seemed impossible for such a tall woman.

"Jesus, it's good to see you again, Mar!" he said.

"Yeah, it is, you old scoundrel. How've you been?"

"Up to my ass, as usual. Look who's here," he uncharacteristically chirped, waving his hand in Mendoza's direction.

"Hi Joe, I didn't see you hiding over there," Mary said with a smile, blatantly checking the Sergeant out from head to toe.

"Hi Mary, it's good to have you here," he replied, beaming. "Listen, this is Sandy Janus. She's working the investigation with us." He nodded in the direction of the woman sitting next to him.

Sandy hopped away from the couch and reached out her hand, nodding a welcome. Mary returned the nod and grasped the smaller woman's hand with a firm, rhythmic shake. "Good. Glad to meet you, Sandy. I hope these two rogues haven't been giving you a hard time?"

"No, not at all. At least, not since I got out of my blues."

Mary broke into a raspy, rolling laugh. "Well, that comment obviously came from the Latin lover over there, right?" she said, pointing directly at Mendoza. Once again, he dropped his head.

"Yeah, it was him. He said he wasn't sure if I was even a woman when he saw me in uniform," Sandy complained with a smile.

"Well, Chris has probably already told you to ignore him. He just thinks he's God's gift to women." Mary said with authority.

Mendoza chuckled but did not raise his head. Chris bobbed his head up and down with a huge smile. It was clear to Sandy that these three deeply cared for each other. They shared a lot of history.

Chris headed back to his desk while Sandy perched next to Mendoza, from where she could keep their newest team member in plain view. To Sandy, Mary Boor looked much more like a cop than either Spell or Mendoza. It wasn't her dress, which was tasteful and soft. It was her bearing and, mostly, her voice. There was nothing uncertain about the tall woman in the dark clothes. When she spoke, she was decisive and frugal. When she spoke, the other two listened and heard what she said. Boor commanded respect in that certain way that good cops do, and it was instantly recognizable. In her late forties, it was obvious that she knew her business and knew it well. Yet, like Mendoza had said a few minutes earlier, she was quiet and unassuming. By Sandy's standards, she was likeable — much more appealing than she had expected.

She was also much older, and that was a relief to Sandy.

"So, Chris, what about Sam? Is he working this one with you?" Mary asked the Lieutenant.

"You bet. I wouldn't have it any other way, right? Listen, Mary, do you know what's going on here?" Chris asked in a hurried voice.

"Well, a little. Marley told me that you've got a serial killer cruising the District. I guess you know that I jumped on it right away."

"Thanks, Mar. What do you know about the murders?"

"Not a lot. I'd like to see the files and talk about it a bit."

"Ok, good, we'll do that. I've got the files here. Why don't we just get out of here for a while? Sandy and Joe both have a lot of work ahead of them and no leads. Spend some time catching up, and then you can work with them. This is Sandy's first homicide, so she'll need our help on some of this. I partnered her with Joe, but it would be good if she could work with you, too."

"Sure," Mary replied. "Is that all right with you, Sandy?"

"Yeah," Sandy said with a genuine smile. "Especially after you told me what a wild guy Joe is."

Mary gave Sandy another large laugh and slyly stared at Mendoza. He, too, was chuckling.

"Ok, done!" Chris announced, clearly pleased. He pushed himself away from the desk, grabbing several files at the same time, and headed for the door. Mary instinctively rose to follow him, as if she had done it a hundred times before — as if the pair knew each other so well that their next move needn't even be discussed. In a moment, they had disappeared from view, down to the second floor hall, off to privately meet and discuss the murders.

Mendoza slapped Sandy lightly on the knee and gave her a tight smile. "I'm not *that* bad," he moaned.

"Bullshit!" Sandy shot back, slapping him hard across the thigh as she stood up and headed for the door.

November 24
Eighteenth Street and South Van Ness Avenue
Evening

Mary Beth Althazar was a regular at Salvatore's Restaurant, especially on Friday evenings. Unlike most of the regular customers of the restaurant, Giovanni Salvatore's three waiters never called her by name and knew virtually nothing about her. They knew her only as a "strange one" — a woman who never spoke, always ate alone, yet tipped them with their preferred cash, even when she used a credit card to pay for her meal. For that, at least, they were grateful. However, as had been the case throughout her life, Mary Beth was easily ignored and quickly forgotten. She was a woman who always seemed apart and aloof from her surroundings.

Located on the frenetic corner of Eighteenth and South Van Ness, just a block from Mission Street, Salvatore's was a bustling, dark, and homey establishment that offered a rare treat to Mission District residents — genuine Sicilian cuisine at reasonable prices. For Mary Beth, who lived just a few blocks away at Seventeenth and Folsom, the restaurant was an enjoyable respite from her usual evenings of eating alone in her flat. At Salvatore's, Mary Beth knew she would always be surrounded by the incessant chattering of other diners, often in pairs, along with the unending clanking of dishes and pans, and the bellowing of waiters shouting out their orders to the sweaty, overwrought chef behind the long mahogany counter. To this lonely woman, none of this smacked of the chaos that others experienced at the crowded restaurant. Instead, it was a kind of important companionship to a person who was without any companions of her own.

A copyeditor, who worked in the Financial District of the city,

Mary Beth was extraordinarily shy and withdrawn. At twenty-seven, she was a short woman with jet-black hair and a slightly plump build — sufficiently rotund to compound her already broken self-image, but far from grotesque. She had a certain passive beauty in her thickening features — the remembrance of a once gentile, petite face that seemed to have been misplaced sometime earlier in her life. It was as if the years of isolation and living in silence had transformed a potentially beautiful teenager into an adult who considered herself unworthy of interacting with others and found a refuge in eating a bit more than she needed. She rarely smiled, seldom spoke, and worked endlessly to avoid the eyes of anyone who tried to speak to her.

At her job, Althazar labored in the same oppressive isolation that characterized her home life. Her office was a windowless, insignificant room – little more than a generous closet – that was secreted away at the rear of a row of expansive, opulent suites belonging to the Rumpart Publishing Company. Her employer specialized in technical and trade journals — cumbersome, expensive, beautifully articulated publications from which the company extracted a worldwide reputation and an enviable cash flow. It was the copyeditor's job to ensure complete accuracy before any journal was published. It was the kind of grueling, painstaking career in which few individuals could survive and only the exceptional minority could excel. The demands for accuracy and speed were often overwhelming; the pressures for deadlines were incessant and intense. Yet, Mary Beth was not only good at what she did, she was superb. In fact, she was the highest paid copyeditor in the history of Rumpart Publishing Company, earning in excess of $65,000 annually when her various bonuses were totaled and added to her salary. However, in order to attain this level of success and reward at her trade, Althazar had made tremendous sacrifices in her life, including the complete absence of friends and companions. The result of this emotionally

Spartan existence was that Salvatore's Restaurant had become the singular focal point of her withered social life.

On this Friday, just after 8:30 in the evening, Mary Beth arrived by a Financial District commuter bus at Salvatore's for dinner. As was her regular habit, she had worked late that night on a crash project that was due in less than a week. Happy with the progress she had made at work, Mary Beth went directly to the restaurant, not bothering to stop by her flat to change from the gray business suit that was her traditional Friday outfit. As she entered the darkened restaurant, she could see that it was crowded with happy, noisy patrons. She was immediately assaulted with the unique, sunny aroma of Giovanni Salvatore's special that night – Petrale Al Fiducci – and instantly decided that she would make it her choice.

For a few moments, Mary Beth stood near the restaurant entrance on South Van Ness Avenue, with her head slightly bowed, unwilling to approach any of the busy waiters for a seat. However, one of them, a young, blonde man in his twenties who had served her before, noticed Mary Beth standing alone by the door and recognized her. He had an open table at the rear of the dining area, near the trade entrance at the back of the restaurant. It was an isolated spot that was unpopular with most patrons because it stood near the worn, chaotic path between the dining area and the noisy kitchen — the single route taken by all the rushing waiters to retrieve meals for their guests. However, he knew Mary Beth's preference for isolation and had often seated her at the same table in the past. The young man ushered her to the table with a smile of recognition and a polite "Good evening, Miss," leaving her with a fat menu to dissect, unaware that she had already made her choice.

In truth, Mary Beth liked this particular table, perhaps for the very reason that other patrons avoided it. Here, there were the constant scurrying, familiar sounds of men and women working feverishly to order, prepare, and retrieve meals. Here, at the small table in the back of the restaurant, she felt a part of her surroundings and, for the time it took to eat her meal, she was not alone.

Mary Beth was in no rush to return home that evening and enjoyed a hearty, leisurely meal at Salvatore's. Her waiter remembered that his guest ordered the special Petrale, including a dinner salad, and finished her meal with two cups of coffee and a slice of cheesecake. It was obvious that she had nowhere special to go and was content with the service, even when her meal was more than a bit slow in coming. According to the waiter, she paid for her dinner with a credit card, slipped a generous cash tip under the water glass, and left the restaurant through the trade entrance at approximately 9:55 that evening.

Salvatore's trade entrance opened onto an unlit, narrow alley behind the restaurant. In turn, the alley connected to Eighteenth Street, very close to its intersection with South Van Ness Avenue. Mary Beth probably decided to use the trade entrance rather than the front door to avoid pushing her way through the crowded dining area to leave the restaurant. The trade entrance was guarded by a heavy, metal fire door with a push arm that released its latch. After the door was opened, it would automatically retract and close securely so there would be no possible reentry from the alley without a key. As Mary Beth left the restaurant through this door, she would have descended two concrete steps to clear the doorway and reach the paved portion of the alley. From there, it would have been a short walk to Eighteenth Street, a well-lit and busy boulevard.

It was at the side of these steps, propped up against the degenerating brickwork next to the trade entrance, that a dishwasher found Mary Beth Althazar's body just before midnight on November 24th.

"Yeah, this is Spell," the Lieutenant grumbled into the telephone on the nightstand. It was 12:25 on Saturday morning and he had just fallen asleep, exhausted and frustrated from another day without leads in the Ruminez and Callohan murders.

"Chris, this is Mary. I'm sorry to wake you up but we have another one," she said excitedly.

"Oh, shit!" he yelped in a hoarse whisper. "When and where?"

"In the alley behind Salvatore's Restaurant, at Eighteenth and South Van Ness. It looks like she's been dead about two or three hours. Chris, her right hand is missing and there's a note stuffed into her left one."

"Christ! Have you seen the note yet?"

"No. I didn't want to disturb it until you got here. The scene is a bloody mess and it's going to be hard not to contaminate it."

"Good, Mary. Good. Listen, have you called Joe or Sam yet?"

"No, you're the first."

"Ok, call Sam right away, then Joe. I want them to get to the scene immediately and have a look before it's disturbed. Has the M.E. made it there yet, or the forensics team?"

"No, just the two patrolmen who responded to the call and me. So far, the scene is pristine."

"Good, great! Try to hold the scene as long as you can. Try to stall the M.E. in case he gets there ahead of me, ok?"

"Sure. I can do that."

"Good, Mary, thanks. I'll be there right away."

Twenty minutes later, Spell arrived at the alley and maneuvered his car so that no other vehicles could approach the crime scene from the Eighteenth Street entrance. He found Mary Boor walking around the body, hopping here and there to avoid pools of blood and frantically writing notes in the three-ring, undersized binder that was her constant companion. Mary must have heard him rushing down the alley toward the trade entrance because she turned quickly to face him.

"Hi, Chris. Jesus, this is an ugly scene..." Inspector Boor pointed at the corpse against the wall with her large right hand and stood back to give him a better view.

Spell nodded at her and began his own inspection of the body. The woman had been propped up against the wall with her legs spread far apart. Generally, the scene was strikingly similar to the Ruminez and Callohan murders. Still, there were noticeable differences. Unlike the other two dumpsites, this scene was a mass of blood. All along the brick wall, across the steps leading to the trade entrance, and scattered around the paved alley, the Lieutenant could see nothing but blood. It was immediately obvious that the victim had been slain in the alleyway, within feet of where her body had been propped against the wall. This was clearly much more than a dumpsite — it was the scene of the murder. Mary Beth's neat, gray suit jacket, along with the white, patterned blouse underneath, had been shredded by the repeated thrusts of a blade. It was obvious that she had received multiple and fatal stab wounds to the chest area.

Spell moved closer to the body, deliberately avoiding her huge, brown eyes, still flung wide open in a grotesque display of panic. He looked carefully around the area of her neck, trying to distinguish any evidence of strangulation that may have been hidden by the thick streaks and splatters of blood. Yes, it was there. This woman had also been strangled, just like the two before her. He immediately let his eyes move farther down her body, searching for her hands, knowing what he would find. Mary Beth's right hand had been cleanly severed and was nowhere in sight. Her purse had been carefully laid against her right forearm. Moving his eyes to her left hand, Spell could see a brown-stained, white piece of paper protruding from between a row of bloody fingers. It had apparently been stuffed into her clenched fist after she died. He could see several lines of block printing on the note, each line comprised of carefully formed characters in blue ink. However, in the darkness of the alley, the words were indecipherable. Worse, the largest portion of the note had been crushed into a small, wet wad by the involuntary death grip of the victim's hand, giving Spell serious concern that it could be extracted without damage.

"Mary, has there been any sign of the press yet?" Chris asked over his shoulder in a worried tone.

"No, but they can't be far away, Chris. The call went out just before midnight, I believe. If they were monitoring, they probably heard it."

As Mary finished her sentence, another unmarked car made its way to the front of the alley and pulled to a stop, punching the bumper of Spell's vehicle from behind and giving it a sharp jolt forward. It was Joe Mendoza. With him, dressed in a white pullover sweater and casual gray slacks, was Sandy Janus. They jumped from the car and trotted down the alleyway toward the murder scene.

"Well, isn't this cozy," Spell said sarcastically to Mendoza as he approached. In return, the Sergeant gave him a sheepish smile and a nod of his head, which answered every question.

"Ok, well, I'm glad you two are here," the Lieutenant conceded. "Listen, Sandy, I want you to make sure those beat cops keep everybody out of this area. I'm afraid the press will be onto this thing any minute and I don't want any information coming out of this scene unless it goes through me, right?"

"Sure, Chris. I'm on it," she said, glad to be away from him for the moment. She raced down the alley and huddled with the two patrolmen who had responded to the initial call. She instructed them to get additional backup and close down this part of Eighteenth Street, making sure that no one – absolutely no one – got near the alleyway, except for the M.E. and the forensics team.

As Sandy finished with the patrolmen, she saw Sam McCannell making his way between the parked cars near the entrance to the alley, struggling in places to squeeze his squat frame between them. With a good deal of effort, he finally worked his way to where she was standing, the usual smile on his face.

"Hey, Sandy. What's going on here?" he puffed.

"There's been another one, Sam. Joe, Chris, and Mary are down there, with the body." She turned to face the trade entrance down the alley and gestured excitedly with her hand. "I want to come along with you, Sam. Is that ok?"

"Yeah, why wouldn't it be?" he replied with a stunned expression.

"Well, Joe and I arrived together and Chris didn't seem too happy about it," she confessed, dropping her head.

The red man laughed and rubbed the upper portion of her left arm with his hand. "Don't worry about it, Sandy. Chris will worry enough for both of you. Listen, kid, let me say something here, ok?"

"Sure," she whispered. "As long as this conversation is between us, right?"

"Right!" he confirmed, wagging his head. "Ok, listen. Joe is an intelligent guy and you're a sharp one yourself. I think you two can decide to do whatever you want to do without anyone else's opinion. The only thing I'd say is, well, just don't rub it in Chris's face. I mean, be discreet. He's got to keep things on track with his crew, so don't give him any reason to worry. When you get to know Chris, you'll find out that he actually leads with his heart. He likes to come off like Mr. I-Am-Tough-As-Shit, but he's really not like that." He finished his advice with another arm rub.

"I appreciate that," she said, too embarrassed to look him in the eyes.

"Ok, good. If you've got things under control here, come on with me and we'll check it out down there," he said, pointing to where the others were standing. She nodded and followed him down the alley.

"Sam, I'm glad you're here," Spell said as he stepped away from the body and stuck out his hand.

"Hi, Chris. I see you've got the whole gang here tonight," McCannell replied, nodding a silent greeting to the others.

Without speaking, the red man moved carefully toward the body, bending at the waist to examine as much of the detail as he could see in the darkness of the alley, watching each step with a caution born of many years at crime scenes. For a few moments, he circled the immediate area, occasionally bobbing his head and pausing from time to time with his eyes closed. When he had finished, McCannell returned to the others, who had grouped themselves several feet away to exchange notes and leave him alone.

"Well, Sam, what do you think?" Spell asked.

"We've got a hell of a problem, Chris. He's changed the game considerably. I mean, this is a very bad crime scene and we'd better rethink what we're going to do with this case."

Lieutenant Spell's face clouded over and became instantly drawn. He had heard Sam say this kind of thing before and he knew what it meant. When Sam used the phrase "very bad," well, he really meant "extraordinarily bad." The Lieutenant took a moment to consider the options, his head down and his hands crossed around the back of his neck. Then, he was ready.

"Listen up, folks, I want everyone out of here right now!" he ordered. "Everyone, that is, except Janus and the black and whites. Sandy, you stay and make sure that the M.E. takes charge of the scene. Then you take statements from anyone inside the restaurant.

Then you leave. If anyone from the press wants to talk to you, tell them that the M.E. already has charge of the scene and they'll have to talk to me for any information.

"Mary, you bag her purse and take it straight to forensics with Joe. I want her identified right away. Joe, you get onto her background, friends, relatives, whatever, as soon as you pull her I.D."

I want everyone out of here in five minutes! The last thing I want is to get into it with the press in this alley with the victim's body here. We'll meet back at my office."

"What about Sam?" Sandy asked, realizing that he wasn't with the group.

Mary leaned over to the shorter woman and nudged her gently on the arm. "Look," she said, pointing down the alleyway. "Sam already knows what he has to do."

Sam McCannell never heard the Lieutenant's orders. He had already started to make his way back down the alley to Eighteenth Street. For McCannell, the Lieutenant's decision had been as predictable as night after day. It had been his only option in a game where the killer continued to hold all the cards.

Still, there *was* the note in the victim's hand and the red man couldn't wait to examine it. That note, he thought, could make all the difference in how the game would be played out.

November 25
Midtown Station
9:40 A.M.

Jane Riordan sat in the hallway outside the ragged private offices that comprised the second floor of the Midtown Station. She waited impatiently, as she had for nearly two hours, endlessly fumbling through the papers on her lap without looking at them. Once again, she glanced at her watch and sighed heavily. Only ten minutes had passed since she last checked. The reporter pushed her lanky body away from the hard wooden bench and walked casually past the glass door marked "Homicide Division," trying to peer as slyly as she could into the inner sanctum.

Beyond the door, on the far side of the wide, dimly lit room lined with rows of cluttered metal desks, she could see the Lieutenant inside his tiny office. Sitting erect behind an ancient wooden desk, she could see him talking rapidly and waving his arms at the others in the room. To one side of his desk was a short, chubby man with red hair, whom she immediately recognized as Dr. McCannell. Next to him, pacing back and forth across the office floor, she saw Joe Mendoza. Unconsciously, a scowl raced across the reporter's face. Mendoza was a pain in the ass. The other two, Spell and McCannell, would at least give her the straight story — when they spoke. But Mendoza was another animal altogether. He hated the press and, particularly, Jane Riordan, who was as tenacious about doing her job as he was about his. Worse, he had a habit of letting his eyes get stuck on her private parts, and that was something she truly hated. Still, she needed Mendoza more than he needed her, so it was the price of the game she played. Jane didn't know the tall woman in the dark clothes standing near the doorway. Somehow, though, she looked familiar. In any event, it was obvious to the reporter that she was a cop.

If only she could hear what they were saying…

"Well, she's out there right now, Sam. I told her I'd give her an exclusive as soon as we had assembled some facts. I promised her something by ten this morning," the Lieutenant said in a plaintive tone.

The red man nodded but said nothing, waiting for the rest of Spell's explanation.

"I think it's better this way. It isn't that I trust Riordan, I don't. But she's usually pretty balanced when she writes this stuff. This way, I can put *some* control into what she's going to say — I hope."

Sam nodded in agreement. "Yeah, that's right, Chris. It's not the best situation, but it's better than letting them all go wild with their reporting. I think she's pretty reasonable, for a reporter. My only concern is that you're giving her first crack at the story. That could get some of the other reporters down your throat pretty hard."

"Yeah, well, they'll all be down my throat anyway, don't you think?"

McCannell just shrugged his shoulders. Spell turned to the others.

"Ok, we need to go around the room on this murder and see what we have. Then we need to make some decisions about what I should give to the press. Joe, have you heard back from Sandy yet?"

"Yeah, by telephone a few minutes ago, Chris. She's at the restaurant. She's still tracking down employees and whoever was in there for dinner last night, along with the neighboring businesses. It's going to be a problem, though. The place was packed and she's having trouble locating people. There was a hell of a lot of folks in there for dinner last night. She could use some help on this, Chris."

"I understand. We'll get her some help when the noon shift comes in. For now, though, she's on her own. What about you, Joe? Got anything on the victim?"

"I've got some preliminary stuff. What I *don't* have is next of kin, though, so you'll probably want to keep her name in your pocket when you talk to the reporter. If the victim's got relatives in the area, I haven't been able to find them yet."

"All right. So, what *do* you have?"

"Her name was Mary Beth Althazar. She was twenty-seven years old and born in Oakland. As far as I can tell, she lived in the City for the past six or seven years, the last four in the Mission District. According to neighbors, she was a real loner and spent her time either at work or in her flat — no social life. No friends, no lovers, no nothing. She worked at a publishing company in the Financial District – a place called Rumpart Publishing – where she was a copyeditor. I'm still trying to track down her coworkers and bosses, so I don't have much on that end of it yet."

"Althazar lived alone on Folsom, near Seventeenth Street. According to Sandy, she was a regular at Salvatore's, eating there at least once a week, sometimes more often. Apparently, her favorite night was Friday. She arrived at the restaurant a little after 8:30 yesterday evening, ate alone at a table near the trade entrance, and left through the back door just before ten. While she was at the restaurant, she talked to no one except the waiter. Sandy told me that she thinks the waiter is clear of any role in this. He was not involved and didn't know much about the victim. I checked our files on this guy, but didn't find anything."

"From what the employees at the restaurant told Sandy, the victim was a real oddball. She always arrived alone, never spoke, and always ate alone. Other than that, Chris, I don't have much on her in the way of background. She doesn't have a record."

"Maybe you'll get some more from her employer or in the neighborhood, right?"

"Yeah, maybe," Mendoza mumbled. Like the others in the room, he looked very tired, very unsure.

"Mary?"

"Well, Chris, I spent the night with the M.E. and the forensics team. Althazar died from stab wounds to the chest. In all, there were eight primary wounds, three of which could have proved lethal. The weapon was probably the same as was used on the others. However, in this case, the wounds were not as tightly clustered as with the other two victims. There were also a number of superficial wounds to the chest area and upper arms. The consensus is that she was moving around – struggling – when she was stabbed."

"After death, she was strangled and her right hand severed. According to the M.E., it was a quick, violent, and as we all saw, a bloody death. The killer was probably covered in blood from the attack and may have left footprints at the scene. The forensics people have some possible imprints. They're working them up now."

"Good, good," Spell interrupted. "Finally, something… maybe."

"Althazar had a note in her right hand. The killer probably wrote it. The note was pretty beaten up and stained but the lab was able to reconstruct it fairly well. I have copies of it here." Mary paused for a moment to hand the photocopies of the note to Spell, Mendoza, and McCannell.

"According to the lab folks, the note was *not* written at the scene. It was apparently prepared earlier, then stuffed into her left hand after she was killed. After the murderer jammed the note into her hand, he crushed her fingers down on it so hard that he broke three of them."

"Shit…" Mendoza yelped as he stared at the photocopy. "This guy's a real fuck!"

"Yeah, Joe, that's how I felt about it, too. It was ugly," Mary whispered.

"Sorry, Mary, go ahead."

She nodded and began again.

"Physically, the victim was somewhat similar to the other two women. She had dark hair, was in her twenties, and was less than average height. However, she was on the heavy side, not petite like the others. The M.E. believes she was killed at about ten, just as she left the restaurant. According to the crime scene, it was a blitz attack with little or no preliminary interaction between the attacker and the victim. The M.E. thinks the whole thing took about ten minutes, including the time needed to quickly stage the body and remove her right hand."

"Now, it was very dark in that alley and there were no windows that opened onto it. I think it's unlikely we'll find any witnesses. Even if someone was passing by the alley entrance, walking down Eighteenth Street, and happened to glance down the alley, there wouldn't be much to see. Unless she yelled out or attracted attention in some other way, there won't be any witnesses. And, even if she screamed, no one inside the restaurant would have heard her — too much ambient noise in there."

Spell again nodded his head from side to side, obviously frustrated. "Jesus! We don't have much, do we? This is getting real old. Mar, do you think forensics will come up with anything useful?"

"Actually, I'm optimistic, Chris. Since the crime scene was more chaotic than the last two, there may be something there – fibers, hairs, shoe imprints, something – but no sexual component. I think this guy wears gloves and takes other precautions, so I wouldn't expect anything definitive. However, this was a quick, brutal, maybe even unplanned attack. He could have left some traces behind. We'll know soon."

"Good, Mar. You'll keep on it, I know."

"You bet," she replied, struggling to send the Lieutenant some kind of a smile.

Spell swiveled in his chair to face the red man. "So, what about the note, Sam?"

McCannell had seen the original note two hours earlier in the medical examiner's office. Since then, he had thought of little else. Now, he was looking at the photocopy that Mary had just distributed. On a heavily bloodstained, wrinkled piece of white paper, approximately six inches square, the murderer had written these words in block printing with blue ink:

FOR DOCTOR SAM MCCANNELL

THE GREAT DOCTOR WHO KNOWS THE MIND
THEY ALL LOVE ME IN THE LAST MOMENT DON'T THEY?
THEY ALL SECRETLY LOVE ME AND WANT TO LOVE ME
BUT I WILL NOT JUST LOVE THEM
I WILL GIVE THEM THE FINAL LOVE
THEY LOVE ME
LOVE ME
THEY LOVE ME

MONSTER

McCannell moved to the couch and flopped heavily into its worn folds, letting out a deep grunt as he did. He closed his eyes and rolled his head from side to side, trying to work the stiffness from the back of his neck.

"Sam, you all right?" Chris asked in a concerned tone.

"Yeah, sure. Just tired, like the rest of you," he answered without opening his eyes. "Ok," McCannell began, "here's what we've got. This guy has been reading about himself. He's been following the case. He's probably been reading *that* woman's articles in the Call," he said, waving his arm in the direction of Jane Riordan, who was still waiting in the hallway. "Now, he's really gotten into the rhythm of his obsession. He's on a roll. Let's start with the note, right?"

"Right, Sam. That's best," Chris confirmed.

"So, he constructed the note very carefully sometime before the murder. He wants it to be a personal note, but he doesn't want us to identify him because of anything *in* the note. So, he used an odd sized scrap of paper, block lettering, and a heavy pen. The construction of the letters is very meticulous and he avoided using any punctuation except for a question mark. That way, he didn't leave much for us in the way of style. In other words, he thought long and hard about his message. He was very careful in constructing it. I know the forensics folks are looking at this note right now, but I'm willing to bet they won't find much. This guy has special knowledge — he knows how to avoid leaving anything behind. That's an important point to remember. He knows how we operate, at least well enough to avoid making stupid mistakes. Mary thinks this guy takes precautions, like wearing gloves. I couldn't agree more. That's exactly what he does."

"Here's another point. The note doesn't refer to *this* particular victim. It doesn't specifically refer to Mary Beth Althazar. It refers to any and all victims. In other words, the note *preceded* the victim and it was more important to the killer than the victim. That means he prepared the note in advance and then went out to kill. He killed to fulfill the message. In other words, it isn't about the woman he killed."

"Sam, that note was directed specifically to you. What's that about?" Chris interrupted.

"I'll get to that, Chris. Now, picture this. The guy prepares a personal note, as you say, a note to me. The note refers to a non-specific victim. He then goes out and murders Althazar and leaves the note behind. But he doesn't just leave it *anywhere* at the scene. He jams it into her fist so hard that he breaks her fingers. So, we have the handwritten note *as well as* another message. To my way of thinking, the note has two parts: the words he wrote and the message he sent. It was almost as if he wanted us to believe that the message was from *both* of them — from both him *and* his victim. Get it? There's a pathological identification process going on here."

"Are you saying that he wanted us to believe that the message came from Althazar?" Mendoza asked.

"No, not exactly. He wants us to believe that his victims feel the same way he does. Read the note carefully, Joe. In his twisted way of seeing the world, he believes that his victims really love him. They join with him at the moment of their death in what he perceives to be an act of reciprocal love or even mutual orgasm. That's the sexual component of the crime. It's a hidden, perverse, sexual component that the murderer only alludes to. He wants us to know that his victims die because of their love for him, but that he, in return, doesn't *need* to love them. He just *needs* to kill them. Why? He *hates* them."

"I'm not sure I'm following any of this," Mendoza grumbled.

"Ok, I know it's twisted. Look at it this way: this guy is murdering women because he views it as an act of love *and* an act of retribution. In his mind, he's not committing murder… he's helping these women to finalize their hidden love for him by *being* murdered. At the same time, he's exacting justice for some wrong that he's suffered, probably at the hands of a woman. To complete the fantasy, he needs to tell us about it. He *needs* for us to know that his victims saw it the same way. That's one of the ways he tries to justify murder in his own mind."

Mendoza nodded his head but said nothing. He was beginning to understand.

"I see where you're heading with this, Sam," Mary said from across the office. "It makes sense, in a way."

"Well, this guy is severely whacked, for sure," the red man continued. "Notice how he signs the note? He refers to himself as a monster. He wasn't very careful with that line. It's the only line that uses both upper and lower case, and he uses an impersonal term when he refers to himself. In reality, he hates what he's doing and he hates himself. He views himself as a monster and he's trying to blame his victims for his own pathology, as well as their own deaths. At the same time, he loves reading about himself, loves the power over life and death, and detests his victims. That's why he mutilates their bodies and strangles them. For him, love, power, sadism, murder, and control are all mixed up."

"The reason he directed the message to me was probably because of Jane Riordan's articles in the Call. Chris, when you talked to the press, you told them that I was working on a profile of this freak. No doubt, that got his attention in a big way. It may have even worried him. Now, he's trying to build a profile of his own — one that he wants me to accept and believe. He's trying to interject himself into the investigation and direct it, just like I warned you he might. So, what he's writing about himself is what he wants us to believe, not necessarily what he is. Understand?"

Chris nodded from behind the table.

"This guy wants to be known, wants attention; but, consciously at least, he doesn't want to be caught. He *wants* to be profiled, but not too accurately. He also wants us to know *why* he's murdering these women, but not the whole truth, which he probably doesn't know or understand himself. This guy is a mass of contradictions — a circus of mixed-up and confused motives, which he probably hasn't even begun to acknowledge or understand. What he understands about himself is only superficial. So, the bottom line is this: he can only tell us what he *thinks* he knows about himself, which isn't much — and, for sure, he'll lie about that."

"Christ, Sam, that doesn't leave much, does it?" Chris asked in a worried tone.

"Well, yes and no. For one thing, I think this guy is not as much of a stalker as a cruiser. Think about this last murder. This was a risky operation. There was no way he could have planned to attack Althazar in the alley, even if he had already targeted her. I mean, her leaving the restaurant by the trade entrance – a rarity, according to the manager, for any patron at the restaurant – was as much a matter of luck as anything else. Yet, he already had the note ready. He knew that he was going to kill that night, but he probably didn't know it would be Althazar. I don't think she was as carefully selected as Ruminez. She may have been more a target of opportunity. In fact, Callohan may also have been the same — a target of opportunity. That's why I told you we have to rethink our strategy. This murder tells us a good deal more about our man. He's changing as he goes and that's going to make things extraordinarily difficult for us."

"Sure, he prefers a certain kind of victim — a certain look. That probably has a lot to do with the woman he blames for his failed life, whoever she may be. I think he may have been very careful in choosing Ruminez as his first victim. In fact, she might be a key to this thing. She was probably stalked and carefully selected. After that though, well, these last two victims, I think, were targets of opportunity. Yes, they fit the physical bill, and yes, he probably had some knowledge about them, but I think his murders are becoming more spontaneous and more symbolic, just like his use of doorways.

"Now, I don't mean to imply that he hadn't already picked

Althazar out in some way. He may have. He may have seen her on the street or known her indirectly in some way. It's just that this attack was far more spontaneous than the other two. In this murder, he took a huge chance. He struggled with the victim and attacked her in an alleyway rather than killing her somewhere private and dumping her body. What if she had survived the attack or managed to get help? He didn't bother to abduct her or take her anywhere else; he didn't take the time to make sure that he was safe. He just murdered her right there. That was a hell of a risk. And, since he was willing to take that kind of risk, I think this guy is looking to make the papers."

"Shit!" Chris interrupted. "I was afraid you were going to say that."

"Well, Chris, you already figured that out, didn't you? I mean, as soon as you saw the crime scene, you knew this guy had moved up to the next level."

"Yeah," the Lieutenant conceded, his face now buried in his hands.

"So, we've got a whacko who wants to see his handiwork all over the place... but isn't ready to give us enough to nail him. That tells me our guy is bright... and he's skilled in the same kinds of things as we are. He's very determined, and he's extremely fucked-up. That's why I don't think this message tells us much about the real personality of the murderer. I think he'll have a lot more to say about who he *really* is. And, when he decides to say it, I think he'll want to make sure that I'm on the receiving end."

"Sam, why is he hacking off their hands?" Mary asked from across the office.

"Well, remember what I said... he believes he has suffered something terrible at the hands of a woman. What if you took that literally?"

With that, McCannell closed his eyes again and laid his head back on the couch. He looked exhausted. For a moment, the room was silent, each of the team working against their exhaustion to consider the possibilities.

"Sam, are you ok about being pen pals with this guy?" Chris asked in a low, worried voice.

"Oh, sure. Shit. I wouldn't have it any other way. Honestly? It's what I live for," McCannell announced with a dry smile.

"Sam, I've been thinking about possible connections among these victims," Mary said. "What if the link here is something other than the victims themselves? For example, what if the link is *where* they were murdered. I mean, each victim was connected with a public place — two restaurants and a bar. What if those locations tie the crimes together rather than the victims' physical characteristics? Does that make sense?"

McCannell moved away from the couch and began pacing rapidly across the floor, his eyes closed and his face contorted in that familiar, far away expression. Suddenly, he whirled around to face her, a huge smile on his face. "Absolutely, Mary. Absolutely! That's a great possibility! There's no reason to assume that the victims are the *only* link. There could just as well be a secondary link in the chain. Great possibility!"

"It is, Mary," Spell affirmed, now standing behind his desk. "I think it *is* a possibility. What do you need to follow it along?"

"Well, Chris, some legwork. Maybe Joe and Sandy?"

"Count me in," Mendoza snapped. "We'd be happy to help with that. Makes good sense to me."

"Good, Joe. Thanks," Spell said. "You two work out the details and see if there's some connection, right?"

"Right, we'll get on it," Mary said with obvious excitement in her voice. Mendoza showed the beginnings of a rare smile, clearly intrigued with the possibilities.

"Ok, in the meantime, I need to deal with the press. So, what do I give our reporter friend out there?" the Lieutenant asked. "Do I tell her we've got a certifiable whacko serial killer cruising the District?"

"As far as I'm concerned, you do just that, Chris," Sam immediately replied. "We don't have any solid leads on the first two murders and I'm willing to bet you won't get too much on this one, despite the forensics possibilities. This guy is very, very good. The only way you're going to play catch up is to increase the number of good guys who are out there looking for him. You need help from the public. Someone out there has seen this guy. Someone knows him. I say, make it hot for him. Force his moves. It may cause him to escalate his murders, but I think he'll kill again anyway. He's ahead of us right now, and we need to even things up a bit... even though that's a risky strategy."

"Well, I don't agree!" Mendoza screeched from near the office doorway. "Christ! If we go full out to the press on this, everyone in the District will be in a panic and the media will shit all over us. I don't think that's a good idea, Chris."

Sam slid back to the edge of the couch to get a better view of Mendoza. "I hear what you're saying, Joe, but consider one thing: What makes you think this guy is going to stop, or even slow down? This sick fuck thinks he's running the world right now. And from our point of view, he might as well be doing just that. If we don't give him some reason to squirm, who will?"

Joe was quick to respond. "Ok, Sam, let's say we do that. Let's say we squeeze him, and ourselves in the process. What makes you think he won't just go underground? What stops him from just disappearing so that we'll never flush him out?"

"Because, Joe, he *needs* to kill and he *needs* to let us know about it. It's all in the note. He won't stop murdering and he won't hide. What I'm hoping is that he'll be more interested in communicating his exploits then doing them. After all, it's a hell of a lot safer that way, isn't it?"

Mendoza nodded but didn't look convinced. He stared at his boss and shrugged his shoulders, unwilling to argue the point any further.

"Mary, what do you think?" Chris asked.

"I guess I agree with Sam. It's a hell of a risk and we're going to take a load of shit, but I can't think of a better way. I trust Sam's instincts on this one. Let's make this freak think we have more than we really do. If he wants to play with us, let's play a little harder and try to draw him out."

The Lieutenant turned to face McCannell, now perched on the arm of the couch. "Sam, are you willing to meet the press with me on this one? Are you willing to take the ride and get raped by these vultures? If you are, you might as well go ahead and give them your best profile. Lay it all out there. Are you willing to do that?"

"Hell, sure. Why not, Chris? After all, I've got a pen pal and you don't, right?"

Chris roared. So did Boor and Mendoza. There wasn't much to laugh about in this case, but somehow, Sam was always good at turning their heads when they least expected it.

"Listen, boss," Mendoza interrupted, "what about the Captain? If you go to the press, he'll come down on you hard, right?"

"Fuck him!" the Lieutenant shouted. "Just fuck him! He's going to stick us with this anyway. I don't give a fuck about the politics of the case. I just want this whacko under the screws."

The room fell instantly silent. Spell was leaning far over his desk, his arms shaking, his face more flushed and twisted with anger than anyone in the room could recall. It was obvious that the Lieutenant was not kidding about this case. For whatever reason, he was hell-bent on nailing this guy and wasn't about to have anyone stand in his way.

"Chris, we're with you on this, you know," Sam said, barely above a whisper. "You're not out there alone on this one, right?"

"Right," Spell mumbled as he sat back down. "Listen, I'm sorry about that. I guess I'm just tired."

"Chris, let me buy you breakfast when you're done with the reporter, ok?" Mary offered softly.

"No, thanks, Mary. I just need to go home and get some rest. Listen, Mary, Joe, why don't you two take off and get a few hours sleep. Joe, you'd better get Sandy off the streets. She must be exhausted by now. We can all meet back here later. I'll hang around for a while and get some of the noon shift folks to help us out with the legwork."

Mendoza and Boor nodded and headed for the door, leaving Spell at his desk and McCannell still on the arm of the couch. For a few moments, neither man spoke.

"Sam, we have a guest waiting out there. Would you like to show her in or should I do it?" the Lieutenant finally asked.

"Oh, well, let me do it. I've always loved taller women — and that's most all of them," he quipped with a huge smile. "And, Chris… better straighten your tie. You look like hell," he said as he moved toward the door.

November 26
The City
Sunday Morning
Midtown Station

Chris Spell stared at the framed photograph of Richard Nixon, prominently hung behind Captain Marley's ostentatious desk on the first floor of the Station. He tried to remember the year Nixon resigned. Was it 1970, 1972? He couldn't remember. He didn't care. What a stupid thing to have hanging on your wall anyway — the face of the only president to resign the job in disgrace. And when was that? Twenty, thirty years? Whatever.

Think of something else. Think of anything else. Don't listen to Marley! Don't rise to the bait!

"Goddamnit! Are you listening to me, Lieutenant?" Marley screamed. Standing behind his desk, nearly blocking Spell's view of Nixon, the Captain looked like he was about to explode. His fleshy face and sagging jowls were beet red and covered in sweat; his eyes looked like tiny blue pinholes that had been angrily punched into the grotesque skin of a Mr. Potato-Head.

"Yes," Spell mumbled, still staring at Nixon, not really listening. "I'm listening."

"Well, shit! You'd better be! I don't know what the fuck you and that idiot shrink thought you were doing. Jesus! Look at this!"

A pudgy hand swept across the Captain's desk with surprising speed, scooped up a page from the San Francisco *Call*, and deposited it in front of the Lieutenant.

A Monster in the Mission?
By Jane Riordan, *Call* Staff Writer

Sunday Edition Exclusive — Crime Watch
November 26, San Francisco:

The question on the minds of SFPD Homicide detectives is a simple one. Who is murdering women in the Mission District?

On Friday, the body of a third murdered woman was found in an alleyway behind Salvatore's restaurant at Eighteenth Street and South Van Ness Avenue. Like the two women before her, the latest victim had been stabbed to death and strangled. The SFPD has yet to release her name, pending notification of next of kin.

Police have also asked that further details of the murder be withheld until the Medical Examiner and SFPD forensics specialists have finished their preliminary investigation.

Lieutenant Christopher Spell is heading the team trying to track down the serial killer, who is prowling the District. According to Spell, the Homicide Division has not identified a specific suspect at this time. However, when asked if he thought that the three murders were committed by the same individual, he said, "Yes, I believe we are dealing with the same individual in all three cases. There is a discernable pattern to these murders and the crime scenes."

Working with Spell on the case is Dr. Samuel McCannell, Forensic Psychologist for the SFPD. Spell and McCannell agreed to an exclusive interview about the status of the investigation, including Dr. McCannell's interpretation of these crimes and the murderer.

According to McCannell, who specializes in profiling unknown perpetrators of violent crimes, the murderer left certain clues behind, which could prove crucial to the investigation. McCannell believes that the killer is a male, twenty-five to forty-five years old, who is very familiar with the Mission District and may live in the immediate area. Both Spell and McCannell confirmed that the murderer specifically targets women who share similar physical characteristics. All three of the victims were between twenty and thirty years old, had dark hair, and were less than average height. All three were residents of the Mission District. However, homicide detectives have not found any direct connection among the slain women.

When McCannell was asked why these murders were taking place, he said, "No one knows, for sure, but the murderer himself. He is trying to tell us why by his actions and in other ways. But, in the end, only he knows. I'm convinced that this man has a deep, pathological hatred for his victims. He communicates with women through fear, domination, control, and manipulation. This guy may not know why he murders. Neither do we — yet."

When asked why the Homicide Division agreed to discuss these murders at such an early phase in the investigation, Lieutenant Spell was forthright. "We need all the help we can get on these three cases. Someone in the Mission District knows the murderer; someone has seen him. The more eyes and ears we have on the street, the more difficult it is for this guy to prey on innocent women."

According to McCannell, the serial killer may stalk his victims or he may choose them randomly. In any event, he favors victims with certain physical characteristics. In two cases, the killer abducted his victims from a public street, murdered them, and dumped their bodies in public view. In Friday's murder, he brutally attacked and murdered his victim in a secluded alleyway behind a restaurant. According to McCannell, the killer may have become careless in claiming his latest victim. However, neither McCannell nor Spell were willing to say why they believed this, except to affirm that they were now in possession of new evidence in the case.

When asked if homicide detectives had any witnesses to the crimes or a physical description of the suspect, Spell was hesitant to comment. "To maintain the integrity of the investigation and the safety of any witnesses, I can't give you any information on that. We are not ready to distribute an artist's rendition of any suspect at this point. However, Dr. McCannell's profile of the suspect does include certain physical characteristics. For example, we know that this individual is of medium height or more and that he is physically very powerful. Also, our forensics unit has some evidence that will aid in more precisely identifying a suspect."

Dr. McCannell confirmed that the murderer has communicated directly with him but refused to comment further. "This man has opened up a line of communication," McCannell said. "That sometimes happens in cases like these. He has decided that he wants us to know more about why he is murdering women. We'll have to see where it leads, but it's important for him to know that I did receive his message and that I took it seriously."

Spell emphasized that unaccompanied women in the Mission District should take reasonable precautions to protect themselves. So far, the murderer has attacked his victims on a Friday or Saturday night, after dark. In each case, the victim was alone at the time of the attack.

When asked if he thought the murderer would strike again, Dr. McCannell said, "I certainly hope not. After all, he's made his point. Now, I'm hopeful that he will tell us more about why he has committed these monstrous crimes. Hopefully, with a greater public awareness of this man's activities, he will be persuaded to stop the killing. Maybe he will rethink the horrible thing that made him kill in the first place."

Lieutenant Spell also had an opinion on the future of this serial killer. "We're not about to look the other way while this guy threatens our citizens. We're going to throw everything we have at this guy — every resource we can muster. There is no one on the Department who is willing to let this monster stay loose in our District. You can bet we will nail this guy."

Readers of the San Francisco *Call* are urged to call the Midtown Station Homicide Division tip line at 555-3534 with any information they may have.

"So, Lieutenant, what *are* you going to do about this!" Marley screamed.

Spell sat back in his chair and slid the newspaper article back onto the Captain's desk. He took another long look at Nixon, then back down at Marley, noticing the similarities in the jowls. "Well, Captain, I need some manpower on this case and I need it right away. If I don't get it, well…"

The Lieutenant let his gaze float easily back to the portrait on the wall, making sure that the fat man in front of him saw the connection. Marley sat down heavily, straining the leather chair and making it squeal. He stared intently at Spell, trying to assess the real meaning of his last sentence. "Chris, seriously now, how bad is this situation? Is it as bad as you made it out to that reporter?"

The Captain's tone was more conciliatory, perhaps a bit fearful. The Lieutenant had made his point. Still, he wanted to make sure.

"Worse," Spell replied, still looking beyond Marley. "Much worse…" He deliberately let his voice trail off into the distance, his face gnarled with worry and concern.

The Captain thrust his plump hands to his face, each covering a fatty cheek, and closed his eyes. He looked like he was about to cry – or shit his pants. "How much help did you say you needed, Chris?"

The Lieutenant didn't answer right away. That would have been too obvious. Instead, he continued to study the portrait of Richard Nixon, wondering if that wasn't a hint of a smile across his otherwise somber lips? Was he smiling?

Now, when was it that he resigned?

Bernal Heights

Herbert Jamieson slipped the two latch bolts to the left and removed the lock chain, letting it dangle and rattle against the inside of his battered front door. He slowly swung the door open, just enough to see the warped, wooden landing beyond.

Yes! It was there.

Like the tongue of a huge snake, his thick arm shot out from behind the door and snagged the newspaper, dragging it inside, and slamming the door behind.

His eyes raced across the front page, looking for something familiar. There, at the bottom of the page, in a single column, was Jane Riordan's exclusive interview with Spell and McCannell. Jamieson raced down the narrow hall to the back of his flat, past the abandoned sitting room whose floor was cluttered with unwashed clothes and scattered papers, past the pink, tiled bathroom that hadn't been cleaned in a year, and into the kitchen. He threw himself into the stiff wooden chair and laid the paper out in front of him on the table. Carefully, he read — and read again.

"…a male, twenty-five to forty-five years old…"

"…very familiar with the Mission District…"

"…may live in the area…"

"…our forensics unit has some evidence…"

"…*why* he has done these monstrous crimes."

"…we will nail this guy."

Jamieson bellowed and pounded his fists onto the kitchen table, directly onto the face of the article, rattling all of the stacked dishes and cups onto the floor and shattering several of them. Suddenly, his arms went rigid and excruciating bands of pain crossed his chest and forehead. He closed his eyes and tried to move, but he could not.

He was frozen to the chair, breathless, in terrible pain, moving away from his own body to another place.

"Marion, you are married to Herbert William Jamieson, correct?" her attorney asked.

"Yes."

"How long have you been married?"

"A little over four years."

"And you are now legally separated from Mr. Jamieson, correct?"

"Yes, since about three months ago."

"Ok. Mrs. Jamieson, at the time of your separation from Mr. Jamieson, did you not also seek and obtain a Restraining Order against your husband?"

"Yes."

"Why did you feel it necessary to seek and obtain a Restraining Order?"

"Objection, Your Honor… relevancy," interjected the woman at the Defendant's table. Her voice was unimpassioned and routine.

"Obviously…" snapped the judge, waving her right hand in a dismissive way. "Overruled."

Her attorney moved closer to the Plaintiff, to within a few feet, as if to stand next to her, and turned to squarely face the Defendant.

"Please, Mrs. Jamieson, tell the judge why you felt it was necessary to seek and obtain a Restraining Order against your husband?"

The woman in the witness box dropped her head and began to shake noticeably. Her right hand rose from her lap, found a tear at the corner of her right eye, and quickly wiped it away.

"I was afraid… I was afraid he would kill me."

Jamieson was back. He felt a thick, sticky sheet of sweat across his neck and chest. His head pounded without mercy. In front of him on the table was Riordan's article. As was his way – according to the ritual – he placed the article in his scrapbook, carefully aligning it behind the other two, making absolutely sure that everything was how it must be.

He moved unsteadily to the front room of his flat, to the edge of the tall, narrow window that faced Courtland Avenue. Slowly, he inched the heavy purple curtain away from the glass, just far enough to provide a slit-like view of the street below. At the curb, directly beyond the stairs that rose from the sidewalk to the front door, Jamieson confirmed that his car was still safe, still where he had hurriedly parked it. It was a maroon, 1988 Ford sedan, adorned with a stubby antenna protruding from the center of the roof. On the far right end of the rear bumper, another antenna was mounted. This was a long, whip-like affair, which rose to a height of three feet above the roof of the vehicle. On the driver's side, mounted just above the outside rear view mirror, a halogen lamp with a shiny handle was in easy reach. To anyone who failed to look closely, to anyone who was unaccustomed to detail, this looked like an official vehicle. It looked strikingly similar to the official vehicle that was once his to drive.

Jamieson let the curtain slide back against the window frame, returning the room to its usual darkness. There was still much to do this morning.

Parkside District

Mendoza dialed the Lieutenant's office telephone and smiled when it was answered by his taped voice asking for a message and a number. This was going to be a good day!

"Chris, this is Joe. It's just after 9:30 on Sunday morning and I'm at my house. I tried to reach you at home but I guess you're back at the station. Listen, I was able to contact Maria Althazar, Mary Beth's older sister, who lives in Fremont. Maria is her only living relative. Their parents died several years ago in an automobile accident."

"Anyway, I informed Maria of her sister's death, so it's all right to release Mary Beth's name to the press. I've also arranged to interview her on Monday over at the Fremont Police Department."

"That's all I have for now, Chris. I'll be off for the rest of the day and I've told Sandy to take it off too. We'll both catch you in the office early in the morning. Take care."

Mendoza set the receiver back on the hook and rolled noiselessly onto his left side. He reached his arms around her, gently feeling her breast with his right hand, and adoring her taut thigh. He pressed his body hard against her back, letting her feel his growing passion.

"Sandy," he whispered, "I know you're awake. I know you heard what I just told Chris..." he whispered in a singsong, childish tone.

She smiled at the wall in the darkened room and tried to breathe as quietly as she could, waiting for him to move just a bit closer, pretending to have heard nothing, wanting to play the game for a while longer — happy that he had lied to Chris.

Bayview District

Mary Boor considered herself one of the lucky ones. She owned her own home in a city that had run rampant with citizens who struggled to pay ungodly rents to faceless, uncaring landlords each month. It was a modest home by San Francisco standards, but it was hers and hers alone. Even better, it was perched on a hill that overlooked the fabulous San Francisco Bay and, on a clear day, afforded a spectacular view of the East Bay hills across the water. Tiny and unassuming as it was, Boor's home was her pride and joy. It was her singular evidence of financial accomplishment in a career whose rewards, both financial and emotional, were unusually sparse.

This morning, she sat in her living room, on her couch, and let her eyes follow the wisps of fog that slithered across the tops of the wharves along the western shore of the bay. She could sense it would be another unusually clear and warm day. This morning the fog was not a thick, deep gray, as it so often was in the Bayview District. Today, it would soon burn off and leave behind a brightness that would warm her home and lift her spirits.

Mary opened the pliable brown cover on her field notebook and searched for a fresh page. When she awoke that morning, the detective could think of nothing but her unknown suspect and his victims. In fact, she'd thought of nothing else since arriving at the Midtown Station to join the Lieutenant's task force. Now, she had a theory. She had a hunch. It was time to organize her thoughts — time to map out a strategy.

Quickly, in a racing, hurried hand, she made her notes.

> *Ruminez, Callohan, Althazar. Location may be the link.*
>
> *Sites located on or near corners. Each was a gathering place — restaurants, bar.*
>
> *Presumably no suspects among patrons, at least not yet.*
>
> *What about tradesmen? What about suppliers? Is there a common link here?*

Check this!

Boor slapped the cover of her notebook against its pages and stood to face the view beyond the wide, curved windows in her living room. The air in the room was still sharp and cool, not yet ready to give way to the warmth that had already won its victory against the dying fog on the bay. She wrapped her beige, terrycloth robe tighter around her thin frame and reached for the telephone at the end of the couch. She dialed. It rang four times.

"Yeah," Mendoza grumbled across the line, sounding out of breath and annoyed.

"Joe, this is Mary... Did I wake you?"

"No."

"Did I interrupt something?"

There was silence.

"Listen, Joe, I'm sorry, maybe I should call back later."

"No, Mary, no. It's ok. I should be up and around by now anyway," he said apologetically. He glanced at the clock on the nightstand. It was 9:55 in the morning. Beside him, Sandy rolled herself into a tight ball and faced the far wall.

"Joe, I think we need to work the three locations where the victims were last seen. I think we need to get on this. Maybe there's a connection here and I don't want it to go cold."

"What kind of connection?" he asked, stifling back a yawn and sitting upright on the edge of the bed.

"Well, suppose our guy is a tradesman or someone who provides supplies or services to these places. What if the three businesses shared this guy in some way? We haven't checked that out, right?"

"Not that I know of. But don't you think this could wait until tomorrow? Let's get some rest," Mendoza said with an edge to his voice.

For a moment, the line was silent.

"No," she replied in a curt tone. There was no room for compromise in her voice.

"Ok, Mary, where and when?"

"Let's meet at the Station in an hour, all right?"

"Ok," he grumbled. He moved the handset away from his ear and aimed it in the general direction of the nightstand. As he did, he heard Mary's voice on the line.

"What?" he asked sharply, quickly replacing the handset to his ear.

"I said, please bring Sandy with you, Joe. We need her help."

Before he could reply, the line went dead.

"Jesus!" he grumbled. "Fuck Sundays!"

Christmas Eve
Mary Boor's Residence
11:30 P.M.

Chris Spell drained the last two inches of Valpolicella from the ornate, black bottle on the coffee table and slouched back into the folds of Mary's decidedly corpulent couch. He grabbed the slender glass by the stem and depleted most of what remained in a single gulp. Beyond and below Mary's living room window, he could see the muted flickering of streetlights along the western shoreline, but nothing beyond. Tonight, the fog was thick, steady, and still, hanging oppressively over the bay and slithering inexorably up the hillside toward her living room window.

Inside, the high-ceiling room had been carefully tidied, but was unadorned for the Christmas season. There was no brightly lit tree, no fragrant wreaths, no indication of the meaning of the holiday. In the background, there was no hint of the impending, joyous celebration that had obviously brightened the rest of the neighborhood. There was only the warbling, complex rhythm of a Rossini opera – *An Italian Girl in Algiers* – to banish the silence.

To Chris Spell and his old friend, Mary, it didn't seem like the Christmas season. It didn't seem like anything at all.

"Chris, how long has it been since you saw Leslie or your daughter?" Mary asked in a whispered, gravely voice. Although she was sitting at the end of the same couch, only a few feet away, she seemed so distant, so removed in her tone. She was struggling to find something pleasant they could share — something other than murder.

"Oh, I don't know…" he mused. "I guess I saw Annie a few months ago when she came through the city on a one-day conference. It could have been around Father's Day. I think she was feeling a little guilty and stopped by my house one night. I really don't remember when. Leslie, well, I guess it's been two, maybe three years. I really don't remember that either, Mar."

She nodded. "Lonely?" she asked.

"Yeah. Well, sometimes, yeah... sometimes no. I guess more yeah than no, though. The nights can get bad, sometimes." Like Mary, his voice was low and hoarse, and he was exhausted, and a little drunk.

"What about you, Mar?"

"Rarely lonely, but it *does* happen. I never wanted to get married and have a family anyway, so I guess you just can't miss what you don't know about, right?"

"Right, I guess not."

Off to the east, somewhere on the shrouded shoreline, the wail of a foghorn knifed through the night. For a moment, they both listened. For a long moment, there was nothing more to say.

"Mar, this case is fucked. It's as cold as a case can be, isn't it?" he finally announced, fumbling to change the subject and working himself back to something safe to share.

"Well, pretty much, Chris. None of the location leads worked out, despite all the help Marley threw our way. I really thought there was a connection in the locations, or the tradesmen, or something like that. I felt good about that. But... nothing. Forensics gave us those shoe imprints at the Althazar murder scene, but they didn't help. Hell, we already assumed our guy was on the large side. Beyond that, the lab was pretty much useless and we went tits up on witnesses. Yeah, I guess that all adds up to a cold case alright."

"Yeah. I thought the tradesman thing was a good idea, too. Are you *sure* there's nothing with that? Anything you could have missed?"

"I'm pretty sure I covered it all. As I said, we had enough help.

We've checked everything out. I don't think there's anything left there to find. The tip line was for shit, too. We logged hundreds of calls, but nothing came of any of them."

She shuffled around on the couch and reached for the Valpolicella. The bottle was empty. Without speaking, Mary padded in bare feet to the maple armoire near the hallway. From behind an unmatched collection of carelessly stacked, chipped dinner plates, she withdrew a fresh bottle and headed back to the couch.

Mary handed the bottle to Chris, along with a wood handled corkscrew and a huge smile. He jammed the bottle between his thighs, gave the corkscrew a few quick turns, and roughhoused the cork from its resting place. She let out a light giggle and stretched her glass in his direction.

"We're getting pretty fucked up here, aren't we?" she asked, smiling at him over the glass.

"Yeah. Just like this case," he grumbled, not smiling.

Inside the room there was silence once again; outside, the foghorn wailed at the unseen bay.

"Listen, Chris, I may have something here." Mary moved to the middle of the couch and leaned close to him, as if to share a long hidden secret. She reached toward the low coffee table and retrieved her notebook. Squinting in the darkness for something familiar, she fumbled noisily through several pages, humming a portion of a Rossini aria to herself.

"Oh, yeah, here it is," she announced, her fingers caressing a certain page. "This is weird... but I don't know if it means anything."

"What?"

"Well, about a month before Alvina Ruminez was murdered, this guy came into the Munoz Grill to talk to the owner, Arnoldo Munoz. He claimed that he was attached to the Presidio Army CID and produced some kind of identification to support the claim.

According to the owner, this guy then showed him an artist's rendition – a black and white sketch – of a young woman. He told Arnoldo that she was an AWOL officer from the Presidio. He asked if the owner had seen a woman fitting the description.

"Munoz told him that he had a waitress who fit that description, but that she couldn't be the same one he wanted. The guy insisted on meeting her, so Arnoldo called Ruminez to the back, to his private office. The alleged Army CID guy never spoke to Ruminez, other than to say hello, but he did take a long, careful look at her. Then, he abruptly thanked them both and left the Grill.

"The guy never came back to the restaurant, didn't leave a card, and Munoz can't remember his name. He couldn't even give me a description other than to say that he was a big guy with a full head of hair, which wasn't gray, but may have been blonde. Munoz didn't notice if the guy left on foot or in a vehicle."

"Well, it's odd enough, Mar, but what makes you think there's a connection?"

"Because the same kind of thing happened with the Callohan murder at Dougall's Bar. A few weeks before Callohan was killed, someone came into the bar and asked Sam Dougall some questions… said he was an insurance investigator looking for the missing beneficiary of a policy. He produced a black and white sketch, filled in some details verbally, and asked Dougall if he knew the woman. Dougall told the guy that the sketch looked like Callohan and gave him her name. When the guy wanted to know where he could find the woman, Dougall told him to check out the boulevard or just wait around the bar… said she would be in, eventually. According to Sam Dougall, the guy got huffy and left, never to be seen again."

"The next night, when Callohan came into the bar, Sam mentioned the guy to her but she didn't seem to know what he was talking about. Like Munoz, Dougall couldn't remember much about the guy except that he was big and was wearing a nice suit."

Mary slumped back on the couch and laid the notebook on her lap. "I don't know, Chris. It just bothers me, and I don't know why. Coincidence? I don't know." She sounded tired and frustrated.

Chris closed his eyes and sniffed hard at the glass in his hand. It was a strange coincidence and the Lieutenant didn't believe in such things.

"What about Salvatore's? Did the same thing happen there?" he asked.

"No," she replied in a dejected voice. "That's what bothers me most of all. If this guy showed up at Salvatore's and pulled the same game, well, we haven't been able to find out who he talked to. The owner doesn't recall any incident like this. Neither do any of the other employees we talked to. It's possible the guy talked to a former employee; the turnover at the restaurant is heavy at the low end."

"Have you checked any of this out, Mar? Any background? Any independent stuff?"

"Well, a little. There's nothing to follow with Sam Dougall. He didn't have a name, or a decent description, and he doesn't recall if the guy ever mentioned the name of the insurance company. I had a similar problem with Arnoldo Munoz. There's just not enough to go on. I *did* call the Presidio Army base to follow up on the lead. They told me that AWOL issues are handled by the military police, not Army CID. In fact, they just about laughed me off the phone when I asked to be connected to Army CID. So, I called the MP station out there and they blew me off, too. Said it never happened."

"Do you believe them?"

"Yeah," she moaned.

"So where's the connection? I don't see it," he asked, obviously interested.

"Not so much of a connection, Chris, as a possibility. Just a wild theory. Suppose this guy has a sketch of his preferred target – a general sketch that physically defines the kind of woman he wants to stalk and kill. Now, he goes to these locations, for whatever reason, until he finds someone who looks like the sketch. He checks these women out. If they fit the bill, he knows where they are, what they look like, and maybe a lot more. Then, he can carefully watch their movements and attack them when he feels safe. The scam gives him sufficient information in a single visit to target a particular woman and learn enough about her to stalk her. More than that, Chris, it may also give him a way to abduct her. Remember that Sam said Ruminez and Callohan *could* have gone voluntarily with their murderer?"

"Yeah…"

"Well, how about this? The murderer is known to the women because he's been introduced to them by their boss or a friend. More than that, he's been introduced to them as a person in a position of authority. He's met them at least once in his role as a CID officer, insurance investigator, or whatever. Now they *know* him… he's no longer a stranger."

"Jesus, Mar…"

"Well…" she interrupted. "What do you think?"

He leaned to his right and gently put his hand to her cheek, giving it a light brush. Even in the darkness of the room, he could see that Mary's eyes were large with anticipation, a smile lurking somewhere behind her taut lips. It was good to see her excited and alive, he thought. It made him feel younger, less tired.

"Ok, Mar. It makes sense for the Ruminez and Callohan murders. In fact, it makes good sense. But, what about the Althazar murder? The pattern doesn't fit there, does it?"

"No," she admitted, dropping her head away from his gaze. "No, Chris, it doesn't fit. But, you've got to remember that the Althazar murder doesn't fit the first two crimes in *any* way, does it? I mean, even Sam said, right off, that the Althazar murder was different than the other two. He said that our guy had moved on and become more brazen and careless. He started taking more risks. Maybe he changed his targeting technique, maybe he didn't. Maybe he didn't have the time to stalk the last victim. Maybe Althazar was just in the wrong place at the wrong time."

"I *do* think it's a good lead. And we should get the word out to the local restaurant and bar owners about this possibility. Maybe he's tried the same tactic at other places. Maybe someone will remember him. The problem is, beyond that, I have no idea where to take it. I mean, you've done what you can, so what do we do now?"

"Chris, I have an idea." She sat upright on the edge of the couch and stared intently at her friend. "This may sound bizarre and risky, but it might work. Suppose we create a situation that duplicates the pattern of the first two murders. I mean, suppose we have a setup that invites this guy to repeat his pattern of the first two murders by inducing him to try to locate a specific victim? Could that work?"

"I have no idea," he mumbled.

"That's the ugly part. We'd have to set up one of our own — Sandy."

"What!" he shouted.

"Hold on, Chris! Just hear me out." She slid a thin, cool hand over the back of his and gave it a few quick pats. He settled back into the couch and drained the remaining wine from his glass.

"Chris, we arrange to have Sandy go under cover for a while. We set her up as an employee of a restaurant, bar, or whatever... something that looks good, something that fits... something right in the middle of the Mission District. After she's established for a while, say a few weeks or a month, we bring her to this guy's attention. We have her save the life of a patron or something impressive like that, something that will get her written up in the *Call*

— maybe even with a photograph. Since she physically matches the murderer's preferred type of victim, and since he's probably a local, he'll likely read about her. He may come to her workplace and go through the same routine as he did with Ruminez and Callohan. If he does, then we'll know who he is. We won't have enough to nail him, but we can start to build a case if we can identify him."

"Jesus, Mar, that's a big risk. Sandy's green as hell," he stammered.

"Come on, Chris," Mary answered in a dismissive tone. "You know as well as I do that she's a sharp woman who wants to get out of her blues. She wants to make this opportunity work for her. Don't you think it should be *her* decision? Hell, she'd be well backed up and you know it. We'd all be there for her."

Chris fumbled for the Valpolicella and refilled both glasses. He leaned forward, squinting into the fog over the bay and rolling the wineglass in his hand, trying to imagine the dozens of ways this idea could go horribly wrong. Still, it was a hell of a good plan and he instinctively knew it. There weren't many options with this case and the pressure was definitely on from topside in the SFPD.

"Ok, Mar, maybe you're right. Maybe it's worth looking at. I certainly agree that it should ultimately be Sandy's decision. I also want Sam to hear about this before we talk to anyone else, right?"

"Sure," she answered, smiling at him in the darkness.

"I sure as hell don't want Joe to learn about this idea until we're absolutely sure that we want to try it. Jesus! He'll come apart if he thinks we're going to jeopardize Sandy's safety. I think he's grown pretty attached to her, don't you?"

"Yeah, you could put it that way." She finished with another light giggle, one that drew his attention from the window to her face and finally made him smile.

"Ok, we'll talk to Sam and then to Sandy, right?" he confirmed.

"Right, Chris. Thanks. If she wants to do it, fine. If not, that's fine too. Whatever."

Once again the room was silent. The wail of the lighthouse seemed more distant now, less plaintive, and he thought the fog on the water seemed less still, less committed to hiding the natural, nighttime beauty of the bay.

"Chris," she whispered. "Do you want to make love?"

"No... but I'd like to stay here tonight, if that's ok?"

"Always has been, always will be," she said without any hint of disappointment. In the darkness, she reached again for his hand and moved close to his side, resting her head on his shoulder.

Chris idly scanned the lights along the near shoreline as he nuzzled his chin to the top of Mary's head. She had washed her thick, brown hair in something mild and sweet, just for him, just for this night.

For some time, he wondered if she was actually lonelier than she led him to believe. In the end, he concluded that she'd told him the truth. She was rarely lonely. Mary was as tough as they came — of that he was sure. *He* was the one who was lonely. And *he* was the one who was afraid.

The fog had finally begun to drift away from the bay, heading somewhere to the south. He could see the first, hazy twinkling of lights from the far shoreline; he could hear the foghorn in the distance, now less insistent, more at ease. Tomorrow would be a better, warmer day. Tomorrow it would be Christmas Day, at least for the rest of the neighborhood. For now, he had nowhere to go and no reason to care about tomorrow.

For now, he had nothing more to do but hold her close and think of anything but murder.

December 26
Midtown Station
9:10 A.M.

"That's fucking crazy!" Mendoza shouted as Mary Boor finished her story. "Christ! You're willing to stake Sandy's life on some fantasy hunch that came from nowhere... some half-baked idea of what this freak *might* do next? What fucking sense does that make?" He threw himself down on the Lieutenant's aging black couch and glowered at Mary standing on the other side of the office, his face lined and flushed with anger.

"All right, Joe, just relax. You're *way* out of line on this!" the Lieutenant snapped, waving his hand sternly in the Sergeant's direction. "Mar's doing what she's supposed to be doing — working on a way to nail this guy. We can discuss our ideas in here without crucifying each other, can't we?"

Mendoza dropped his head and grunted. "Yeah, we can," he mumbled, unwilling to look at his boss. "Sorry, Mary."

"That's ok, Joe. I understand completely. I know it's risky. I know it's not based on anything solid. That's why we're talking about it," Mary said in a soothing tone.

Mendoza bobbed his head up and down but said nothing.

"Well, I like the idea and it's *my* safety we're talking about here," Sandy announced, looking directly at Mendoza. "I think Mary's idea has merit. In fact, it sounds like the best thing we have going right now."

Mendoza grunted once again — a dismissive, disbelieving sound that still rang with anger.

"In fact," Sandy continued, ignoring his mood, "I even have a place in mind... Pento's Restaurant at the corner of Mission and Twenty-third. It would be perfect." She moved to the couch and sat down next to Mendoza, trying to get his attention with her last statement.

"Why Pento's, Sandy? What have you got going there?" Spell interjected.

"The guy who owns it, Rich Gariblaz, has talked to me a few times about working nights there as his dinner hostess. The restaurant is on my beat and I eat there pretty regularly. He doesn't have a night hostess. Well, actually, his wife does it and he doesn't like that arrangement. Anyway, he offered me the job, if I was interested. As of two days ago, he still had his wife doing the night gig, so I guess it's still available. He needs someone to work from four in the afternoon until they end the dinner business around nine."

"Well, Sandy, the location and the hours would be perfect," Mary added.

"Yeah, that's what I thought. It's on the boulevard and right on a corner. It would fit our guy's first two murders perfectly, at least for location and timing." She sneaked another look at Mendoza seated next to her. He was shaking his head from side to side, obviously not wanting to hear any more.

For a moment, the room was silent, except for Mendoza, who was making light clicking sounds with his lips and still shaking his head from side to side.

Chris watched McCannell drift around the periphery of his office in that special way, his eyes closed, his feet shuffling rhythmically like paddles in the water. There was obviously something on his mind. "Sam, you haven't said anything about Mar's idea yet. Want to now?"

"Yeah, I do," Sam replied, opening his eyes and focusing on Mary. "I think the idea is terrific. In fact, it's better than that..."

"Oh, Christ!" Mendoza grumbled. "Jesus! Not you, too!"

"Ok, Joe, I understand how you feel about it," Sam explained in a soft voice. "I agree that there's a risk here. The bottom line, though, is that it should be *Sandy's* decision, not yours, mine, or anyone else's. That's the way things work."

Another grunt from the couch.

"Anyway," the red man continued, now talking to the Lieutenant, "I think Mary's plan fits the facts of the case. The murderer has been quiet for a month now and I think there's a good reason for that. I think he got scared with the Althazar attack and Riordan's exclusive in the *Call*. He took a risk, made an unplanned attack, and now he's afraid that we're hot on him. He doesn't know that we're going nowhere on the case. That's probably why he's been so quiet. But, you can bet your ass he won't *stay* quiet. This guy *has* to kill. It's not something he can control. He can't just turn it off and on like a light switch. I think he'll be more careful in the future. I think he'll go back to a safer way of picking his targets and murdering them. In other words, I think he'll go back to the method he used with Ruminez and Callohan. If that's the case – if my hunch is right – then Mary's plan is perfect. It anticipates this guy's next move and gives us a proactive way of getting back into the game."

McCannell turned his attention to Joe, trying to pull some reaction from him. There was nothing.

"Joe, listen, don't you see that?" Sam said in a scolding tone.

"Christ, yes!" Mendoza yelped. "I'm not stupid, Sam. I just don't want Sandy's ass out there! I know you're right. I just don't like it, that's all."

Sandy looked at Chris, then at Sam. They were both looking down, obviously worried. "Chris," she said in a determined voice, "I *want* to do this. I think it's the right move and I *want* to do it. Ok?"

"Yeah, Sandy. I agree," the Lieutenant conceded. "Joe's just worried about you. So are the rest of us."

The others nodded in unison.

"Go ahead and set it up, Sandy," Spell confirmed. "Work out the details with Mary and Joe. Let me know when you're ready to start working at Pento's. We'll arrange backup, a wire, whatever you need to make this work. But I don't want anyone outside this room to know about it, right? I mean, just us, no one else. Not even Marley, right? That's not optional."

Again, they nodded, but only Sandy was smiling.

"Ok, let's get on it then," Spell said, indicating with his hand that the meeting was over. "Sam, will you stick around for a minute?"

McCannell nodded and waited in the far corner of the office until the others had left. When they had gone, he moved to the door and pushed it closed with his foot.

"Problems, Chris?" he asked, turning to face the Lieutenant.

"Yeah, Sam. We go back a long way, right?"

"You bet."

"Straight up, Sam. I have two questions. First, how risky is this?"

"Not as bad as it sounds, Chris, depending on how far you let the ruse go. If we *do* lure this freak out into the open, we can pull the plug on him after he targets her but before he attacks. If we do that, you may blow the case but Sandy will be ok. The real risk is *after* he targets her... if you let it go that far. We know his *general* tactic, but there's no way of knowing how he'll react the next time around. Maybe he'll grab her off the street, maybe he'll try to manipulate her into his vehicle, who knows? If you play the game all the way – if he takes the bait and then tries to attack her – she may wind up being out there on her own."

"Well, Sam, we'll have backup. We'll wire her and do all the right things. That should help."

"Maybe, maybe not. I believe he attacks his victims very quickly. You may not have all that much time to intervene."

"So what do we do about it, Sam?"

"You go with the plan. It's the best you've got right now. Sandy believes in it and she wants to do it. She told you so."

Chris stood up from behind his desk and moved to the couch, sinking back heavily with a sigh. "I don't know. I like the plan but Sandy's green as hell and this guy is a fucking freak. This could be bad." He closed his eyes and rolled his head from side to side, trying to think out the possibilities, trying to assess the risks. He decided there were just too many to eliminate all of them.

"All right," he said in a tired voice. "I guess we go with it. As you said, we can always pull the plug if she gets in too deep."

Sam nodded. "What was the second thing, Chris?"

"Mendoza. He's out of control when it comes to Sandy. I've never seen him like this. Sure, he screws around with the help now and then, but I've never seen him so tense about it before."

The red man slapped his hands together and let out a rolling laugh. "Jesus, Chris, don't you remember what it's like to be in love? Can't you see that in Joe? He's just met his match with that little cop. He's been knocked on his ass by someone half his size! It's love — remember that Chris?"

A tight, forced smile drifted across the Lieutenant's face as he turned toward his friend. "Well, to tell the truth Sam... no — I don't remember."

"Then try it sometime, Chris! It's good for the soul. Unless I miss my guess, you've had your chance very recently and you'll probably have it again," McCannell said with an enormous glint in his eyes.

"Fucking shrink!" Chris roared back with a wide smile.

"Fucking, mick, know-it-all shrink!"

"Scot!" the red man yelped as he headed for the door. "There's no 'O' in front of McCannell!"

The door closed with a rattle — and immediately opened again. A huge, red, smiling face popped through the opening and stared intently at the Lieutenant. "And, Chris, her preference is Italian. Did you know that?"

Spell grabbed the yellow notepad lying next to him on the couch and launched it at the partially opened door. McCannell instantly retreated and slammed it shut, bellowing a laugh through the glass at his friend.

"Fucking, *Scot*, know-it-all, shrink!"

January 5
Forensic Science Laboratory
10:30 A.M.

Sam McCannell slid the photocopy across the polished meeting room table, sending it in Spell's general direction. The Lieutenant snagged it with his right hand and, with his left, reached for the brass, gooseneck lamp nearby, adjusting it to illuminate the paper in front of him. He looked carefully at the handwritten message, squinting at the block printing and working hard to absorb every nuance:

FOR DOCTOR SAM MCCANNELL
FOR JANE RIORDAN

NO ONE WANTS TO BE A LONE
NO ONE WANTS TO BE LEFT BEHIND
I DO NOT LIKE IT EITHER
SHE WANTED TO LEAVE ME BEHIND
BUT NOT ME
THE NEXT ONE WONT LEAVE ME BEHIND
I KNOW WHO SHE IS
SHE WAS

MONSTER

"Ahh, shit!" Spell mumbled as he examined the message for the first time. Once again, without speaking, he read the words, his lips moving silently in sync to the syllables. When he finished, the Lieutenant grimaced at McCannell across the table. "Where's the original, Sam? How did you get this message?"

"The lab folks have the original next door," Sam replied, gesturing with his large head in the direction of the forensics lab adjacent to the meeting room. "I received the note in this morning's mail, addressed to me at my office. It was written in the same style, with the same kind of paper and the same color ink as the last one. There's no doubt in my mind that it's the real thing, Chris."

"Shit!" the Lieutenant repeated, shaking his head from side to side. "Now he's gone to the press with his insanity! He's gone right to Jane Riordan and the *Call*. We've got a hell of a problem here!" the Lieutenant moaned.

"I'm not sure about that, Chris," McCannell said in a far-away, sleepy tone.

"What! Come on, Sam! If Riordan has this note, we're in deep shit! If she prints it, we're screwed! In the public's mind, we've just lost any semblance of control over this freak. This guy will make fools of us in the press. We'll look like absolute idiots!"

"Maybe not, Chris." McCannell shuffled away from the table and moved to the thick picture window that separated the darkened meeting room from the brilliance of the forensics laboratory. In the lab area, just beyond the glass partition, he could see a young, blonde woman working with the original note, carefully manipulating it by the edges with a shiny, long-handled instrument.

"For one thing, Chris," he continued, "we don't know, for sure, if he *really* sent a copy of this note to Riordan. It's possible that *we* have the only one. It's possible that he just wants us to *believe* that he sent it to the *Call*. That would be consistent with the way he's tried to manipulate the investigation so far. It could just be a bluff — a way to get us to contact Riordan ourselves and tip her off to the fact that he's communicating with us."

"For another thing, even if he *did* send it to Riordan, she may be willing to cooperate with us and not print anything that could hurt the investigation. If that's the case, she'll want something in return for her cooperation — that's for sure. Even then, she may just decide to cooperate with the investigation. She's a straight-up reporter, in my opinion."

Spell moved to the window to stand next to the red man. He didn't look convinced. For a moment, his eyes followed the lab technician as she worked with the note. "Well, I don't know about that, Sam. If he wants everyone to know about his exploits, why not just send the message directly to Riordan and be done with it? Why the extra step? Why not go right to the *Call*?"

"Because it would be too simple to send it directly to her, Chris. That would be too obvious. Nothing this guy does is simple or obvious. Everything is well planned and carefully considered. He may be a whacko, but he's a whacko who plans meticulously and enjoys working out all the details. Besides, I'm sure he wants to keep the pressure on us. He wants us to look like fumbling idiots. He wants to prove to everyone that he is superior to us in every way. What better way to do that then to have *us* tip the press off and bring more pressure on ourselves? Listen, tell me this: have you heard from Jane Riordan? Have you received any messages from her?"

"No, nothing."

"Well, don't you think she would be on the phone to you immediately if she received something like this note in her mailbox? She'd want verification of some kind, wouldn't she? She'd want to know that it was the real thing and not just a hoax. Riordan is much too careful to accept something like this at face value. She wouldn't just assume that the note was the real thing and print it. She would check first, right?"

"Yeah, I agree with that, Sam. She would check."

"And don't you think that she would do it *immediately*? She would call *you*, right?"

"Yeah, I agree with that, too." The Lieutenant moved back to the oak table and sat on its edge, his eyes scanning the note once again, his mind on the reporter. "Yeah, Sam, she would have been on the phone to me *right now*. You're right. There's no way she would move on this without verification. I see where you're heading, Sam. It's perverted as hell but it does make sense for this guy, doesn't it?"

McCannell nodded. "Chris, you know you have to call her or meet with her, right? I mean, that's the only way to know for sure whether or not she has a copy of his message. It's the only way to reassert some control here, right?"

"Absolutely, I see that. And I know I'm going to have to admit to some form of communication from this freak, even if she hasn't received a copy of this note. I can see where this is heading, Sam. This guy is good, isn't he?"

"Among the best I've seen, Chris. He's a master."

"So, if your theory is right, this creep forces me to trust a reporter whose business it is to pry into my investigation. Shit!" A disjointed, twisted smile swept across the Lieutenant's face. He looked over at McCannell, still standing across the room, and saw that he, too, had a strange, awkward grimace on his face.

"What a lousy deal this is," the Lieutenant grumbled, angrily pushing the photocopy far away from where he was sitting.

"It sure is, Chris. Not only are we going to have to trust Riordan – not only are we still being manipulated by this guy – but there's even worse news. Have you read the message very carefully?"

"Sure, Sam. Let me tell *you* this time. He's going to kill again and he's already selected his victim, hasn't he?" Spell said without looking at his friend.

Sam nodded, his face dark and grim. "And there's more. As far as the murderer is concerned, his victim is already dead. That means he's already determined who, when, where, and how. He has the next killing already planned out and he's telling us that in his message.

We probably don't have long, Chris. He'll strike soon."

McCannell moved toward the table, once again shuffling his feet like an arthritic duck. He had that familiar, dreamy look on his face. Spell knew there was more to come.

"The guy is also trying to tell us *why* he does what he does. For him, there's nothing worse than being left behind — nothing more painful or abhorrent than being abandoned or forgotten. This guy is absolutely alone in life. He's been stripped of all meaningful relationships. Now, after this message, we know that for sure. He's a loner and he can't stand it. The way he copes with that kind of intense, unacceptable loneliness is by demanding attention — the very special kind of attention that a serial killer gets from people like us. He's also telling us that there was a particular woman in his life who left him alone — someone who hurt him badly and abandoned him. When she left him alone – completely alone – he turned to murder."

"Does that help us, Sam? I don't see how…" Spell answered his own question in a frustrated voice.

"Well, it does. For one thing, we know about his preferences for certain types of victims. Now we know his motivation: to lash out against the loneliness — to castigate others because he was hurt in some profound way. We know he is punishing his victims for the way in which he was treated when that special woman abandoned or rejected him. There's no question in my mind that he's attacking these women because he sees them as substitutes for the particular woman who hurt him so badly."

"Then why doesn't he just attack the one woman he hates so much, Sam? Why all the others? Why not just whack this woman and be done with it?" the Lieutenant snapped back.

"Maybe she's already dead, Chris. Maybe that was how he was abandoned. Maybe there's another reason. The point is that he *can't* attack that special woman, for whatever reason, so he murders substitutes who fit her general physical description."

"Ok, so he's already selected his next victim, right?" Spell asked in a leading way.

"Yeah."

"Then we need to intervene before he actually attacks her, right?"

"Ideally, yes. But that's not likely?"

"Why not, Sam?"

"Well, for one thing, we don't know when, where, or who. Remember, Chris, this guy has switched up on us between the first two murders and the last one. He's changed the rules of the game. The best you can do is try to work on his method for the first two cases, to see if he's been snooping around the area with sketches and questions. If he's scared and more cautious, he may go back to his old ways. If he's not, he may try something entirely new. But, I assume you're already following up with the local businesses, right? You're working on the method he used on Ruminez and Callohan, right?"

"Yeah, but it hasn't turned up anything. There's a lot of ground to cover and we haven't talked to *every* restaurant or bar owner yet. So, there's still hope, I guess."

"I guess so," McCannell said in a dejected tone. "But I don't really believe it in my heart."

"Why not, Sam? Shit! Until this morning you thought this whacko would go back to his old ways. You thought he had been scared by the Althazar murder and would go back to something safer, something more familiar. Now, you're telling me that he might not?"

"Because, Chris, I think it's *possible* that he will change his tactics again. This time, he may not use the old sketch and question routine. After reading this message, I'm not all that certain he is *really* afraid of what we know. In fact, I think he's more whacked out and committed to violence than ever. Honestly, Chris, I'm surprised we've heard from him *before* the next murder. I hadn't expected that."

Spell looked like he was ready to explode, his face flushed and tight. "Oh, shit! Our entire investigation is predicated on this guy going back to the pattern of the Ruminez and Callohan murders. Sandy's undercover gig is based on that! Why are you saying this, Sam? I don't want to hear this!"

"I could be completely wrong on this," McCannell answered in a slow, methodical tone. "And I hope I am. Maybe he *is* using the sketch and question tactic. Maybe he *is* going back to his original pattern. I just don't think so after this morning. He's telling us that his next murder has already been planned. He's saying there will be no random elements in it... no loose ends, whatsoever. Nothing will be left to chance. That's his answer to being threatened by our investigation. He's essentially telling us to go fuck ourselves — telling us that he can overcome our investigation by being more precise in his planning."

The Lieutenant dropped his head and shook it slowly from side to side.

"Listen, Chris," McCannell continued, "the bottom line is that I don't know. Maybe I'm wrong about this. Maybe he'll go back to the old ways. I think you should go ahead on the assumption that he'll use the same method he used with Ruminez and Callohan. After all, there's nothing else I can give you that's any better. It's just a feeling..." McCannell's voice trailed off to nothing. He stood motionless at the glass partition, his unseeing eyes following the pretty woman on the other side.

Spell slid from the edge of the table and walked back to where McCannell was standing. He gave the smaller man a light slap on the back. "Sam, you're probably right. You usually are. My problem is that I have no idea what the fuck to do next." The Lieutenant banged his head lightly against the glass partition several times in frustration. On the other side, in the lab, the young technician turned toward the glass and gave him a big smile. He tried to return the greeting, but it was strained and meaningless.

"You need to call Jane Riordan, Chris. That's what you do next," the red man said in a determined, serious voice. "You try to control as much of this bullshit as you can. That's all you can do until you get some kind of break in the case — or until this guy screws up."

"Jane Riordan," she answered in a snappy, hurried voice.

"Jane, this is Chris Spell at the SFPD," he announced. There was a noticeable pause while Riordan flipped to a fresh page in her notebook and positioned it in front of her, pen in hand and handset up against her chin.

"Hi, Chris, nice to hear from you. What's up?" Her voice was more relaxed now, more willing to be patient. This was a call she had not expected. This was something very special and she knew it the instant she had heard his voice.

"Jane, I need your help on something here. I need your cooperation..."

"Wait a minute, Chris," she interrupted, "Before you go too far on this, whatever it is, you need to know that I have a job to do here. Do you understand what I mean?"

"Sure," he said with an edge in his voice. "Of course, I understand. Listen, Jane, I'm not going to ask you to run anything wild or wrong. In fact, I'm not going to ask you to run anything at all. All I want from you is to listen to what I have to say and possibly help with my investigation. I won't ask you to withhold anything that I tell you on the record."

"Ok," she said slowly. "Is this about the serial killer, Chris?"

Her heart was pounding fast now. She knew the next answer, as good reporters usually do.

"Yes."

Riordan began to write. She noted the date and time of the call, and the subject: "Mission District serial killer."

"All right, ask away," Riordan said in a serious tone.

"My next question is off the record — it's just for you, right?"

"Umm-hmm..."

"Have you received any kind of communication from this guy?" he asked in a deliberate way. For several seconds, the line was completely quiet. She was obviously thinking the question through. It wasn't that she didn't have an immediate answer — she did. It was the meaning of the question that she was probing in her mind.

"No, Chris, I haven't received a call or letter or anything else. But, I suspect you have or you wouldn't be calling me with *that* question. Am I right?"

Another long, uncomfortable pause.

"Off the record, Jane?" he asked in his most official tone.

"No," came the instant response.

"Come on, work with me here, will you, Jane?" He wasn't pleading — yet.

"Chris, don't ask me to walk away from my responsibilities. You wouldn't do it and I won't do it. Either you confirm a communication from the killer or you force me to speculate about it. You know that I don't like guesswork but, if I have to, I'll use it. I haven't asked you anything *about* the communication yet. All I've asked you is whether or not you received something from this guy."

Spell tried to picture the reporter at her desk, writing furiously in her notebook, working out her next headline. In his mind, he raced though her articles over the years; how she had handled guesswork and speculation in the past, how she had approached her subject, how she had treated the SFPD in print. It was true. She was not one to speculate unless forced into a corner. That was something he wouldn't do.

"Yes, we have a handwritten message from the killer," he said tersely. "I can't give you any specifics about it, though. We'll need to hold that back for the investigation."

"All right, Chris. I see the problem. I won't push you on that. Did he address the message to me? Is that why you're calling?" she asked.

"Yeah, you were one of the addressees."

"Who were the others?"

"Sam McCannell was the only other."

"Chris, is this the first message you've received or were there others?"

"I can't tell you that."

"Ok…." She paused to make another note.

"Listen, Jane, I know that you're going to print this but I *really* need your help. We need to work together on this." His voice was more pleading than she could ever recall.

"Why is that?" she asked in a wary, cool tone.

"Because this guy obviously wants to manipulate the press *and* the SFPD. He wants to be a front-page headline, Jane. That's part of the game he's playing with his victims and us. It's about power, control, and manipulation. This guy doesn't give a damn about the women he murders — they're just a means to an end." His voice was impassioned, and to the reporter's practiced ear, unusually animated. It was clear that he wanted to nail this guy — badly.

"All right, Chris. I'll work with you on this, but not at the expense of doing things my way. *I'll* decide whether there's anything worth printing or not. Can you at least tell me *something* about the message? Can you give me something to work on here? If we can agree on something along those lines, I'll work with you before I write anything that could hurt your investigation. But I have a condition. If I work with you on this – work with you *my* way – I get the exclusive when the shit hits the fan. Is that fair?"

"Yeah, good, Jane. That's fair," he replied hurriedly. "Listen, if you have some time this afternoon, why not come down and meet with Sam and me. We can go over the general details of the message and he can give you some background. Then we can agree on what you go with, right?"

"No!" she said definitively. "We'll meet, we'll talk, but *I'll* make the call on what gets written and what doesn't. That's the deal. I'll give you a preview and give you a chance to tell me how you feel; but, in the end, *I'll* do the writing. That's the way it has to be, Chris. I hope you understand that."

"Yeah, I do," he said quietly.

"Ok, how about lunchtime then? Will you and Sam be available? Maybe we can get something to eat and talk?"

"Sure, we'll be here, Jane. See you then."

She was still writing furiously as the line went dead, still wondering what in the hell was really going on — but loving every moment of it.

January 12
Mission District
6:30 P.M.

He raced through each page of the San Francisco *Call*, harshly snapping them back upon each other, looking for any article, any mention of the serial killer. There was none. Nothing! It had been a week to the day since he had sent the note to McCannell — an entire week since the shit *should* have hit the fan. What had McCannell done? Where was Jane Riordan's article? Why was she ignoring him? What the fuck was going on? He was furious.

He angrily crumpled the newspaper and threw it over his shoulder, onto the cluttered floorboard behind the passenger's seat of his car. He glanced at his watch. It was time to make the call — it was time. He had warned them and they had done nothing. Now, it was *his* turn. If they wanted to play *their* game instead of his, well, he had an answer to that. He had an answer to everything.

He jumped from the maroon sedan and walked quickly to the telephone booth at the corner of Folsom and Twenty-fifth. He dialed her number.

Joanne Callin curled up on the end of her brown velveteen couch and cradled a glass of pleasantly chilled white wine between her hands. She was exhausted. She had stripped off her work clothes and flung a flannel robe around her petite frame. Her feet and calves throbbed miserably from an endless day of showing commercial properties from one end of the Mission District to the other. Now, finally, it was *her* time. In a few hours, her fiancé, Roy Dunover, would be knocking at the door and expecting her to look her very best for dinner. In the meantime, she desperately needed to relax, recharge, and think of anything else but trying to sell real estate in an area of the city that was infested with cutthroat property agents and brokers.

Callin was a dynamo in the real estate business and had the credentials to prove it. For the sixth quarter in a row, she had managed to surpass twenty-one other salespeople at the Mission Best Real Property Company — the largest, most active commercial real estate agency in the District. And her rewards had been worth the effort. In the previous year, Callin had earned over $300,000 in brokerage commissions and had finally achieved the lifestyle she had always wanted. At the age of twenty-seven, she was successful, pretty, well regarded, and unquestioningly dominant in what had traditionally been a man's world of intensely competitive commercial real estate sales. The only complaint that Joanne Callin had about her life was time — there was never enough of it.

She closed her eyes and put the chilled glass to her lips, trying to extend the pleasure of the moment, sucking in the welcome silence of her spacious flat along with the crisp bouquet of Chardonnay. Life had been good to Joanne Callin and now there was nothing to stop her — except time.

In the middle of her first, delicious sip, the telephone next to the couch rang out rudely, startling her eyes open and sending an unexpected shudder down her arms. For someone other than Joanne, this would have been an unacceptable intrusion — something to be ignored after a long, tiring workday. But she had learned to never question the telephone. It was the lifeblood of her success and the most important connection to keeping what she had worked so hard to attain. No phone, no leads. No leads, no lifestyle. She reached for the receiver instinctively, without hesitation, still holding the wineglass in her right hand.

"Hello," she said in a practiced, pleasant voice designed to mask her exhaustion.

"Ms. Callin... Joanne Callin?" the man asked. His voice was full and deep, pleasing to the ear, she thought.

"Yes, this is Joanne."

"Oh, good. Ms. Callin, I'm very sorry to bother you at home. Brian Silverstein gave me your number and said it would be all right to call you at home." He sounded unsure and apologetic, as if he had noisily intruded on a Sunday service.

"Sure, it's fine. Ah, Mr., ah... sorry, I didn't get your name," she said softly.

The man on the line laughed in a good-natured way. "Oh, sorry. My name is Ron Vintini. Please, just call me Ron." He pictured her in his mind. Dark, small, attractive — just as he had seen her in the photograph in the agency window, the one captioned "Salesperson of the Quarter."

"Ok, Ron, well, call me Joanne. So, Brian asked you to call me?"

"Yes. He said you were the best agent he had. Well, you know, Brian and I are old friends. We did several real estate deals together in the Mission District, years ago. Anyway, he said you were the best and that you could take care of selling one of my properties."

Joanne instantly perked up and slipped to the edge of the couch. She quickly set the wineglass on the coffee table in front of her and picked up a yellow notepad near the telephone. He had said the magic words. Now, she was no longer tired, she no longer ached — she had caught the irresistible scent of a sale.

"Sure, I'd be glad to help. What can I do for you, Ron?" she asked in a snappy tone.

"Thanks, good, Joanne. Well, I live in Southern California now. I still have a few properties up here and I want to divest. Right now, I have a vacant commercial piece. I'd like to list it and get rid of it as soon as possible. It's a bit off the beaten track and it's been vacant for several months. Since I live so far away, I'd like to cash it out and use the proceeds in other ways. So, Brian said you could take the listing and work the property for me."

"Sure, that's my specialty, Ron. Where's the property located?"

"It's on Folsom, near Twenty-fifth Street."

She thought for a moment, bringing up the images of that block in her mind. Yes, she remembered. "Right, I know the storefront you mean. That was a Chinese restaurant that went under about a year ago, right?"

"Yes! Wow, I'm impressed, Joanne. That's remarkable! I can see why Brian thinks the world of you." He could imagine her blushing. He could picture her petite features broadening with a huge, wonderful smile. He could see her brush the straight, black hair from her face as she began to take notes.

"Thanks," she said with a happy voice. "That's my business, so I work hard at it." She wasn't exaggerating.

"Good, good. Well, I don't have a lot of time to spend on this deal, so I'd like to just turn it over to you and we can work out the details on the telephone as necessary. Brian mentioned that all I'd need to do was show you the property, sign a listing agreement, and give you the keys. He said you could take care of the details. Is that correct?"

"Sure, we could do it that way. I could work with you on the telephone, once we have a listing agreement. That would be no problem at all. When would you like to get together?"

"Well, Joanne, as soon as possible. I'm only in the city for a few hours, then back off to Los Angeles. Would it be possible to get together tonight? We could meet at the property, you could see it, and I could sign the listing agreement then and there?"

Her face and shoulders dropped. She suddenly realized how

much her feet hurt, how much she looked forward to her dinner date that night. But, business was business. "Sure," she said in her best agent's voice. "Let's do it tonight. I don't live far from the property, so it's not a problem to meet you there."

"Good, great!" he said, sounding genuinely thankful. "You're terrific! How about eight o'clock? We'll meet at eight, ok?"

"Sure, fine."

"Ok, good — very good. You can avoid the parking hassles on Folsom if you park behind the store, in the alley there. Do you know about that?"

She thought for a moment, once again searching for an image. "Ah, no..." she hesitated. "Well, yeah, I know there's an alley there but I didn't think you could park in it."

He laughed pleasantly. "Well, technically, you can't. The area in the alley behind the restaurant is a loading zone. But go ahead and pull in there. You'll see my car. There's plenty of room and no one will bother you at night. When you get there, just come in the trade entrance. I'll leave it unlocked and I'll wait for you inside. I have a few things to do there anyway."

"Good, Ron. That's fine. I'll meet you at eight then."

"That's great, Joanne. I really appreciate it. You're wonderful!"

"Ok, see you then." She hung up the telephone, still feeling the blush on her cheeks. He sounded nice enough, although a bit thick on the complements. Well, anyway, it sounded like an easy deal — quick and profitable. Just the way she liked them. She made a note to talk to Brian in the morning, to thank him and buy him lunch as soon as possible.

Callin made a call to Roy Dunover's answering machine and explained that she would be late for dinner. The message was simple enough. She had to follow up on a last minute real estate deal for her boss. It shouldn't be more than an hour and she would be home by nine o' clock. Sorry, love you, sorry.

For now, she still had enough time for that glass of wine, a bath to cure her aches, and a change of clothes.

At 8:05 that evening, Joanne Callin turned east down Twenty-fifth and carefully maneuvered her year-old, steel blue Lexus into the alleyway that ran parallel to Folsom. Less than fifty yards from the entrance to the alleyway, she could see a large, dark sedan parked very near one of the several trade entrances that punctuated the dim, vacant street. The sedan was facing the Twenty-fifth Street entrance, as if it had been backed into position, leaving just enough room for any other vehicle to squeeze by on the right. It was the only vehicle in the alleyway and Callin was sure that it belonged to her new client, Ron Vintini, although it looked nothing like any rental car she had ever seen. She drove slowly beyond the maroon sedan, noticing that it sported several official-looking antennas, and inched her car into a cutout on the opposite side of the alley, about thirty feet past the trade entrance to the defunct restaurant.

Joanne snatched her brown leather briefcase and matching purse from the seat beside her and made sure the car door was locked. She walked quickly in the direction of the sedan across the pavement. The alleyway was poorly illuminated by a single, aging street lamp nestled near the Twenty-fifth Street entrance. Buttressed by the high brick walls of antiquated commercial buildings on the south side, and the rears of windowless, wood-planked, post-Victorian flats on the north, the alleyway gave the impression of a narrow, dank gorge hewn from the density of the neighborhood in an era when automobiles were the exception, not the rule, for this part of the city. Not a single window opened onto the dark street, on either side, and the only trade entrance that appeared to be open was the one that beckoned her into what had once been the kitchen area of a Chinese restaurant.

As she reached the two concrete steps that led to the open tradesman's entrance, Joanne paused at the bottom of the threshold and instinctively checked her wristwatch. To her pleasure, she was less than ten minutes late. Acceptable, she thought.

"Mr. Vintini?" she shouted in a high voice through the open doorway. Inside, she could detect a faint, beige flicker of light from somewhere beyond the kitchen area. "Ron?" she shouted again, "This is Joanne Callin." She waited a few seconds, but heard nothing. She decided to step up to the threshold and try again.

Standing just outside the doorway, she yelled once more — louder, this time. "Mr. Vintini, this is Joanne Callin. Are you in there?"

"Oh, yes," answered a deep, affable voice from somewhere inside. "Come on in, Joanne, I'm in the kitchen here. Be sure to stay on the tarp, Joanne. The floors are wet and dirty."

She stepped over the threshold and felt a slight movement underneath her right foot. Looking down, she saw that she was standing on an enormous, heavy cloth tarp that stretched ahead of her. She smiled and made a mental note that the owner must be making *some* effort to renovate the interior of the store. That was a good sign. That would help with the listing price.

Joanne stepped forward carefully, making sure that the high heels of her shoes did not catch in the random wrinkles in the tarp. To her left, even in the dim light, she could see the outline of a huge commercial stove and the gleam of a long, metal worktable against the adjoining the wall. Directly in front of her was a wooden swinging door, which had been propped open. In its center was a circular window, a porthole affair, that desperately needed cleaning. This had obviously been the door that separated the dining area of the restaurant from the kitchen, she decided. Beyond the battered door was the source of the diffused light she had seen from the tradesman's entrance. That must be where her client was waiting.

She stepped in that direction and stretched her head forward, squinting toward the room ahead. "Ron?" she asked in a normal voice as she paused in front of the swinging door. "Are you in there?" She cocked her head a bit to the right, straining to hear any reply.

Instantly, an enormous opaque figure appeared in the doorway, positioning itself between Joanne and the source of the light beyond, leaving her in almost complete darkness. The figure was that of a large man, tall enough to fill the frame of the doorway nearly to the top, sufficiently broad to leave behind only small crevices of light from the dining area in the distance.

"Mr. Vintini?" she said in a halting voice. "I'm Jo..."

Joanne felt an enormously powerful thrust to her chest, like a white-hot rocket exploding directly over her sternum. Instantly, she heard a sickening rushing of air coming from deep inside her breast, exiting unnaturally away from her body in his direction. She involuntarily dropped her head and tried to speak but realized that she could not take a breath. She felt the grip of a huge hand around the back of her neck, forcing her to stay on her feet despite the pressure on her chest, preventing her from falling backward or escaping. She could taste the stale heat of his rapid, shallow breathing on her face and thought she glimpsed his arm move rapidly toward her for a second time.

There was another tremendous blow to her chest, this time penetrating her left breast and sending her reeling backward into the arm and hand around her neck, again breaking her fall. She felt a hot rush of blood come to her throat and gurgle through her mouth and down her chin. She gagged violently and tried again to scream, but could not. A crushing sensation across her chest told her that the air for which she struggled was escaping from in front of her — from two deep, mortal wounds. In that instant, she knew that she would die, her last conscious thought a flood of undefined and profound sorrow.

Her eyes rolled involuntarily upward and her head snapped sharply to the left. She let out a stifled, plaintive whimper, like that of an abandoned child. There came an unexpected, fleeting millisecond of painless calm and wondrous resignation to the moment, followed by the eternal, impenetrable darkness.

Mercifully, Joanne Callin felt nothing more. She was unaware of the next six thrusts of the eight-inch blade to her chest or the pain of her back and head crashing sickeningly to the kitchen floor with his final, furious blow. There was no agony when he momentarily propped her body up to a sitting position, wrapped the thick rope around her lifeless neck from behind, and snapped the ends together with such force that it crushed two of her vertebrae. She felt nothing as he lifted her right arm by the fingers, raised back the bloodstained knife, and severed her hand at a single stroke.

Her death had been horrifying, but mercifully quick.

Jamieson quickly wrapped her severed hand in several thickness of white cotton cloth and placed it into a red plastic toolbox that waited nearby. He picked up her purse and briefcase from where they had fallen and laid them next to the toolbox. With rapid, determined movements, he pulled his large frame from the translucent, disposable plastic jumpsuit. He was careful to not remove the surgeon's gloves, calf-high rubber boots, plastic goggles, or seaman's cap he was wearing. Jamieson wrapped his discarded, blood-spattered clothing inside a green trash bag and quickly knotted it at the top.

Moving alternatively to each end of the tarp, the murderer made several passes across her body with the cloth, covering the bloody remains with the unnatural shroud and arranging it so that any evidence of his presence would be captured within its folds. He rolled Callin's body over several times, encasing it in several layers of the thick tarp and making sure that as little blood as possible would be left behind. With surprising ease, he lifted her thin, light body, now concealed inside the tarp, and stepped out to his car. There, he flipped the unlocked trunk lid open with his left hand and gently laid his cargo inside.

Jamieson hopped back through the doorway and grabbed the plastic toolbox, purse, trash bag, and briefcase. Pausing on the spot where his victim had fallen, he meticulously scanned the kitchen with his eyes, searching for any obvious evidence of his presence. There was none.

The murderer stepped outside and tried to close the battered metal fire door behind him but found that the broken lock and shattered jam made the effort impossible. It was clear that the door would not stay fully closed in its present condition. He moved to his car, opened the passenger's door, and laid the grim remnants of his crime on the seat. Using the flashlight, he scanned the floorboard and poked around in the debris for something suitable to hold the tradesman's door closed. His hand found a small wedge of pine that looked like it would do. Raising it to eye level, he examined it for any markings — anything that could lead back to him. There were none.

Jamieson stepped back to the metal door and pushed it closed again, this time using the wedge to make sure it would stay secure. As he turned to leave, he saw Joanne Callin's Lexus parked across the alleyway. Quickly, he moved to the driver's side of the shiny automobile and reached for his keys. He pulled the key ring from his pocket and selected a thick, stout house key. With a quick series of deep, thrusting motions, he carved two letters into the driver's door. That was for McCannell. When he had finished, he stepped back to his own vehicle, slid behind the wheel from the passenger's side, and started the engine.

He slowly directed the maroon sedan toward the alleyway entrance and turned onto Folsom Street, patiently waiting for the oncoming traffic to clear. Jamieson then drove three blocks south, to Twenty-eighth Street, and turned left onto Androni Parkway Drive. He drove a few hundred yards into the unlit urban park until he located a familiar dirt spur, which led to a stand of trees off the main drive. There, he pulled the sedan another fifty feet onto the spur, to a place where it was impossible to be seen by motorists navigating the main parkway drive.

He left the engine running and the headlights off. He stepped to the trunk of the car and lifted the tarp and its contents onto his shoulder. He turned southeast, back toward Androni Parkway Drive, and began to walk rapidly. Without the benefit of anything but ambient light, the murderer worked his way to a forgotten wooden bench that was stationed about fifteen feet from the main drive, in a cloistered grove of tall, pungent eucalyptus trees. There, he unwrapped Joanne Callin's body and carefully positioned it on the park bench. He laid her left arm serenely in her lap, palm down; he spread her delicate, bloodless legs far apart in a gross display that mocked her death. When he was sure that the position of the body was just as it should be, he raced back to his car and retrieved the victim's purse and briefcase. He ran back to the park bench and laid the bloodstained articles next to the woman's right arm, where her hand should have been.

Tonight, there would be no note to McCannell. That had already been taken care of. He had a different surprise in mind — something fresh and new.

For a brief, extraordinary moment, Jamieson surveyed the horrific scene, trying to make sure it was absolutely perfect, assessing every gruesome detail of his handiwork. Yes, it was just as he had seen it so often in his mind. He smiled in the darkness and felt an indescribable flood of power and satisfaction race up his spine, orgasm-like in its intensity. This was his moment. This was what it was all about.

He whispered her name, "Joanne... Joanne... Joanne..." in a rhythmic, ritualistic prayer that would ensure she would never be forgotten — as he had been. Then, he finished his secret ceremony with the words that would complete his mission and resolve all things: "Fuck them all! Forever... fuck them all! Especially him. Now they are alone, too!"

Like the careful man he was, Jamieson did not linger a moment longer than was necessary. He ran back to his car and backed it down the dirt spur and onto Androni Parkway Drive. From the moment of the first thrust of the long blade, which had crushed her chest and punctured her left lung, until he drove away from the bench in Androni Park, less than twenty-five minutes had elapsed. It had been an efficient, meticulous, wondrous kill.

In less than ten minutes, he would be home, back at his Bernal Heights flat, working to relieve himself and his maroon sedan of the remaining evidence — free to relive this very special moment in his own, private way.

January 13
Mission District
Morning

Androni Park, 8:15 A.M.

"Chris, I think I've got something here," Mendoza yelled to his boss as he pulled a yellow piece of paper from Joanne Callin's blood-spattered purse.

The Lieutenant backed away from the secluded park bench and moved toward his colleague, motioning for the waiting forensics team to begin sweeping the scene.

"Yeah?" he asked Mendoza as he approached the Sergeant's car. Mendoza had spread various articles across the hood of his automobile, each encased in its own plastic evidence envelope. He was working his way through the contents of the victim's purse as the Lieutenant joined him.

"I found this in her purse, Chris. It was just jammed in, like it was the last thing she put in there" Mendoza said, holding the wrinkled page by one end and carefully shaking it open. Both men leaned forward to focus on the note in the dusky grayness of the morning. On the lined page, in neat script, they read:

- Ron Vintini
- friend of Brian's
- commercial property, vacant restaurant
- 25th and Folsom
- list right away
- 8:00 tonight

"Joe, do you have an approximate time of death yet?" Spell asked, rereading the last line of the note. "Was it after eight o'clock?"

Mendoza shook his head from side to side. "I can't say for sure. Best guess... I'd say she died last night; that the body has been on the bench all night. Are you thinking this is the guy — the guy she was going to meet?" he said, lifting the note.

"Maybe," Spell mumbled. He pulled lightly on Mendoza's arm to steady the moving note and bring it closer to his eyes. He stared at it again for a few seconds, trying to assess its meaning to the dead woman. "Was she a real estate agent?"

Mendoza fumbled among the articles on the hood of the car and selected a small, square, translucent evidence bag with a green strip across the top. "Yeah. She was a commercial real estate agent at the Mission Best Real Property Company on South Van Ness," he said, handing the baggie over to the Lieutenant. Inside the evidence bag was one of Joanne Callin's business cards. On it was her picture – smiling, so alive and obviously happy – along with her work and home telephone numbers. "I have no idea who 'Brian' is, but I've got to think that her eight o'clock appointment may be the guy who whacked her. Don't you?"

Spell hunched his shoulders and nodded his head in a stiff, uncertain way. "Maybe, I don't know... I don't know much about this guy anymore..." He studied the card for a moment, holding its container close to his eyes, then handed it back to Mendoza. "Do you know how the body got here, Joe?"

"Not yet, not for sure. Still working on it. But I have an idea. There are some fresh vehicle tracks on the spur down there, about fifty feet of them, but the ground may be too hard for good impressions. He could have come in here that way, though," Mendoza replied, nodding toward a destination behind the park bench and deep inside a stand of trees.

Spell searched the stand of trees with his eyes and saw a pair of officers inspecting the ground in the area. In the morning light, he could clearly see how the dirt spur separated from the main drive at a sharp angle and disappeared among the trees. At night, it would be impossible to see a vehicle among those trees from Androni Parkway Drive. Mendoza was probably right. This was a likely place to hide a vehicle long enough to remove the victim's body without any fear of interruption. Spell judged the distance from where the murderer may have parked his car to the bench. It was fifty or sixty feet. If that was how it came down, the Lieutenant thought, then the killer must have selected this place in advance. He must have worked out all the details, just like Sam said he would.

"Have you talked to Mary or Sandy yet? Do they know about this?" the Lieutenant asked.

Mendoza thought for a moment before he answered. "No, neither," he said unconvincingly. He pictured Sandy asleep, still in his bed. Perhaps she was awake by now, wondering when he would be back, curious about why he had disappeared so abruptly. "Well," he quickly retreated, "I haven't talked to Mary this morning."

"Ok, Joe. I understand," Spell said in a soft voice. "I want you to get Sandy onto the background of this one. Have her start checking on friends, relatives, coworkers, right?"

The Sergeant nodded, looking down at his feet.

"Joe, is Sandy working tonight — at the restaurant, I mean?"

"Yeah. She starts at four, Chris."

"Ok, well, tell her I'm sorry to screw up her afternoon off. Please call Mary and have her check on the victim's employer — the real estate company. You work the victim's residence, right? I'll call Sam and we'll check on her appointment last night."

Mendoza nodded again, still unwilling to look at his boss.

"Listen, Joe," Spell said in a loud whisper, leaning closer. "I'm not stupid. I can see what's going on with you and Sandy. Just take it easy and keep it straight with me. And don't bring it to work, okay?"

Another nod — more silence.

Spell had no stomach to pursue the matter any further and was in no mood for lies or excuses. He headed back to his car, struggling to pull the cell phone from his overcoat pocket as he walked. When he reached the driver's door, he paused. The number he dialed was Sam McCannell's home telephone.

"Yep," McCannell answered in a crisp tone.

"Jesus, Sam, you sound chipper for this early on a Saturday morning," Spell announced in a somber voice.

"What's not to be chipper about? Things were fine until you called," Sam shot back. "Now, you're going to take me away from a well-planned day doing nothing, right?"

"Yeah, Sam, sorry. We have another one."

The line went silent for a long moment.

"Where?" McCannell asked in a curt tone.

"Where was she killed or where was she found?" Spell asked.

"Oh, I see... Found."

"In Androni Park, on a park bench. Her body was staged, sitting position, legs spread. It was the usual, Sam — strangulation, severed right hand."

Again, the line was silent for too long. "Ok, Chris. Where do we meet?" McCannell finally asked.

"Let's meet at Twenty-fifth and Folsom, Sam. I think she may have been murdered in that area last night. It's only a few blocks from the park and she had an appointment with some guy in that area. I'd like to get there before the forensics team and check it out. If there's nothing there, well, we can get some coffee and talk, right?"

"Right," Sam snapped back. "I'll be there in ten minutes. Bye."

Twenty-fifth and Folsom, 8:50 A.M.

McCannell slipped his canary yellow Fiat convertible into a red zone, and walked quickly down Folsom to the corner of Twenty-fifth Street, passing in front of the telephone booth that Joanne Callin's murderer had used the night before. As he arrived, the Lieutenant appeared from around the corner, looking harried and concerned.

"Sorry to take so long, Chris. I couldn't find a damn place to park," McCannell complained.

Spell nodded and tried, unsuccessfully, to smile. "Well, the victim didn't have the same problem, Sam. Her car is parked in the alley behind the second store there." The Lieutenant pointed to an abandoned building that had once been a bustling, family-owned restaurant when this part of the Mission District was still considered a neighborhood. The windows of the vacant store had been painted over from the inside with several thick coats of white latex. The door had been secured with a rectangular piece of plywood nailed across its face and affixed to the frame. Over the doorway hung a battered, hand-painted sign with faded red and gold lettering that read "Chin's Three Dragons."

"Oh…" McCannell mumbled as he headed for the front door.

"Don't bother, Sam," the Lieutenant snapped in a harsh tone. "Come around back with me and take a look at something. That's what you need to see."

Spell quickly disappeared around the corner and headed down Twenty-fifth with McCannell in tow. They turned into the alley and walked a short distance to the trade entrance of the restaurant. The metal fire door had been pushed open during Spell's earlier inspection of the premises. Across the alley, deep in the shadows of the old buildings, McCannell could see a shiny blue Lexus parked snuggly against the windowless back wall of a private residence. The condensation on the windows and body of the vehicle told him that it had been parked in that same position over night.

"That's the victim's car, Sam," Spell said, pointing in the general direction of the Lexus. "You may want to take a look at it before the forensics team works it over. It has writing carved into the driver's door that may have something to do with our guy."

The red man stepped quickly down the pavement and stood next to the driver's door, moving his head from side to side to study the markings. After a few seconds, he stepped back into the middle of the pavement and stared for a while longer at the door. Then, with his head down, he shuffled his way back to the Lieutenant.

"It looks to me like two letter 'M's," Spell said. "It's like 'M' and 'M', or 'MM', right?"

"Yeah, Chris. It's definitely two 'M's all right. What was the victim's name?" McCannell asked, probing for some connection with the carved letters.

Spell reached into his overcoat pocket and pulled out a thin, black notebook. He rifled through the pages, slapping a certain page with the back of his hand. "Her name was Joanne Callin, according to the identification in her purse. She was apparently a commercial real estate agent and may have been here at eight o'clock last night to meet a client by the name of Ron Vintini. We don't have anything else on her yet, except that she was physically similar to our other victims and was nicely dressed when she was killed."

"She didn't meet a client here," Sam shot back. "That was our guy. And this," he said, pointing to the metal doorway, "is where he killed her. He left her car and took the body away in his. He marked her car as a message to us." McCannell started up the concrete steps to the trade entrance when he felt a sharp tug on his right arm.

"Wait, Sam!" the Lieutenant yelped. "Put these on before you go in there. The forensics team hasn't been here yet." Spell thrust a pair of cotton booties and surgeon's gloves at McCannell. The red man sat on the top concrete step, slipped the booties over his shoes, and pulled the latex gloves over his chubby fingers.

"Ok?" he asked the Lieutenant with a tight smile, holding his hands away from his body.

Spell nodded. "I'll wait out here, Sam. I've seen it already. Be careful in there. Don't disturb anything, right?"

McCannell grumbled something and disappeared into the darkened kitchen. For several moments, Spell waited on the pavement, anxiously pacing between the trade entrance and Joanne Callin's Lexus. Finally, McCannell appeared at the doorway, pulled the gloves from his hands, and stared silently at his friend.

"Well?" the Lieutenant asked with a drawn, worried look.

"This guy is good, Chris. Do you have any idea how good?"

Spell nodded back and forth. He didn't want to consider that question. "What happened in there, Sam? I didn't see much visual evidence; just some blood smears on the floor — not nearly enough for the way she died."

"He killed her in there, for sure," McCannell answered, his face flushed. "He lured her here and murdered her in that room," he continued, pointing over his shoulder at the abandoned kitchen. "He had everything ready. That's why there isn't much to see. I'll bet we have very little on forensics, too. He lured her here, killed her here. Jesus! It must have been awful, Chris."

McCannell stepped down to the pavement and began to make small, circular scraping motions with his right foot. He was far away, trying to summon up an image of her last few moments alive, trying to put together some picture of her murderer.

"The real question is how and why he targeted her. He's changed up again, Chris. This one was different," McCannell said.

Spell's face looked lifeless and desperate. "We're nowhere on this guy, Sam. We're nowhere…"

January 14
Bernal Heights District
Sunday Morning

Herbert Jamieson rested his left arm on the kitchen table, directly across the headline of the newspaper article he had meticulously clipped from the Sunday morning edition of the *Call*. With vacant, distant eyes, he scanned the words without concern for their meaning. With his right hand, he tried desperately to masturbate, to find the magical rhythm of the moment — but nothing was happening.

Nothing *ever* happened.

Mission District Monster Claims Fourth Victim
By Jane Riordan, *Call* Staff Writer

Sunday Edition—Crime Watch
January 14, San Francisco:

Yesterday morning, homicide investigators discovered the body of Joanne Callin, a resident of San Francisco and well-known commercial real estate agent with the Mission Best Real Property Company on South Van Ness Avenue. Callin was the fourth victim of the Mission District Monster — a serial killer who remains unidentified and at large. Like the previous victims, Callin had been repeatedly stabbed in the chest and strangled. Investigators believe she was murdered around eight o'clock Friday night. A shocked tourist from San Diego found her body on a bench in a secluded area of Androni Park. Callin was twenty-seven years old.

When reached by telephone for his comment,

Callin's employer and friend, Brian Silverstein, said, "This is the worst news I've ever had. Joanne was not just an outstanding saleswoman and colleague; she was a dear personal friend. She was someone who had so much life in her. She was loved by everyone."

Roy Dunover, Callin's fiancé, was hospitalized from shock after learning of her death from SFPD officers. He had reported her missing around midnight on Friday. Dunover is not a suspect in the case.

According to investigating officers, Callin had no other close relatives still living. She was a resident of the Mission District since 1988 and lived alone.

Lieutenant Christopher Spell and Dr. Sam McCannell head the SFPD homicide investigation team that is responsible for solving the murders of four young women since September of last year.

"We are making headway, but it's slow," Spell said. "This man is very determined, very lethal, and very intelligent. But we are also very determined to put a stop to his activities."

An unusual aspect to this case is the fact that the murderer has been in direct communication with Dr. McCannell, a Forensic Psychologist with the SFPD. According to McCannell, the serial killer has written to him on more than one occasion regarding the murders. Although unwilling to disclose the details of the communications, McCannell did confirm that the murderer is in contact with him and is providing valuable information to investigators.

"He's trying to tell us why he does these horrible things," McCannell said. "He wants us to understand his motives and his reasoning. Personally, I believe this man would like to stop killing. From his communications, I think he hates what he is doing but cannot find a way to stop. Hopefully, he will keep in contact with us and we can work with him to end the killing."

McCannell said that serial murderers occasionally communicate with investigators in an effort to draw them more deeply into the case, although it is not a common aspect of the crime.

"This kind of thing happens, in a few cases," McCannell said. "It's a hopeful sign when the murderer wants to communicate with us. We are always optimistic that he will see the horror of what he is doing and let us work with him to put a stop to it."

According to Lieutenant Spell, all the victims were slain in the same manner. Each was stabbed repeatedly in the chest and strangled. All the women were between twenty and thirty years of age.

"This man stalks and murders a particular type of victim," Spell confirmed. "They were all similar in physical appearance and all of them lived and worked in the Mission District."

When asked if investigators were closing in on a suspect, Spell refused to comment, but said that investigators were pursing all leads. "We're getting closer all the time," Spell said. "We're throwing everything we have at this case in an effort to stop this senseless killing as soon as we can."

Jamieson pushed himself away from the kitchen table and rolled his naked body along the frigid, filthy linoleum floor. He lay on his back, the muscles in his right forearm throbbing from their useless effort, his arms limp by his sides. An involuntary stiffness came across his chest, back, and head.

His eyes rolled upward, but did not close.

"When did you first come to fear your husband?" Marion Jamieson's attorney asked.

"A few years after we were married," she answered in a halting voice, her whitened fingers interlaced tightly on her lap.

"So, you were married just over four years, correct?"

"Yes."

"And you came to be afraid of Mr. Jamieson shortly after you were married, correct?"

"Yes, maybe two years afterward."

"Please tell the court why you were so afraid of your husband, Mrs. Jamieson."

"Objection, objection…" The woman at the Defendant's table rose abruptly and waved her right hand angrily in the general direction of the witness. "This matter has already been considered in my client's criminal trial, Your Honor. Charges related to this issue were dropped. This material is not relevant and should not be admitted in a civil trial such as this."

"Overruled, counselor," the judge said in a stern voice. "Even though the charges against your client were dropped for *insufficient evidence*, that does not make the underlying issues irrelevant to these proceedings. Sit down."

She turned to face Marion Jamieson's attorney, standing to her left. "Proceed," the judge ordered.

"*Why* were you afraid of your husband, Mrs. Jamieson?"

The answer was slow in coming. "Because he would make me do things I didn't want to do," she whimpered, fighting to hold back the tears.

"All right. I understand this is difficult for you. Can you continue?"

"Yes," she mumbled.

"What *kinds* of things did your husband make you do, Mrs. Jamieson?"

The witness dropped her head and did not immediately answer. Her slight frame seemed to stiffen and grow more determined as she sucked in a large breath. Without looking up, she said: "He made me do sexual things to him — things I did not want to do. Things that were not right, or normal."

"What *kinds* of sexual things, Mrs. Jamieson?" her attorney quickly repeated.

"Objection!" the Defendant's attorney shouted at the judge, leaping once more from her chair.

"Overruled!" she snapped back. "Sit down and stay down, counselor! We *will* hear this testimony."

"What kinds of things?" her attorney asked again, this time more deliberately.

The witness raised her head and looked directly at the judge. There were massive pools of tears in her eyes and her face was strained and pale. "He would make me do things to him sexually. We never had normal sexual relations. I mean, he never made love to me — ever. He would make me do things to him with my hands. He would hold me around the neck and make me do things to him with my hands. If I didn't do it right, he would squeeze my neck and threaten to kill me. He said I could never leave him or he would kill me. He would tell me that his mother did it right, so I should just learn to do it right. He would say…"

"Fucking bitch!" the Defendant screamed. "Bitch!" He pounded both fists on the table, threatening to overturn it. With a sudden ferocity, Jamieson thrust his body to the left, away from his attorney, and hurled himself to the floor. Immediately, he jumped back to his feet and rushed unsteadily in the direction of the witness. A burly SFPD officer, who had been standing near the judge's bench, jumped in front of the Defendant and tripped him with a quick movement of his leg, sending him crashing to the floor. The officer briefly struggled with the large man before he was able to force his arms behind his back and snap on a pair of handcuffs. The Defendant rolled angrily around on the courtroom floor, unable to bring himself to his feet, screaming "Bitch!" and "Fuck you!" to the sobbing woman in the witness box.

"All right! All right!" the judge yelled, slapping her hand noisily on the bench in front of her. "That is enough!" She waited for a moment while the police officer dragged Jamieson to his feet. The Defendant's attorney sat back down at her table, shaking noticeably and rubbing her forehead with her right hand. On the witness stand, Marion Jamieson was crying uncontrollably and being comforted by her attorney, who looked at least as pale and afraid as the witness.

"Bailiff, sit that man down!" the judge demanded, pointing her finger directly at the Defendant's face. The officer pulled Jamieson by his arm toward a wooden bench to the right and in front of the judge. As the struggling pair arrived at the bench, the officer thrust Jamieson down with a massive crash, holding him in a sitting position with a firm hand on his shoulder. The prisoner began mumbling incoherently to himself and shaking his legs uncontrollably.

"Counselors, approach," the judge ordered, still glowering at the man in handcuffs.

The two women quickly moved to the front of the bench. The judge stared down at them and shook her head in disgust. "I've had enough!" she said in a low, whispered voice. "After two days of this, I've seen enough and I've heard enough." Turning to Jamieson's lawyer, she said in a menacing voice, "Your client has severe problems. That's obvious, isn't it?"

Jamieson's attorney nodded and dropped her head. She had done all she could do.

"All right. Do either of you want to continue with this mockery?" the judge demanded of both lawyers. Both shook their heads. They, too, had had enough.

"No, I certainly don't want to go on with this," Jamieson's

attorney confirmed without looking up.

"All right. I want you to go back to your places and immediately rest your cases — both of you," the judge instructed the attorneys. "I will then issue a ruling and we can get the hell out of here. I want this man out of my courtroom and out of my sight!"

The lawyers returned to their respective tables and sat down, both still shaken from the chaos of the past few moments. In the corner of the courtroom, the Defendant was writhing on the bench where he sat, a glowering, blank expression on his face.

"Your Honor, we have nothing further for this witness," Marion Jamieson's lawyer said in a weak voice as she rose from her seat. "We have no further witnesses and we rest our case." She immediately sat down and let out a huge sigh.

The judge turned to the witness. "You are excused, Mrs. Jamieson," she said softly.

As Marion Jamieson left the stand, the woman on the bench wheeled around in her chair to face the Defendant's table. "Anything more?" she demanded in a harsh voice.

"Your Honor, we are finished. We rest," his attorney croaked without ever moving from her chair.

Jamieson tried to struggle to his feet but was again thrown back by the officer. "Fuck you!" he shouted at the judge. "Fuck yourself, bitch!" he shouted at his attorney.

"Enough!" the judge ordered. "Herbert William Jamieson," she said in a loud voice, looking directly at the Defendant, "Based on your outburst here today and the record of these proceedings, I am ordering that you be placed in custody for a period of thirty days observation at the Brisbane Psychiatric Hospital. During that time, I will advise the City prosecutor to consider charges of contempt and assault against you. The temporary restraining order against you in favor of Marion Jamieson is hereby made permanent. In addition, the

Plaintiff's request for judgment against you in the amount of $100,000 is sustained and so ordered."

Immediately, the judge rose from behind the bench and disappeared into her chambers.

Jamieson threw himself forward with tremendous force and began to writhe on the floor screaming, "Bitch, I'll cut your head off... bitch, I'll cut your hands off..."

A second officer appeared at the back of the courtroom and rushed to where Jamieson was struggling with the bailiff. The two officers grabbed the prisoner by his arms and dragged him, face down, across the floor of the courtroom, to a side door that led to a holding cell. His face bounced along the planked floor, his head banging up and down in rhythm to the jerky steps of the officers.

As they pulled him across the threshold that separated the courtroom from the holding cell, his face bounced especially hard against the floor and he noticed that the surface had changed from wood to concrete. The officers threw him into the holding cell and removed the handcuffs, leaving him lying on his back on the cold, unyielding floor. He felt dizzy and far away. He thought he heard the clanging of a cell door, somewhere in the distance.

His mind rushed away from his prone body — a dream within a dream.

No... It was the clanging of the *noon bell* that he heard — not the cell door!

Yes, it was the bell!

He was young again. He was thirteen. He was back at St. Boniface's Seminary.

It was time for the noon prayers — it was the noon bell calling him to prayer.

Jesus! They would be late! Jesus! What if they were caught

like this — in the seminary! Oh, Christ!

Jamieson angrily pulled the man's sweaty hand from around his erect penis and flung his arm to the side. Using both hands, he shoved the Brother's undernourished body from beside him, off the cot, and sent him crashing to the stone floor. The young man in the brown robe looked hurt and insulted but said nothing. He leapt to his feet, tightened the cloth robe around his ashen frame, and rushed toward the door.

"Get out!" Jamieson screamed. "Get out! I don't want to do this anymore! Get the fuck out!"

Brother Franklin ran from the tiny guestroom and scurried down the hallway in the direction of the chapel. Jamieson fumbled with his pants, trying desperately to pull them over his spindly legs as quickly as he could, but it was too late.

At the threshold of the open door to his room stood Father Amando, glowering down at him.

"What was going on in here, Herbert? What were you doing in here? Who was with you?" His voice was stern and unyielding; his questions came in a rapid, demanding staccato. To the young boy, the aging, fattened priest was incredibly large and frightening. He seemed like a dark, misshapen angel who had magically, unexpectedly descended into the stone cradle of Jamieson's guestroom to exact a holy revenge. The priest stepped inside and closed the door behind him, moving slowly toward his charge.

The young boy threw himself face down on the hard cot. He could smell the dusky, woolen bedcover against his cheek. He began to cry, uncontrollably.

"Herbert," Father Amando whispered as he sat down on the edge of the cot. "I know that you're only here until there's a new home for you, but you've made a wonderful impression on us. Some of us have grown very fond of you, Herbert. We hope you will decide to stay with us — forever. To join us — forever."

The priest laid a fleshy hand on the boy's upper back and began to rub it in a circular motion. Herbert fell quiet, his sobbing replaced by short, thick, fearful breaths. Father Amando slid his hand underneath the boy's white pullover shirt, now stroking his sweating, shaking back with firm, thrusting movements.

"We are very fond of you, Herbert..." he repeated, as he gently rolled the boy onto his back and raised his shirt to a tight clump around his neck. The priest gazed at the pale skin and began to stroke the boy's chest in short, rapid movements.

Jamieson closed his eyes and waited. He felt Father Amando's tight grasp on his frail right hand. Slowly, the older man led the boy's shuddering fingers to that secret place beneath his sacred robes. The boy felt the heat of the priest's erect organ and allowed his hand to be wrapped around it, to caress it. He waited and said nothing as the priest guided Herbert's hand in just the right way, with just the right rhythm.

Finally, the holy man let out a whimpering sigh. The boy felt a series of warm, wet, pulsating movements in the palm of his right hand. When it was done, an enormous pain shot instantly across Jamieson's fingers, up his wrist, up his arm, and into the kernel of his brain. He closed his eyes tight against the pain and tried to pray it away.

In the blackness behind his closed eyes, the young boy saw an angel of God enter the confines of his narrow, dank cell. Dressed in God's silver armor and radiating brilliant red, yellow, and white light in all directions, the Holy Messenger smiled lovingly upon the young boy — his face resplendent with understanding and determination. The Angel reached down, raised Herbert's right arm above his head, and instantly severed his hand at the wrist with his flashing silver blade.

The boy smiled. The pain had vanished. The evil had been excised. It was done.

Slowly, an impenetrable, infinite stillness filled the darkened room. Father Amando had gone. The angel had left him. Now, there was only the unsettling peace born of a boy's vanquished guilt — the intense hatred of the men in robes and the women who bore them, and the loathing of his mother for her unforgivable act of abandoning him to this unspeakable place.

January 15
Midtown Station
Noon

Sam McCannell snatched his third slice of pizza from the greasy box on Lieutenant Spell's desk and began nibbling on it like a voracious rabbit. "Come on, Mary," he mumbled through a mouthful of his lunch. "Give it a try — it's great!"

"Yeah, it's better while it's warm," the Lieutenant added. "Lots of garlic…"

Mary Boor wrinkled her nose and shook her head slowly from side to side. "No, thanks. I'll pass." She stared at the two men devouring thick slices of pungent pizza and laughed sarcastically. God, what she wouldn't give for a salad right now!

Her forlorn expression was not lost on the Lieutenant.

"Listen, Mary," Chris said between gulps, "how about if I make this up to you with dinner?"

"Sure, that would be good," she quickly answered. "Why don't you come over to my place tonight and have some *real* Italian food for a change?"

There was something coded about her statement — or at least she intended it that way.

Spell shot a quick glance at McCannell. He had that impish, know-it-all expression pasted all over his round, red face, highlighted by random streaks of tomato sauce across his chin. "Yeah, Chris," he chirped. "Why not get a *real* meal," he echoed with a smile.

The Lieutenant nodded and pretended to move some papers around on his desk. "Sure, Mar, I'd love to."

"Hey, did you leave any for us?" Mendoza said as he strolled into the Lieutenant's office with Sandy Janus in tow.

"Sure, Joe. Help yourself," Spell answered, pushing the box to the edge of his desk. There was still almost half a pizza left, despite McCannell's frontal assault on it.

Mendoza and Janus took their usual places on the couch in front of the Lieutenant's desk. They each attacked the pizza without a word, obviously preoccupied with their stomachs. Spell wondered what they had been doing to create such an appetite.

"Ok, now that we're all here, let's talk about Joanne Callin, right?" the Lieutenant announced.

"Well, Chris, I know how the murderer found his victim," Mary said from the corner of the office. Immediately, the chewing stopped. Inspector Boor had managed to refocus everyone's attention with her simple, understated pronouncement.

"Jesus!" Mendoza whispered, still dangling a slice of pizza from his right hand.

McCannell moved very close to Mary and stared directly into her face. "Oh, Mary, I certainly want to hear this!" he exclaimed, instantly relieved of his hunger.

She blushed intensely and looked away from him, her eyes examining the chaotic collection of memorabilia on the bookshelf behind the Lieutenant's desk. "Sam, it wasn't that big of a deal. I mean, it was actually pretty obvious," she said to the bookshelf.

Mary turned to face the Lieutenant at his desk. "After I got the call from Joe, I started checking on the victim's employer. I hit the jackpot on my first trip to her real estate company on South Van Ness. Right in the window of the office was a huge poster with Callin's photograph on it. She had won some kind of sales award. Not only was her picture up there for everyone to see, they also put her office and home phone numbers on the poster. In fact, the poster looked like a blow-up of her business card."

"Did it look like this?" Mendoza asked, sliding a plastic evidence envelope from the top of the Lieutenant's desk and holding it up in her direction.

Mary moved toward the couch, took the envelope from him, and held it close to her eyes. It contained Joanne Callin's business card.

"They must have just blown it up for the window display. Right there in plain view... he knew all he needed to know — what she looked like, how to get in touch with her..."

"Not everything," Sam interrupted. "He would still have to gain her trust... lure her to the place where he killed her."

"Yeah, right, Sam. Based on the note in her purse that Joe told me about, I'd say he probably impersonated a friend of her boss... Brian Silverstein. It'd be easy to find out his name and then use that to lure Callin, right? I mean, so long as Callin didn't check with Silverstein, our guy could say he's an old friend, former business partner... or whatever. If the murderer called her in the evening, after the business closed, which I'm sure he did, well, she probably wouldn't check with Silverstein. All he had to do was give her a good, convincing story to set the hook. She probably didn't even suspect anything."

"Absolutely!" McCannell said with a hearty shake of his head. "I think that's just the way it probably happened, Mary. Great work!"

"You bet, Mar," Spell added. "That's terrific! So, the guy finds his mark because everything he needed was there, right in the store window. She fit the physical requirements and he had everything he needed to get in contact with her...."

"And from there," Sam finished, "all he had to do was come up with a believable story. The murderer would have known that she was a top salesperson. It would have been obvious from the storefront display. And everyone knows that a good real estate agent is available twenty-four hours a day. So, he told her he had this piece of property and lured her to look at it. When she arrived to meet him and look at the property, he had everything ready to whack her."

"Makes sense," Chris mumbled to himself. "It's fucked, but it makes good sense... Sandy, what have you come up with on Callin's background?"

"As Mary said, Brian Silverstein is the owner of Mission Best Real Property. Callin worked for him for about five years. In the last few years, she was his number one salesperson. They were good friends but nothing more. Silverstein checks out clean, Chris. He knew nothing about a new listing on Folsom and had never heard of a guy named Ron Vintini."

"Callin's boyfriend, Roy Dunover, is also clean. He's a financial analyst for the Federal Reserve Bank. Actually, the guy is a real social loser, in my opinion. He had a date with the victim for dinner on Friday night. When he got home from work he found a message from her on his answering machine. She said she had a last minute real estate deal for her boss, Silverstein, and that she'd be late for their eight o'clock dinner date. He waited at his apartment to hear from her but she never called. He repeatedly telephoned her flat but got no answer. Apparently, she didn't leave her answering machine on that night. At around midnight, he was completely freaked out and tried to file a missing person's report here at the station. The next morning, when he heard from us about Callin's murder, he went into shock and wound up in the hospital. Bottom line here is that he's not involved."

"The victim had no other relatives that we've been able to locate. I did talk to her neighbors and they all said that she was a hard-working, good person. From their point of view, she was *always* working. Her only recreation was apparently a pretty intense relationship with Dunover."

"Joe, what did *you* get?" Spell asked.

"Some pretty good news, actually, Chris. The forensics team

picked up a few shoe imprints that *could* belong to our guy. The way it plays out, he had to carry the victim's body from his car to the park bench. From the scene and the imprints, it looks like he had the body in the trunk of his car. From the car, he had to walk about fifty feet across a stretch of uncut grass and dirt to get to his destination. Along the way, he may have left three usable imprints because of the extra weight of carrying the body. Now, we don't know for sure that these are his prints, but it's a good possibility."

Mendoza pulled three black and white photographs from a manila envelope next to him on the couch and handed them to the Lieutenant. They each showed a distinct imprint in dark, damp dirt. Spell briefly examined the photographs and passed them to Mary, who was standing close to him, looking over his shoulder. He nodded to Mendoza to continue.

"Ok, so the imprints tell us a few things. If this is our guy, he wears a size eleven shoe and probably weighs between 180 and 220 pounds, allowing for the extra weight of Callin's body at about 100 pounds. From the pattern of the imprints, it looks like he may have been wearing reasonably new rubber boots. Given what we have, a good guess at his height would be around six feet or a bit more. A strong guy…"

"Oh, excellent, Joe!" Chris yelped. "Anything else?"

"Yeah, it gets better. We also found some tire tracks."

The Sergeant pulled four more photographs from the manila envelope and handed them to the Lieutenant. "We have good tread imprints on these. The tires are the size and style that would be used on a heavy, American sedan… a Cadillac, a Buick, a big Chevy, or an old Pontiac. The position of the tracks and the shoe imprints indicates that our guy probably parked his car in a stand of trees, removed the victim's body from the trunk, and carried it over to the park bench. That would account for the evidence at the scene."

"Fan-fucking-tastic!" Spell said, almost shouting. "Finally…"

"Chris, I have some forensics from the murder scene that may also help," Mary said in a quiet voice.

"Yeah?" Spell asked in an excited tone.

"The lab team found several fibers from a cloth tarp at the scene. Some of them were saturated with blood of the same type as the victim. They think that the victim was murdered while standing on this tarp and then her body was wrapped in it. According to their analysis, that would account for the lack of trace evidence and blood at the scene. Since the medical examiner found the same wounds and same style of attack with Callin as with the others, that may explain how he was able to sanitize the crime scenes as well as he did. Basically, he takes the evidence with him when he leaves. He probably wraps everything up in a tarp, including the body. That's how he transports the corpses from place to place."

From the corner of the office, McCannell let out a guttural sound and began to nod his head up and down. "Oh, man. This is beginning to make sense. This is right. It fits…" His voice trailed off.

Mary moved to where the red man was standing and gave him a delicate nudge on the arm. "Ok, Sam, I can see you've got a picture in that fluffy head of yours. Want to share it?"

"You bet I do!" McCannell shot back.

For the next ten minutes, the red man shuffled back and forth across the office, waving his arms excitedly and filling in the details of the Mission District Monster as *he* saw them. It was obvious to the others that he had assembled the facts in his mind and put them together in that special way that few others could do. True, there was much assumption and some guesswork mixed into the story he told. But, to his colleagues, it was a red-hot tale that fit the few facts well. It was the first moment since the murder of Alvina Ruminez, back in September, that Chris Spell actually felt like he was close to knowing something concrete about the murderer.

"All right," the Lieutenant said as McCannell finished, "What do we do with this information?"

"I have an idea," Mary offered. "Why not let Sam tell his story to Jane Riordan? Why not use the information that we have to draw the guy back to us — to get him to communicate directly with us again? Would that work, Sam?"

McCannell thought for a moment, his eyes shut tight in their usual way. "Yeah, Mary, that *may* work. We *could* let our guy know what we know — up to a point. We could begin to personalize our relationship with him through the press and try to draw him closer. It's worth a try."

"I like it," Spell announced from behind his desk. "I like it a lot. It's proactive. Joe, what do you think? Sandy?"

They both nodded. They had long ago forgotten the pizza.

"Ok, that's what we'll do — if you're comfortable with that, Sam?" Spell asked his friend.

The red man nodded. "Hell, yes! I really like that Jane Riordan lady. She may be a foot taller than me but she sure smells good up close!" He winked at Chris so hard that the entire side of this face seemed to pucker up.

Mary leaned over and gave McCannell a delicate kiss on the cheek. "You know, Sam, if I didn't have anything better going on in my life, I'd steal you away from your wife for a long weekend. I'd take you somewhere down the coast and I'd work some of that chub off you in a hurry." With that, she gave his fleshy cheek a tight squeeze with her long fingers.

The others roared a laughing approval at their traditionally demure, quiet colleague and stared at McCannell for his reaction. He was crimson – not just the usual red – but a deep, bright crimson. His head hung on his chest and his arms dangled uselessly at his side.

Although they couldn't see his round face, the jerky movements of his well-fed frame told them that he was also silently laughing — very hard. It was a rare moment when their in-house Dr. Freud was bested in a conversation, and the others in the room were not about to let it pass unnoticed.

Today, McCannell had clearly finished in second place — and he was loving it.

January 17
The San Francisco *Call*

Understanding a Monster
An Exclusive Interview with Dr. Sam McCannell of the SFPD
By Jane Riordan, *Call* Staff Writer
January 17, San Francisco:

I met with Dr. Sam McCannell, Forensic Psychologist for the San Francisco Police Department, in his office at the Midtown Police Station late yesterday afternoon. The purpose of our meeting was to learn more about the serial killer who has been haunting the Mission District for the past five months. It is McCannell's job to help investigators identify unknown perpetrators of serious and violent crimes — a job that is emotionally trying and often very frustrating. Despite the intensity of his work, McCannell is a jovial, pleasant, middle-aged man who is quick with a smile and direct in his answers.

Hidden away in a tiny, cluttered office on the second floor of the police station, he works virtually alone, surrounded by case files and documents that seem to span the range of human depravity. To many at the SFPD, McCannell is a legend — one of the rarely seen crimefighters whose work is vital but who often goes unnoticed in the press or by the public. It is a situation that does not seem to bother this interesting man at all.

Since the murder of Alvina Ruminez last year, McCannell has been working with the SFPD Homicide Division to identify and apprehend the serial killer known in the media as the *Mission District Monster* — an individual who has claimed the lives of four women in a series of exceptionally brutal attacks. Now, for the first time in the case, Dr. McCannell has agreed to provide us with his assessment of the serial killer who has occupied his thoughts for the past several months.

Riordan: In the media and on television, we often hear the term "profiler" as someone who tries to identify a criminal through the psychological aspects of his or her crime. Is that what you are? Is that your job here at the SFPD?

McCannell: Well, in a one way it is and in another it's not. It's wrong to assume that I can somehow identify a criminal by some mystical means. That's television fiction. In fact, identifying perpetrators of crimes is not even my job. The investigators are the individuals who identify and apprehend perpetrators. It's my job to reduce the possibilities – to increase the odds – so that the investigators can better focus their efforts and therefore apprehend a suspect more quickly and efficiently. In other words, I look at the facts of the crime and try to narrow the pool of potential suspects. The investigators rely on me to help them narrow the field of suspects down to a manageable level. But they also turn to me to better understand why an individual does what he or she does. In many cases, if an investigator can understand the "why" of a violent crime, he or she can more quickly answer the "who" of it.

Riordan: And you have been working on the case of the Mission District Monster?

McCannell: Well, I don't like that term, "Mission District Monster," but, yes, I've been working with homicide investigators on this case since the first murder, last year.

Riordan: By any standards that I can imagine, this man *is* a monster. He has committed four, very vicious murders. Why do you object to the phrase I just used?

McCannell: You're right in saying he has

committed monstrous acts. But, despite his horrible crimes, this is a *man* we are talking about. He is flesh and blood — a man with some serious problems, obviously, but he is still a man. Unfortunately, men, and sometimes women, are capable of monstrous crimes, like those that have occurred in the City over the past several months. To call him a "monster" is to give more to him and his actions than they deserve. Yes, these are monstrous crimes, but they've been committed by a man — nothing more. I don't believe that sensationalizing these crimes adds to our ability to put a stop to them.

Riordan: Then, you know, for sure, that the murderer is a man?

McCannell: Yes. We've known that from the first murder. There's no question about it.

Riordan: How do you know that, or how did you come to that conclusion so quickly?

McCannell: Every crime has a signature, a kind of imprint at the crime scene that is apparent to the trained eye, even if the perpetrator of the crime isn't aware that he has left that signature behind. In the case of a serial killer, the *method* of the murder may change but the *signature* of the crime does not. There are elements in each of these murders that make it obvious that the crimes were committed by the same individual — a man. In addition to that, in this case, we have received communications from the murderer that confirm his gender. There is no question that this serial killer is a man.

Riordan: What can you tell us about the murderer? What have you learned about him through his crimes and communications?

McCannell: This man targets his victims in a very specific way. For one thing, the victims share similar physical characteristics. He prefers women who are below average height and have dark or black hair. In three of the four cases, one could describe the victims as slender or of delicate build. The murderer does not choose his victims in a random way. In fact, he is very careful about selecting them. That tells us that these victims are proxies, that they are representatives of the person who is the *real* target of his wrath and venom. When he attacks these women, he has someone very specific in mind who is the genuine target of his hurt and anger but whom he cannot or will not attack directly.

Also, this man is intelligent and careful. He plans his crimes in great detail and sticks to the plan when he attacks. In three of the four cases, we are convinced that he communicated with the victim before he attacked her. In other words, he arranged the details of the murder and drew the victim into his plan. In one of the cases, we are uncertain if he did this or not. One of the murders may have been spontaneous. Generally, however, he works out each detail of the crime, accounts for possible scenarios, and lures the victims to their deaths. In other words, he is able to create a situation in which the victim participates, to some extent, in her own murder.

Riordan: What can you say about the murderer himself? What is he like?

McCannell: He is angry and he has been hurt terribly in the past. I believe he suffered some significant psychosexual trauma in his childhood or youth. Most likely, he is between the ages of thirty and forty-five, judging by the sophisticated planning and care that he takes in each crime. He probably lives alone and may hold a job at which he works weekdays, leaving him free to commit the murders on Friday nights or weekends. I cannot say too much on this issue because the homicide investigators have some important evidence along these lines. However, we know that he is on the large side, probably about six feet tall or a bit more, weighing somewhere in the range of 180 to 200 pounds. He may drive a relatively late model American sedan or a similarly heavy vehicle. It's possible that the murderer impersonates someone in an official capacity or presents himself as an individual who could be trusted by his victims. He has an intimate knowledge of the Mission District and probably lives nearby or in the District itself. Most important, he is intelligent, manipulative, articulate, and resourceful.

Riordan: And, I assume, he is also crazy?

McCannel: No, I doubt it. Without getting too technical here, this man is an organized murderer, not a wanton, crazed killer. There is little about him that is disorganized. Now, that is not to say that he isn't suffering from some severe psychological problems — he probably is. But that does not make him "crazy," as you put it. He knows what he is doing and is able to function effectively in society. If you were to meet him on the street, you would not suspect him of being a murderer. In fact, I believe that he can be very articulate and charming. In other words, like many serial killers, he is a master at manipulation and quite capable of highly intelligent, effective actions.

Riordan: Not to belabor the point, Dr. McCannell, but how can someone commit these kinds of atrocities and *not* be insane?

McCannell: I suppose that depends on your definition of "insanity." That term has both legal and medical implications. From a legal point of view, it's a rare event when a murderer is determined to be insane by a judge or jury. From a medical perspective, it's a bigger question. There's also the issue of "how" insane. It's not a simple thing to define; it's not a black-and-white kind of thing. Certainly, from a general perspective, it's hard to imagine someone who has committed these kinds of crimes as being "normal." But, in the end, I doubt very much that this man is insane.

Riordan: Then *why* does he kill and *what* is he

trying to accomplish?

McCannell: That's also a very complex question. At one level, he is exacting retribution against a particular individual who has hurt him deeply. Unfortunately, he is taking out his aggressions against innocent women. At a deeper level, he is playing out a sexual fantasy that involves violence. In his mind, sex and violence have become intertwined in an abnormal, perverse way. He views sex and violence as inseparable. So, he is both violating his victims and joining with them in a substitute form of sexual release. In a bizarre thought process, he may believe that his victims are willing participants in their own deaths. In fact, I have reason to believe that the murderer operates within a fantasy that his victims are somehow in love with him at the moment of their deaths. In other words, they surrender themselves completely to him by giving up their lives. To the murderer, this is a kind of sex act.

Riordan: I was under the impression that these were not sex crimes. It is my understanding that none of the victims were sexually violated in any way. Is that correct?

McCannell: You're correct. None of the victims were sexually violated. However, that does not mean that the murders were not sexual homicides. In fact, these murders were definitely sex crimes. Again, I cannot disclose all that I know about these cases, but I can tell you that certain elements at the crime scenes indicate that the murders had a sexual component. But now, none of the victims were raped.

Riordan: Then how did you arrive at the conclusion that there was a sexual element to the murders?

McCannell: I cannot discuss specifics here. Let me say this: the murderer made it clear that there was a sexual component to the murders. He wanted us to know that fact and made an effort to make that fact clear at the crime scene. He also alluded to that fact in his communications.

Riordan: How has this man communicated with you and what has he said?

McCannell: I've received written communications from him. Part of the SFPD case against this man will rely on those communications, so I cannot disclose the specific content of what he wrote. I can tell you that the purpose of his communications was to explain *why* he was murdering. He wanted me to know that he was not acting in a random, wanton way — at least not to his way of thinking. It was important for him to make it clear that he had a plan and a reason for his actions, no matter how bizarre and disgusting that may seem to anyone else. In my opinion, he wants to keep these lines of communication open. So do I. I believe that this man does not take pleasure in murder. In fact, he detests what he has become and would like to stop the killing. I believe he has tried to communicate that with me.

Riordan: If he truly wants to stop, why doesn't he just turn himself into the SFPD?

McCannell: I think there's a part of him that would like to do just that. However, there's another part of this man that *needs* to kill — a part that cannot resist the compulsion to murder. The part that needs to kill is stronger than the part that wants to stop, at least right now. The part of this man that needs to kill hasn't yet finished with his work.

Riordan: Are you saying that he will continue to kill?

McCannell: At this time, I think that he will kill again, yes. More than that, this man, like many serial killers, enjoys engaging law enforcement personnel in a "cat and mouse" game. This man is a natural manipulator and finds power in his ability to lead us around by the nose. Much of what he does before, during, and after the murders indicates that this man thrives on the entire killing scenario, including interaction with law enforcement officials or other public figures. There's a part of this man that needs to be engaged in this kind of life-or-death power struggle. For him, it has become an irresistible addiction.

Riordan: You said, "part of this man" several times in your last two responses. Does that mean you think the murderer has a psychological problem like schizophrenia or multiple personality disorder?

McCannell: Not necessarily. In fact, probably not. All of us have conflicting personality traits, but most of us are able to manage effectively and without violence. Still, we each feel many things in many different ways and at times experience tremendous conflicts within ourselves. We all have good qualities and bad qualities, beautiful parts and ugly ones. For this man, the darker side has taken over and driven him to incredible acts of violence.

Riordan: Are you saying that anyone has the potential to be a serial murderer?

McCannell: You must realize that serial murderers are relatively rare, even in a society as obviously violent as ours. Their crimes get a lot of attention from the press because their activities are so vicious and frightening. However, genuine serial murderers are relatively rare. This man is a genuine serial murderer. He was created by the sum total of his experiences and his environment. He didn't spring from the cradle as a serial murderer. That just doesn't happen.

Riordan: Are you ever afraid when you have to deal with a man such as this? I mean, you have invited him to keep in contact with you. Does that prospect frighten you?

McCannell: Well, I'm like everyone else on this planet. Sometimes I'm afraid, sometimes I'm not. I can tell you this, though: I would be in much greater fear doing nothing about stopping this mayhem than I am doing something about it, even if that means working directly with this man to get him to stop the killing.

Riordan: You said earlier that the murderer might have suffered some form of abuse when he was a child. Could you explain that in more detail?

McCannell: There are a few things that make me believe this. First of all, most serial killers have suffered periods of physical, psychological, and sexual abuse as children and adolescents. This fact has been proven through a number of outstanding studies over the past two decades. So, the odds are great that this man has suffered those same kinds of trauma. Second, the signature of his crimes and the selection of his victims points in that direction. Last, there are his communications. They, also, lend credence to the possibility that he suffered significant abuse when he was younger. I would guess that, in his case, the abuse was sexual and psychological.

Riordan: Putting together what you have said, is it possible that he suffered abuse at the hands of a woman when he was younger and is now attacking victims who remind him of the abuser?

McCannell: No, not necessarily. He could have just as easily suffered abuse at the hands of one or more older male figures in his youth and blamed his mother or another older female figure for not protecting him or putting a stop to the abuse. In other words, even though the target of his fundamental obsession is a woman, she may not have been the fundamental abuser. She may have been a co-conspirator by her silence or her unwillingness or inability to protect him against a primary, male abuser. Most abusers are male, not female, so it is more likely that he suffered at a male's hands. Also, you must realize that it takes a long time to become a serial murderer. You just don't wake up one day and say to yourself, "Ok, today I am going to be a serial killer." In fact, the process leading up to that first murder is a long and painful one. However, once an individual commits that first murder, well, there's really nothing to stop him or her from committing another.

Riordan: So many children are abused and yet there are so few serial killers. Doesn't that fact strike you as strange or contradictory?

McCannell: Not at all. You have to make a careful distinction in what I just said. I said that many, even most, serial killers have experienced abuse in their childhood. I didn't say that childhood abuse leads to serial murder. In fact, it obviously does not. Childhood abuse is just one of the characteristics that are common to serial killers.

Riordan: Does the SFPD have eyewitnesses to any of these crimes or has anyone seen this murderer and lived to talk to investigators?

McCannell: I'd rather not discuss that.

Riordan: Given the complexities of this murderer and his tactics, how can one be safe from him? What can you say to our readers that would help them protect themselves against such a person?

McCannell: Well, there are ways to be careful. For one thing, this man usually communicates with his victims before he attacks. When he communicates, it is under the pretense of something safe or necessary to the victim. In other words, he approaches his victims in such a way that he is able to lure them into a place where he feels comfortable and they're at a disadvantage. That is a tremendous key to his behavior. Regardless of how safe or normal a contact may appear, it is important to realize that this murderer succeeds because he is able to convince his victims that they are safe in his presence or by meeting him somewhere. Now, since there is no evidence to indicate that any of the victims knew this man before they were murdered, he must lure them by creating a situation in which they felt safe. That's a key. If someone approaches you with that kind of scenario, no matter how routine and safe it may appear, you must give some thought to it. Why is this man contacting me? Can I verify what he tells me? How do I know that he is telling me the truth? If in doubt, just don't cooperate.

Now, having said that, I must add one disheartening piece to the puzzle. In one of the murders, we're not sure how he managed to select his victim. It is possible that his third victim was coincidental — a spontaneous murder. We just don't know what happened and we may never know... unless he tells us.

Riordan: Dr. McCannell, how can this murderer be stopped? What will make the killings end?

McCannell: He will eventually be caught. It's just a matter of time. The SFPD is building a case and the case gets stronger all the time. There's no question about it. Beyond that, he may die or be incarcerated for some other crime. That's another way that the killings can end. Or, he may just stop killing on his own or turn himself in to the police. In other words, he may just decide that it's time to stop his terrible crimes.

Riordan: Is it likely that he will just stop killing or turn himself in to the SFPD?

McCannell: Likely, no. Possible, yes. If I am right about this man, he doesn't want to keep on doing these terrible things. He may have an agenda to fulfill or he may just be sick and tired of the horrors of his life. It's possible that he will just stop on his own. I certainly hope so.

Riordan: It is also likely that he will read this interview. If he does, is there anything that you would like to say to this man?

McCannell: Yes, there is. I understand your pain

and suffering. You've made that very clear to me in your communications and through your actions. To my way of thinking, you don't want to keep killing, but you feel that you must. It's very important for you to keep the lines of communication open. You know, and I know, that you must pay for the crimes that you've already committed. I know that you're willing to do that. What's important now is that you recapture that part of yourself that hates what you are doing. If you are willing to work to find that part of yourself, I am willing to help you. It's not too late to get back what you've lost, and you don't need to murder anyone else to get that. Please, contact me and let me know what I can do to help you.

January 19
Midtown Station
9:15 A.M.

Sam McCannell burst into the Lieutenant's office and brusquely handed photocopies of the letter to Mary Boor and Chris Spell. The pages he carried were still warm to the touch, fresh from the photocopier in the outer office at the Homicide Division. It was clear that McCannell was exceptionally excited, moving much more rapidly than his customary, first-gear pace, his hands and arms flailing in front of his torso in an animated series of pokes and parries.

"I received four letters after Jane Riordan ran the interview piece," McCannell announced at breakneck speed. "Three were from freaks who needed to get something off their chests and thought I was their man. They were nothing. Then, there was *this* one," he said, curling his upper lip into a half-smile and waving his copy over his head. "This is a knockout! Take a look at it, you two. The original is in the forensics lab, but I suspect they won't be able to tell us much more than we already have here."

He jabbed repeatedly at the air in front of his face with a chubby finger, indicating that the other two should immediately begin reading their copy and hold their questions until they had finished.

Spell pulled his chair tight against the oak desk and leaned over the message to bring it into focus, his head cradled in his hands. Like the others, this note had been constructed with neat, block letters and no punctuation. Undoubtedly, this was a note from their man.

DOCTOR SAM MCCANNELL

OUR PROBLEM IS MUTUAL

NEITHER OF US CAN BACK AWAY NOW

I CARVED MOTHER MARION INTO THE
DOOR OF HER CAR SO YOU WOULD KNOW WHO
AND UNDERSTAND WHY

I HAVE THE HANDS THAT HAVE HARMED
ME AND I WILL MAKE THEM YOURS SOON
WHEN I NO LONGER NEED THEM

UNTIL THEN THEY ARE SAFE AND
IMPORTANT TO ME

YOU HAVE CONFIRMED I AM NO
MONSTER AND I WILL NEVER WRITE TO THAT
FEMALE REPORTER AGAIN

I APPRECIATE THAT

YOUR ASSESSMENT IS GOOD BUT YOUR
INVESTIGATION IS NOT WORKING

WE WILL MEET FOR THE END OF MY
WORK VERY SOON

MONSTER HA HA

"Yeah, it worked, Sam. I mean, he's responding directly to the
Riordan piece, isn't he?" Mary asked with a concerned expression.

"Not only that, Mary, but this message is very different from the
previous ones. Check it all out carefully. Check each line," he said
hurriedly. "Also, look closely at the last line before he signs off. The
guy is telling us that he's working up to some kind of finale, and one
way or the other, he wants me to be a part of it." The red man began
pacing back and forth across the office, the photocopy dangling
loosely from his left hand, his feet shuffling in tiny steps.

"I don't like the sound of that," the Lieutenant snapped from
behind his desk as he finished reading the message. "What are you
saying, Sam?"

"I'm saying that he'll kill again and somehow he wants me
involved in it. At least, that's the way I read it," Sam mumbled, still
pacing.

"Who's Mother Marion, Sam?" Mary asked, holding the message close to her face and studying the lines over and over.

"My guess is that it's *the* woman – or women – who he's really after. It's hard to say, Mary. Maybe it's one person, two people, or just his twisted-up fantasy of all women. I don't really know. What I do know is that Mother Marion is his *real* target, whether or not she – or they – are *real*."

"Jesus!" Spell moaned. "I'm confused. Run that one by me again, Sam, will you?"

McCannell moved quickly across the room and slid onto the Lieutenant's battered couch, resting his head heavily on its leather backrest, his eyes half closed and dreamy. "Mother Marion is *the* woman, Chris. She is the *reason* why he kills. She *may* exist in reality, or she *may not*. She may be one person, two people, or many people. She is a symbol — an archetype of the person against whom he has focused all his anger and hatred for so long. You know, Chris, it really doesn't matter who she is at this point. He's working his way through the substitutes at his own pace and in his own way. It really doesn't matter…"

McCannell suddenly opened his eyes wide and slid to the edge of the couch, once again staring at the photocopy in his hand. "This message troubles me, Chris…" he began.

"Christ! Me, too!" the Lieutenant interrupted in a frustrated, fearful tone. "Now he's involving you *directly* in his craziness, Sam. That's not what I wanted to have happen here."

"Well, in a way, I think it's a good thing, Chris," Mary said cautiously, stepping closer to the couch to stand near McCannell. "We wanted this guy to focus on us – on Sam – to lead us back to him without any more killing. At least, I thought that's where we were heading with this. That was the purpose of Sam's interview with Jane Riordan."

"That's right, Mary," Sam offered without hesitation. "That's right. We *want* him to communicate. That's not what's troubling me. You two need to read this message very carefully. This one is different," he emphasized, waving the photocopy excitedly in the Lieutenant's direction. "For one thing, this message doesn't have the disorganized overtones of the previous ones. This one is logical, direct, and to-the-point. He's told us a hell of a lot here. But, he's not a stupid man. He put most of what he wanted to say between the lines and in the *feeling* of the message. You've got to get into the *feeling* of what he is saying if you're going to understand what he wants us to know."

McCannell stood up from the couch and began to pace again. "In *this* message, he's taken responsibility for the murders. Our guy didn't bother to blame anyone else here. Instead, he just came right out and said it was him, in so many words. That's a kind of confession. He's telling us that he's collecting their severed hands as trophies but, later, he won't need them any longer. That's a plan and a promise. He's telling us that he left us the message on Joanne Callin's car door so we would know who his true target was. In other words, he not only told us *why...* he told us *who*. He's saying that we've nailed him psychologically, but that we are nowhere in terms of putting him away. That's telling us where we stand. In other words, he's letting us play catch-up by giving us more than he's ever given us before... but he still wants to retain control of the situation.

"I mean, it's a strange message, isn't it? It's not just lines of crazy rambling without a point. This thing hangs together, tells us about a plan, and even smacks of a guy who is near the end of the line in terms of coping with what he's done. This one is *very* different, Chris."

The room grew quiet as McCannell finally stopped pacing and stood silently facing the wall, his back to the others, his head hung low. It was Mary Boor who broke into the reverie that had carried the red man so far away.

"Ok, he's planning another murder, Sam, right?"

"Yeah," McCannell mumbled in a barely audible whisper. "I think it'll be his last — one way or the other..." His voice trailed off into nothingness.

"What does *that* mean?" the Lieutenant demanded, clearly upset by what McCannell had said.

"I think what Sam means," Mary answered in a protective tone, "is that this guy will stop after the next murder, Chris. Right, Sam?"

McCannell barely nodded.

"What! You mean that this guy will just walk in here, sit down on my couch, and roll over on himself? He'll just walk in here, introduce himself as the Mission District Monster, and ask for a cozy cell? Is that what you two are trying to tell me?" Spell demanded incredulously.

McCannell turned his head to face Spell behind the desk, his tone low and confident. "No, not exactly, Chris. I think he'll kill *twice* more. His last victim will be himself. I think that's what he's trying to tell us. But before that's happened – before he's finished what he set out to do – he wants to make sure that I'm involved. I think that he wants me to view his work firsthand. I think that's what he wants. And that presents a problem, doesn't it? I mean, if we're going to do our jobs, we need to save his life, too. That's probably why he wants me in the mix."

"Oh, Christ! That's not going to happen!" Spell yelped. "That's out of the question, Sam!"

"I agree, Sam," Mary said softly, moving closer to McCannell and gently touching his arm. "That's crazy. Don't even think about it."

For a moment, McCannell was silent, his eyes again closed.

"To tell the truth, I'm not sure that I'll have anything to say about it, Mary. He'll drag my ass into his next move, one way or the other, if he can. He needs some kind of validation and I guess he thinks that it should come from me. As he said, my assessment was right on the money. We've reached a certain level of understanding about each other. So, from his point of view, the missing element is validation for his actions. After all, what good is a fantastic painting if it's never seen by anyone? What's the value of a brilliant piece of music if there's no audience to hear it? You see, Mary, this guy hasn't told his *whole* story yet. He tells his story through his murders. They are his works of art. But, since we only see the final chapter at the crime scene, it's not good enough for him. He wants me to see the *whole* story. That's what he's planning – a way for me to see his whole story before he ends it."

"That's not a tune we're going to dance to, Sam," the Lieutenant announced sternly. "That's just not going to happen."

"You weren't listening, Chris!" the red man snapped back at him, an unusual tone of anger in his voice. "That may not be our decision. That may be *his* decision."

"Bullshit!" Spell screamed. "You will *not* be in this guy's sights, Sam. That *won't* happen!"

McCannell turned sharply to confront the Lieutenant with a determined, stern expression of his own. In an obvious and exaggerated expression of frustration, he moved his large head deliberately from side to side. "We'll talk about this tomorrow, Chris. For now, I'm off for the rest of the day," he announced, allowing no room for further negotiation or discussion. McCannell immediately swung his pudgy frame away from Spell's desk and strode quickly out the door, slamming it noisily after him.

"Jesus..." Spell mumbled. For a moment, he stared open-mouthed at the office door, the fading ring of its harsh rattle still sending ripples of anger and concern across his chest and stomach. Then, his eyes settled on Mary in the corner of his office. She looked troubled — much more so than he had seen her since she joined the investigation.

"What the fuck is going on here, Mar?" he whimpered in her direction.

"You weren't listening to him, Chris," she scolded, hunching up her shoulders and turning her back to him. "We'll talk later — at my place," she mumbled over her shoulder as she headed for the door.

January 19
Mary Boor's Residence
11:45 P.M.

Mary gently laid her head across his chest, listening dreamily to the steady, reassuring rhythm of his breathing and staring idly out the bedroom window. Across the narrows of the bay, to the East, the hills were still visible through a thickening, silky haze of fog, made luminescent from the rows of street lamps that snaked their way along the crooked streets to the very top of each elevation. Below this disorganized chain of distant, luxurious homes, the bay waters were unusually still and glassy, without any hint of movement. It was a rare, beautiful night in the Bayview District — both inside her home and on the bay.

Unwillingly, her eyelids began to shudder and close, made heavy from an exhausting day at the station. The calves of her legs still ached from the endless hours of movement that was the mainstay of her daily routine. Still, tonight, despite her exhaustion, despite the aching of her aging body, things were good for Mary Boor. She felt uncommonly satisfied and relaxed. Chris had taken his time with her, and in return, she had given back all that she could. It had been an hour of silent, easy, sensual pleasure, which neither of them had bothered to question or analyze. It had just happened. It had been just the way she liked it — simple, unplanned, and undemanding.

"Mar, you awake?" he asked in a careful whisper.

"Umm... yeah." Mary nodded her head lightly against his chest to make the point. She was too comfortable to do much more than mumble.

"I really screwed up with Sam today, didn't I?" he asked in a plaintive, childlike way.

She thought for a moment, reluctant to disturb this special time with any conversation. Still, she knew the issue was important to him — very important. The guilt was thick in his voice.

"No, Chris, I don't think so. It was obvious you were concerned about Sam. He knew that and I knew it. Maybe you just let your concern get ahead of hearing what he was trying to tell you. It was a tense moment. No big deal."

Now it was Spell's turn to be quiet, to think about what had really happened. He rolled his head to the left and scanned the bay waters and the hills beyond, searching for something that wasn't there. For a few moments, he silently replayed his meeting with Sam that morning, substituting a half dozen scenarios for how it *should* have turned out, for how he *should* have reacted to what his friend had said. Now, none of them mattered any more — it all came out the same. Spell was at the end of his rope on this investigation and desperately afraid for Sam's safety. He just could not bring himself to say it out loud. It was an old problem for a cop growing older by the minute. All that emotional stuff on the inside just never seemed to make it out in the right way or at the right time.

"Mar, I'm going to retire," Chris casually announced. He closed his eyes to the view outside her bedroom window and tried to settle something in his mind — anything.

Mary pressed the full length of her lean body against his side, wrapping her long right arm tightly around his stomach and nuzzling his chest with the side of her head. That was all the answer she was willing to give him — at least for now. Anyway, she told herself, there was nothing she could say that would make a difference, one way or the other. He *was* coming up to the end of the line. She had seen it a few weeks ago. He was tired, frustrated, and afraid. They all were.

For a few moments, she listened once again to his breathing and wondered what he would do if he really *did* retire. As desperately as she tried, Mary could not imagine her friend doing anything else but what he had done for so long. He was too set in his ways, too much a loner — too much the detective in his soul. Retirement was out of the question.

Still...

She tried to picture the couple together in some warm, easy-paced place where detectives were unnecessary, murders unheard of, and doors devoid of locks. She tried to conjure up a truly happy place for two. Despite her best efforts, nothing seemed real – nothing except the inevitability of tomorrow, and she knew what that would be like for both of them. There was just no hope of holding onto the moment for either of them. She knew that.

Retirement began to sound more like an option than it ever had before. In the end, she found *herself* thinking about it, wondering what *she* would do.

Well, she *had* to say something. He was expecting *something*.

"What would you do, Chris?" she finally whispered into his chest. "I can't see you mowing the lawn on Saturday morning or feeding the pigeons in the afternoon. Matter of fact, I seem to recall that you don't have a lawn and you hate pigeons."

His chest rippled with a small, unexpected laugh. She felt his hand on the side of her face, stroking her hair in an easy, familiar way. "You're right, Mar. I have no idea what I'd do. I just know what I *don't* want to do. I *don't* want to do this anymore. I feel *fear*, Mar. I don't remember feeling it before... but I've got it now."

She nodded in that way that told him she understood. "Well, Chris, I can't remember when I *wasn't* afraid in this job. Maybe what you're feeling isn't so unusual. Maybe your *lack* of fear for all those years was the unusual thing."

He gave a gurgling grunt and dismissed her suggestion

immediately. That answer was far too philosophical, even if it made sense. He had fear now and he didn't like it. That was that.

Time to change the subject. There was something else on his mind.

"I really do like you, Mar," he said, wrapping his right arm around her shoulder and pulling her even closer to his side. "I have for a long time, you know."

"I know that, Chris. I've known it for years," she said in a low, confidential tone. "It's good to hear you say it, though. It's especially nice when you *do* something about it… like you did tonight." She ended with a coy, girlish giggle.

Once again, his chest rumbled with a welcomed laugh, jiggling her head to his rhythm. "Ok, Mar, I got the message…"

The harsh, tinny rattle of the telephone on the nightstand made her head and arms jerk unexpectedly, sending a jolt of surprise across her chest. "Shit!" she complained in an angry, harsh voice.

Mary struggled to unwind herself from his grasp and laid her upper body across his chest, stretching her arm toward the nightstand to snag the receiver. "Yes," she spat at the mouthpiece, obviously unhappy about the intrusion.

"Mary, is that you?" the caller said in a concerned, rushed voice.

"Mendoza?" she asked, surprised at hearing his voice.

"Yeah. I'm really sorry to call you so late, Mary. I'm trying to get a hold of Chris. He's not at the station and he's not answering his phone at home. I'm really sorry. Do you know where he is? I really need to talk to him." The Sergeant's tone was unusually high-pitched and troubled.

Mary turned away from the telephone and glanced up at Chris, searching carefully for his reaction to the call. He had an anguished look on his face and was shaking his head slowly from side to side. Silently, with her eyes and a certain movement of her head, she prodded him to take the call, indicating that is was important.

He nodded reluctantly.

Without speaking, Mary swung the receiver over her head and handed it to him. She could hear Mendoza repeatedly calling her name on the other end, probably wondering why the line went silent so suddenly and for so long. He sounded scared.

"Yeah, Joe," Chris grumbled into the receiver. For a moment, there was no reply. The Lieutenant could feel Mendoza's surprise at hearing his voice. No doubt, he was scrambling for something appropriate to say — something that would make the intrusion at least somewhat acceptable to his boss.

"Jesus, Chris! Glad I finally got you. We've got a real problem," Joe rattled. "Sandy's missing! She left Pento's Restaurant just after nine tonight and she's missing, for Christ's sake! You know what I…"

"All right, Joe. Hold it!" Chris ordered in a stern voice. "How do you *know* she's missing?"

"She was supposed to come here, to my place, Chris. She should have been here hours ago. Anyway, I called Pento's to find out what happened. She left just after nine and never made it here. There's no answer at her place and she hasn't been seen at the station. Chris, she was supposed to come here. I *know* she's missing! I *know* it, for Christ's sake!"

It was clear that Joe was in no mood to be questioned. He was panicked.

"All right, Joe. You're at home, right?"

"Yeah."

"Ok. We'll meet at the station in a half-hour and decide what to do from there. Ok with you?"

"Yeah, good," he answered in a hurried voice. "Yeah, a half hour."

"Joe, take it easy, right? We'll take care of this, right?"

For a few seconds there was silence on the line — then it went dead.

"Shit!" Chris yelled as he slammed the receiver back onto the cradle. "Mar, we've got to go, *now!*" he demanded, trying as gently as he could to move away from the bed.

Mary said nothing. She knew all she needed to know. Quickly, she rolled off the bed and rummaged around on the floor, gathering up her clothes, running through the possibilities in her mind.

None of them were good, she decided.

January 20
Pento's Restaurant
Earlier that evening

It was nearly nine o'clock and Sandy's feet ached miserably from twelve hours of her two-job existence. Like most evenings, Pento's had seen a chaotic flurry of business between six and eight o'clock — two intense hours of endless movement that had stretched the restaurant's crew to the limit of their endurance. But, now, things were quiet in the dining area and the employees were already well into their nightly clean-up ritual of clearing tables, sanitizing the kitchen area, and preparing for the next day's opening. This was the most grueling part of her shift — those moments just before the end of her workday, which always seemed boring, pain-ridden, and interminable.

Sandy stood stiffly at the hostess station near the front door of the restaurant, bracing herself behind a chest-high, ornate mahogany pedestal from where she could survey the entire dining room. Leaning delicately on the pedestal, she shifted her weight from foot to foot, trying to ease the throbbing as best she could and shuffling her feet in and out of her low-heeled shoes. Across the long, narrow floor of the dining room, she could see only three occupied tables — two with couples lingering in intimate conversations over their last cups of coffee and a third occupied by a single man sipping on a cappuccino and studying the evening edition of the San Francisco *Call*. These would be the last of her customers for the night. She had already hung the "closed" sign in the restaurant window and was more then ready to leave for the night, looking forward to a hot bath and a warm bed at Joe Mendoza's.

From the rear of the dining area, where the kitchen was located,

Rich Gariblaz, Pento's owner, motioned at Sandy with a subtle wave of his hand, silently asking her to join him. She slipped away from her station and moved in his direction, being careful to maintain a discreet distance from the remaining patrons and smiling in her customary way as she passed.

"Sandy, you look tired," Gariblaz said in a concerned, intimate tone as she approached. He was a thoughtful, sincere man. Middle-aged, dark, and naturally suave, Gariblaz had been in the restaurant business all his life and knew the demands it made on those who worked for him. He had not forgotten how to bus tables or work tirelessly for a ridiculous wage and inadequate tips. Rich Gariblaz was a man who cared deeply for those around him and they, in turn, cared for him.

"Yeah, Rich, I'm beat…" she confessed, looking plaintively up at his lean, smiling face.

"I thought so, Sandy. It was a hell of a night. Well, why don't I watch the front and take care of these folks," he offered, motioning with his head in the direction of the remaining customers. "I can deal with them if you want to take off. It's not a problem."

Sandy thought for a moment — mostly about the pain in her feet and calves. "No, I don't mind, Rich. It looks like they're all finishing up anyway. I'll see them out and then go home."

He smiled down at the small woman dressed in her best black pants suit and nudged her gently on the side of the head with the back of his hand. "Ok, kid, I appreciate that," he said as he turned and disappeared into the inner sanctum of the kitchen. For a moment, Sandy stood where he had left her, trying to decide if she dare sit for just a moment at a nearby table. No, that wouldn't do. She had a station up front and that's where she belonged. It just wouldn't do for the customers to see her sitting, even though they probably didn't care. She would be there, at her pedestal, at the front door, to send them away with a pleasant smile, a cheery "goodnight," and a feeling that she *really* wanted them to come back to Pento's again. It didn't matter that she was exhausted.

For a few seconds, Sandy rocked back and forth from the heels to the balls of her feet, trying to renew some of her lost energy. Reluctantly, she started down the line of tables, working her way toward the front of the restaurant. The dining area was softly lit and intimate, despite its long, narrow shape and high, ornate ceiling. Overhead, three enormous brass chandeliers, each fitted with a dozen light bulbs formed into the shape of deep pink, flickering flames, added their luminescence to the wicker oil lamps on the tables. The floor was carpeted with a brownish, tweed pile, which neatly offset the warm beige tablecloths and dark, rounded mahogany chairs. The walls of the dining area had been decorated with rich wood paneling, punctuated here and there by watercolor paintings depicting unnamed chaparral and high desert scenes. Omnipresent was the thick aroma of spicy, exotic dishes from the Mexican Sonoran desert, wafting throughout the room and beckoning Pento's patrons. It was a classic, established, mid-city restaurant that thrived on a combination of excellent food and intimate surroundings.

As she made her way back to her station, Sandy passed by the two couples at the rear of the dining area, once again smiling in their direction. Neither pair seemed to notice her — both were still chattering away in quiet, secret tones, savoring the last of their coffee. Closer to the grand front window of the restaurant, the well-dressed man sat at a table against the wall, hovering over his newspaper, as he had for nearly an hour. His head was hung low to the table to catch all he could of the soft, uneven light from the wicker lamp. Like the other patrons, he held fast to the remnants of a last cup of cappuccino, apparently oblivious to the hostess's growing impatience to be free of the restaurant for the night.

Sandy had nearly reached her station when she heard an unsettling, muffled gurgling and the shrill clattering of tableware from behind her. Instinctively, she whirled around to her left, in the direction of the unexpected uproar, and saw the large man at the table against the wall reaching toward his throat with one hand while the other flailed desperately in mid-air. It was obvious that he was choking and excitedly trying to get someone's attention to come to his aid.

Sandy pushed her way past the intervening tables and raced in his direction. She could see his eyes fixed on her, wide with fear and anxiously following her progress. From the rear of the dining area, Sandy could also see Rich Gariblaz rushing in her direction. He, too, had heard the commotion. Peering into the dining area from where he stood in the open doorway to the kitchen, the owner had instinctively realized that one of his customer's was in some kind of trouble.

When she reached the table, Sandy quickly positioned herself behind the man's chair and tried to wrestle him to his feet. It was no use. Not only was he a huge, bulky man, but the wild, erratic movements of his burley arms made it impossible for her to grip him without the danger of being hit.

In a matter of seconds, Rich Gariblaz was at her side, also looking wide-eyed and ashen. "Shit! What's wrong, Sandy?" he yelled.

"The guy is choking! We need to get him to his feet... NOW!" she ordered.

Gariblaz stepped next to Sandy and slid his arms around the man's torso, grasping him firmly and anchoring his grip under the man's arms. He quickly pulled the gasping patron from his chair and lifted him to his feet, overturning both the chair and the dining table at the same time. Immediately, Sandy wrapped her arms around the man's waist from behind and nudged Gariblaz away from where he stood. She clasped her hands together to form a tight ball and laid her head across his back, struggling to hold onto the writhing, panicked man. Quickly, she moved her hands along the center point of his abdomen and upward toward the narrow of his ribcage, feeling for just the right point of pressure. Within a few seconds she had found the right spot and pulled back as hard as she could, sending her clenched fists deep into his upper abdomen. Without speaking, she repeated the movement again and again, each time pulling as hard as she could against his bulk, with each pull forcing her clenched fist upward and inward against the man's upper abdomen.

Finally, after four or five intense thrusts, she heard the man emit a deep, rattling, painful cough and felt him exhale with tremendous force. She could also feel his weight slacken against her grip and the muscles along his ribcage begin to relax. Whatever had obstructed his breathing had found its release in a life-restoring, deep gush of air.

The man slid through her arms and sat down hard on the floor, resting his shoulder against the wall. Sandy could feel the sweat pour from the sides of her face and neck; her arms throbbed from the pressure with which she had held him and the repeated intensity of her movements. Quickly, Gariblaz retrieved the overturned chair and gently helped Sandy into it. She was exhausted and unable to speak between the gasps for air that her effort had brought on. Still on the floor, the large man was also breathing heavily, his head and shoulder now resting against the paneled wall and his thick legs spread out in front of him.

"Oh, God," Gariblaz mumbled in Sandy's direction. He reached down and lightly touched the customer's right shoulder to get his attention. "Are you ok, sir?" he asked in a frightened, shaky voice. The man said nothing but slowly moved his head up and down, signaling that he would be all right. "Let me get some water!" Gariblaz yelped as he turned to sprint in the direction of the kitchen.

Sandy glanced down and to the left at the man on the floor. She could see that his breathing was beginning to return to normal and the color in his cheeks was becoming more full. "Are you all right?" she asked between gasps, wiping the sweat from her cheeks and forehead with the palm of her right hand.

"Uhh... yeah, thanks..." he croaked in a hoarse, broken voice. "Thanks, miss..."

She said nothing, waiting for her own heavy breathing to subside. In a moment, Rich Gariblaz returned with two glasses of water. Both Sandy and the customer took the glasses with a nod and began to sip. For a few moments, neither spoke. Finally, the man on the floor looked directly at Sandy with a broken smile and obvious gratitude in his eyes.

"Thank you, miss. I'm very sorry," he said in a deep and shaky voice. "I don't know what happened there. I guess..."

"That's ok," Sandy interrupted. "Are you sure you're all right?" she asked in a concerned tone.

"Yeah, fine... embarrassed... glad you were here," he answered in a croaking staccato.

She smiled and moved away from her chair, dragging it behind her to make room for the man to get back to his feet. He braced himself on the wall and worked his way upward, finally standing erect. Next to her, he was enormous — easily over six feet tall and 200 pounds or more.

"Would you like to sit down, sir?" Gariblaz asked, moving a second chair next to where he stood.

The man nodded again and sat down, throwing his weight heavily on the back of the chair. "Thanks. I'm very sorry about this scene. Please don't be concerned. I'm fine," he said sheepishly.

"Good, good," Gariblaz responded in a hurried, excited tone. "It's a good thing Sandy was here."

"Yes, it was. Thanks again, miss," the man said softly, with a struggling smile.

Sandy blushed noticeably and smiled back. She felt winded and sticky with sweat but good about what she had accomplished. It had been a moment that proved the value of her training. There had been no hesitation — no concern, except for the man in trouble. But now, all she wanted was to be out of the restaurant and back with Mendoza. She had had enough for one night.

"Ok," the large man said to her. "If I can have my bill, I'm ready to leave. You two have had enough of me for one night, I'm sure."

"No! No..." Rich Gariblaz shot back. "There will be no bill for you, sir. I'm sorry about what happened. I certainly hope you are all right." His voice was plaintive and sorrowful.

The patron looked embarrassed, and for a few seconds, speechless. "That's very kind. I assume you're the owner, right?" he finally asked.

Gariblaz nodded sheepishly.

"Well, that's very kind. It seems I will owe this young woman my life and you the price of an excellent meal. But if you both agree it's fair, how could I refuse?"

They both nodded.

"Thank you, then," he said with a broad smile. "I'll be back often, I'm sure." With that, the man rose gingerly from his chair and nodded at Sandy, giving her a parting smile that seemed genuinely warm. He stretched his arms and brushed the front of his shirt, unsuccessfully trying to remove the wrinkles that had accumulated from his ordeal. Without speaking, he made his way to the front door of the restaurant. As he pulled on the door to swing it open, he turned for a final time in their direction and nodded gratefully before slipping out into the night.

"Oh..." Gariblaz moaned, sliding his tall frame into the chair just vacated by his customer. "I don't know what to say, Sandy. I'm sure as hell glad you were here."

Sandy reached out and gave his shoulder a squeeze, letting him know that everything was fine. "Look, Rich, I need to get out of here. I'm exhausted." Her face was drawn and still glistening with sweat.

"Oh, sure, kid. Go now... Go! I'll take care of things," he announced, gesturing with his hand toward the door.

"Thanks, Rich."

Sandy turned and headed for the front of the restaurant to retrieve her black cotton overcoat from the open closet in the corner. She slipped her aching arms into its warmth and made for the front door. As she pulled on the handle, she turned back to view the dining area once more. Rich Gariblaz was still sitting in the chair, his head in his hands, obviously still shaken.

"Goodnight," she mumbled as she, too, slipped out into the night.

January 21
Midtown Station
3:05 A.M.

Sam McCannell staggered sleepily through the open office door and slumped noisily onto the Lieutenant's couch. He looked unusually pale and lifeless.

"Sam, I'm really sorry to drag you down here in the middle of the night," Spell said apologetically from behind his desk.

McCannell nodded uneasily. "What happened, Chris? What happened with Sandy?" he answered in a hoarse voice.

"I'm not sure, Sam, but it doesn't look good. She left work around nine last night. She was supposed to go straight to Joe's, but she never got there. Mendoza called me just before midnight and he was in a real panic. He's convinced she was grabbed by our guy, and I'm thinking he might be right."

The red man closed his eyes and slowly moved his head from side to side. "What's the evidence, Chris? Why have you two come to *that* conclusion?"

The Lieutenant leaned across the desk and stared intently at his friend. "What has me convinced is that her car is still parked in the alleyway behind Pento's. She walked out of the restaurant, onto the street, and vanished. Doesn't that sound just a bit familiar to you, Sam?" he asked sarcastically.

McCannell pushed himself away from the couch with an audible grunt and began to shuffle across the length of the office. "Yeah..." he mumbled. "That sounds *too* familiar, Chris. I suppose you've checked all the obvious, like..."

"Sure, we did that," Spell interrupted. "Mar and Joe went to Pento's and then to interview the owner, Rich Gariblaz, at his home.

They were going to meet us here about now. They should be back here any time, Sam."

McCannell suddenly stopped his rhythmic pacing and swung his stout frame around to face the Lieutenant. "Listen, Chris, did you check my message recorder? Was there anything on my recorder?" he asked in an excited voice.

"I thought of that, too, Sam," Spell replied in a low tone. "There was nothing there."

"Well, if you're right about what happened to Sandy, there will be. There will be..." McCannell mused in a dreamy, distant voice.

"Will be what, Sam?" Mary Boor echoed as she rushed into the Lieutenant's office with Mendoza behind her. "You got something, Sam?" she pressed. Like the red man, she looked haggard and worried. Mendoza looked even worse, with a dark, drawn expression that, to the Lieutenant, looked dangerous.

"No, nothing, Mar," Spell interjected. "Sam and I were just throwing around possibilities. What do you two have?" he asked, looking alternatively at Boor and Mendoza.

Mary grabbed Mendoza by the arm and pulled him toward the couch. They both sat down hard, obviously exhausted. Mendoza flung his head back and tightly closed his eyes. Mary looked from McCannell to Spell and back again, giving each a tight, forced smile.

"Well, nobody saw Sandy after she left the restaurant, Chris. She never made it to her car — it's still in the alleyway..."

"So, he set her up *inside* the restaurant, Mary," McCannell interrupted. "That's the way he did it..."

Mary looked down at her feet and nodded solemnly. "Yeah, Sam, that's how I think it went down."

"No shit!" Mendoza spat, his eyes still closed and his body rigid with tension.

"Ok, Mar, let's hear the rest of it," the Lieutenant said in a stern voice, trying his best to ignore Mendoza's angry outburst.

Mary shuffled rapidly through her notebook, pausing at a particular page for a few seconds and rubbing her fingers across its scribbling. Spell thought he saw the signs of a growing dampness in the corners of her eyes and sensed that she really had no need for those notes. What she needed was time to compose herself. He didn't press the issue. When Mary finally spoke, it was with the practiced tone and rhythm of a disinterested homicide investigator — a sure sign to her friends that she was very, very worried.

"According to the owner of Pento's, Mr. Gariblaz, there was an incident in the dining area just before Sandy left work last night. One of the male patrons began choking and Sandy intervened to help him. The incident was over in just a few moments. Less than five minutes later, the patron left the restaurant. He was fine. A few moments after he left, Sandy also left the restaurant..."

"And you think this is our guy, Mar?" Spell interrupted. "You think he grabbed her outside the restaurant?"

"Christ! Of course!" Mendoza yelped before Mary could answer. He sat straight up on the couch, his eyes open and glaring into the space above the Lieutenant's head. "That sick fuck nailed her by turning the tables on us! He hooked Sandy the way we planned on hooking him! Ask Sam there," he raged, jabbing his arm in McCannell's direction. "Ask Sam if that doesn't fit this sick fuck's profile. Ask Sam!" Mendoza gave a few more thrusts in McCannell's direction and finished by launching his back hard against the couch.

Spell and Boor stared at the red man, silently asking him the same question. For a moment, he stared back, waiting for more from Mendoza. There was none. McCannell hunched up his shoulders and shook his head back and forth.

"Could be, could be..." he mumbled. "Mary, let me ask you a few questions, ok? For one thing, did the owner or anyone else at the restaurant know this guy?"

"The owner thought he had been in there a few times, Sam, but he wasn't a regular. No one seemed to know him very well."

"So, he was alone, right?" McCannell began to pace again, his eyes half-closed, waiting for her answer.

"Right," Mary replied, her eyes following McCannell back and forth across the office.

"He paid in cash, right?" the red man asked.

"Well, he didn't pay at all, this time. Gariblaz gave him a free meal to smooth the situation over."

"Well, ok," McCannell snapped. "He hasn't paid there, before, with a credit card? I mean, in the past he's paid with cash, right?"

"They weren't sure, Sam. Probably cash."

"Did he sit near the front of the restaurant, Mary? Did he sit near Sandy's station?"

"Yes."

"Did he come in late? I mean, was he among the last to leave?" Sam's eyes were open now, his voice higher in pitch and more animated.

Mary nodded. Like the red man, her eyes were now wide with anticipation.

"I suppose he fits our general description, right?"

Mary nodded again.

For a moment longer, McCannell paced back and forth. As he approached the office door, he changed direction and shuffled to the couch where the two detectives sat. McCannell reached out with his left hand and placed it gently on Mendoza's right shoulder. Mendoza gave a slight shudder and looked up at the red man, his eyes tight and fearful.

"Joe, you *know* this was the guy, don't you? You *know* it in your gut, right?" McCannell asked in a whispered voice.

Mendoza nodded uneasily, his eyes beginning to glisten over. He said nothing. For a moment, the room was intensely quiet.

"Mary, did he talk to Sandy?" McCannell asked, his hand still resting on Mendoza's shoulder.

"Yeah, he talked to her, Sam. He didn't say much, but he did talk to her. He was polite and apologetic about what had happened. He expressed some embarrassment. According to Gariblaz, this guy appeared to be in real trouble. He was very convincing, Sam."

McCannell felt another pulse of anger and fear jolt through Mendoza's body as Mary finished her sentence. The red man raised his hand to the back of Mendoza's neck and gave it a warm squeeze. After he had finished, he turned away from the couch and began to pace again, up and down the office floor.

"We've got to do *something*, boss!" Mendoza said in a pained, plaintive tone to the Lieutenant. "We've got to…"

He couldn't finish.

Chris Spell looked down at the papers strewn across the face of his desk but didn't see them. He had no answer to give. He had only questions.

"Sam, what do we do?" Spell asked his friend.

"We wait, Chris," came the immediate and sharp reply. "If we want to get Sandy out of this, we wait."

"She's probably already dead," Mendoza moaned from the couch. "We're too late, I think…"

"No!" McCannell yelled, sending a start through the others. His voice was angry and determined. "Fuck no! She's alive, Joe! This sick fuck hasn't killed her yet. He won't do that until he gets what he wants from me!"

January 21
Bernal Heights District
3:40 A.M.

From within the murkiness of Jamieson's filthy flat on the hill, beyond her own slowly awakening consciousness and intense pain, Sandy Janus looked down upon her own image standing alone on the Boulevard. From above, wrapped within the indescribable emptiness of incorporeal unfeeling and timelessness, she saw herself at the restaurant door, wrestling with her thick, dark coat against the whipping swirls of fog that raced northward along Mission Street. There, from above the street, as in a bizarre, unhinged *film noire*, she saw the delicate woman with dark hair and pale skin standing unsteadily at the restaurant door, her hand still resting on its ornate, curved handle. Within this surreal vision, her consciousness set adrift between dreaming and reality, she knew the horror that the victim below must soon face.

The woman dropped her head against the biting wind and strode with determination down Mission Street, moving in quick steps toward the corner. As she walked, she passed no one. She heard only the muffled whine of an occasional automobile on the Boulevard and saw only the irregularly cracked concrete of the damp sidewalk directly in front of her. The walkway was unusually quiet and desolate, abandoned by would-be strollers in favor of the warmth and preserve of dozens of Victorian, second-story flats perched over darkened and muted storefronts. It was growing late and cold — there was little reason to be on the Boulevard that night. The woman in black, anguished by her aching feet and calves, became distracted by the warming lure of her lover's bed, and she moved eerily below the sculptured, inadequate street lamps. She was alone, witnessed only by her floating soul from above, seen only by her imprisoned self, which watched mutely from inside his dank, crypt-like room.

At the corner of Twenty-fifth Street, the woman turned east. She dragged the thick collar of her coat up against the side of her face, working with chilled fingers to protect her ear from the onrushing, impelling sting of the southerly wind. Across the street, an unseen door slammed noisily and sent a hollow echo in her direction. A deep, grumbling voice mouthed something unintelligible and angry. The woman's head swung instantly to her right, in the direction of the unexpected sounds, and an involuntary spasm of tension overtook her forearms and back. Inside her coat pocket, the woman's left hand instinctively clenched into a taut fist. She peered deeply into the darkness across the street, scanning each of the doorways that lined the way, but could see nothing out of the ordinary.

Inside her coat pocket, her hand slowly relaxed its intense grip, now drained of her instinctive unease. From above, Sandy's soul could see the woman shake her head imperceptibly from side to side, silently scolding herself for the unfounded fright, rationalizing her reaction against a mosaic of exhaustion, frustration, chill, and desire. Once again, she dropped her head and snuggled her chin against the warmth of her coat. She moved down the street with quickening steps, now close to the alleyway where she had parked her car hours before.

From above, from within her black imprisonment, Sandy's soul screamed out to the woman in black, to warn her of what was to come. But there was no sound to be heard. The woman below only moved more rapidly toward the alley entrance, unaware of the warning and untouched by fear. From her secret place of ethereal terror, Sandy's soul had no voice to be heard, no substance — no will to be imposed on the victim below, even at the risk of her life. From above, from somewhere inside Jamieson's room, she had only the sure knowledge of what was to come. To the woman in black, who now turned into the alleyway, who stretched her pretty head forward to locate her car, there was only the silence of the night and the overwhelming drive to be in her lover's home — warm and safe.

Sandy Janus stretched out her fingers and reached into the narrow depth of her coat pocket, searching for the thick silver ring that held her keys. She felt their jagged, reassuring shapes and hooked the ring with her left forefinger, dragging the keys into her palm and holding them at the ready. She walked carefully now, keeping some distance between the row of cars parked parallel along the west side of the alley, wary of anyone who might be lurking unseen between each. As she moved silently down the alleyway, she again lifted her head and stretched her neck forward, scanning the long line of cars in search of her own.

Yes, it was there — five or six cars ahead, just where it should be.

Between where she stood and her destination, a pale triangle of light snaked upward from a partially opened car door just ahead of her and to her left. She paused for a moment, scanning the interior of the car through its crusty back window, searching for any evidence of occupants.

There were none.

The woman moved forward, directing herself to the middle of the alleyway while she kept a wary eye on the dark sedan with its open driver's door. As she neared the vehicle, she could see that the door had been stopped from fully opening by its proximity to the weathered brick façade that lined the western wall of the alleyway. As she passed close by the sedan, she saw no evidence of a driver or passengers and decided that the car had been abandoned with its door ajar.

It was then that she heard the sickening, gurgling noises from the far side of the automobile, coming from somewhere close against the alley wall.

Sandy stopped immediately and turned to fully face the sedan from the passenger's side. Carefully, she bent at the waist to peer into its interior, still searching for any evidence of life. There was none.

Once again, the sickening, guttural sounds came from a place near the driver's door, low to the street. Instinctively, she held her breath and stood frozen, trying to assess the situation and unwilling to give away any evidence of her presence. For a long moment she listened, still leaning forward from the waist, still straining to hear any sound or catch any movement with her eyes.

"Oh, God..." came the grinding, gurgling voice from the far side of the sedan. "Oh, Christ..." Then, more rumbling and hacking — sounds of fright and agony. Then, silence.

She moved cautiously forward, very close to the passenger's door, and peered through the dungy window and across the front seat of the vehicle. The floor of the sedan was littered with debris, as was the back seat. Her eyes carefully scanned the length of the vehicle, finally coming to rest on the open driver's door. There, propped with his back against the mottled, ripped fabric of the door, wedged into a damp, narrow crevice between the vehicle and the brickwork, was the man she had seen moments before at Pento's Restaurant. His head hung limp against his chest, his chin wet from the saliva that had gathered in his mouth and trickled across his blue, unmoving lips. She could see that his breathing was irregular and heavy, coming in unpredictable bursts and accompanied by an audible rumbling sound from deep inside his chest.

For a moment, she stood motionless and stared intently at the large man on the ground. Mentally, she tried to pace his breathing, while she scanned his face carefully for any sign of movement. There was only the sporadic heaving of his chest and the low, sickening rumble that accompanied each gasp. It was clear — he was unable to regularize his breathing. He was dying.

From afar, Sandy watched the woman in black move rapidly to the rear of the sedan and squeeze her small frame between its bumper and that of the car parked behind. She worked her way between the two vehicles and moved quickly along the brick wall toward the open driver's door, approaching the prone man from the front. From above the darkness of the alleyway, Sandy tried again to scream her warning. But the woman in black heard nothing and sensed no danger.

Sandy stepped gingerly between the large man's outstretched legs and withdrew her left hand from her coat pocket, releasing the grip on her silver key ring and letting it drop silently into the folds below. She stretched her hand toward his face and gently felt for a pulse on the side of his thick neck with two chilled fingers. To her touch, his skin seemed warm and alive, his pulse surprisingly strong and regular. She bent further forward and tried to look more carefully into his face, searching for any evidence of consciousness.

"Sir, are you..." she said in an artificially loud voice, as if to wake him from an unexpected sleep. But she never finished her question. From below and to her right, from where she thought his burley left arm lay limp next to his body, came a lightening sharp movement against the right side of her face and neck. She saw a bright flash of yellow and gold as the handle of his huge metal flashlight crashed against her temple.

The world narrowed, darkened, and disappeared.

From deep within Jamieson's lair on the hill there came a final, whimpered, unheard warning as the woman in black fell forward into his chest, unfeeling and beyond fear.

Sandy felt a cool dampness against her right temple — a soft, welcomed caress that brushed across her pounding cheek and head.

Her eyelids fluttered involuntarily and struggled to open but could not. She worked furiously toward consciousness, trying to focus her gaze somewhere in front of her body. She tried to orient herself to some familiar point, but she could not. There was only obscurity and uncertainty. The vision of the woman in black had gone and Sandy was now within herself.

She tried to wiggle her fingers and toes, to bring some life to the vacant, pervasive numbness that seemed to encapsulate her entire body. No longer was she apart from the unconscious, prone body in the alleyway. Now, there was no distance to protect her from his presence. She was *in* the moment; no longer reliving the earlier horror. Now, she was *in* the moment, waiting at the threshold of abomination that comes just before the full consciousness of horror.

"Marion?" he whispered in a deep, melodic voice. "Marion..." His voice trailed away to nothing as she drifted closer to wakefulness.

Sandy felt the damp cloth move slowly across her right cheek, softly massaging her swollen and bruised skin. She involuntarily moved her head to the right, nuzzling against the cool touch of the cloth and drinking in its soothing strokes. Once again, she tried to open her eyes; she tried to force herself back to full consciousness. Through partially opened eyelids, she saw the dim blur of his living room, cluttered, frightening, and foreign. Through her unsteady wakefulness, she sensed a horrifying scene, intermittently blocked by the bulk of a thick, shirted arm that moved across her unsteady vision in rhythm to the caresses against her cheek.

"You're all right now. You're fine..." came the husky voice. "Just be still now..."

In a second of wrenching, white-hot panic, Sandy became fully aware of her surroundings. Her eyes bolted open in absolute terror and began to focus more clearly.

Yes! It was no dream! Christ! He had her!

Sandy instinctively heaved her torso forward in an effort to leap to her feet. Instantly, she felt an insurmountable tautness across her chest that prevented her from moving. Quickly glancing down, she realized that she was held in place by several strands of thick seaman's rope — bindings that had been wrapped and tightened around her trembling frame with great determination. The thick rope crossed her breasts repeatedly and held her upper arms fast against her body, the strands arranged in such a way that even a slight shifting movement caused them to wrench painfully against her.

"Oh, shit!" she moaned as she tried again to move forward from her sitting position. With her second thrust forward, she felt a large hand push harshly against her chest, sending her backwards. Her back slammed hard against the wall that had been her support, momentarily shocking the breath from her chest.

"Marion, don't struggle!" he ordered in a bad tempered tone. "There's no point in doing that! Just relax!"

She felt an instant bolt of anger and fear race through her stomach — an overwhelming urge to both flee and fight. Sandy jerked her head back and to the right, her eyes searching wildly for the source of the voice. Looking into his broad, pale face, she spat her unthinking reply.

"I'm not Marion! I'm Sandy…" she yelped, her tone somewhere between uncontrollable wrath and complete desolation.

A disgusting, inscrutable grin passed across his face, accompanied by an easy nod of his enormous head. "I know that," he said in a slow, determined voice. "I know that, Sandy. What *you* need to know is that this is *my* house, *my* game, and *my* rules. So, tonight, I say you're Marion. Tomorrow, well, maybe you're someone else — or maybe you're dead. We'll just see, won't we?"

His smile dropped away and was replaced by a dark, ominous curling of his upper lip. With a heavy sigh, he lifted himself from his knees to his feet and moved quickly toward the door at the far end of the room. Standing at the threshold, he turned momentarily and looked back at the bruised woman propped against the wall, bound so tightly that she could no longer feel the natural warmth of her arms or legs. She stared back in anger and fear, trying to study his face in the dim, reflected light of the room, searching for a sign of humanity or compassion, pleading silently for some understanding of her pain and fear.

There was none.

In a moment he was gone, the scarred wooden door slamming menacingly behind him.

January 21
Midtown Station
4:40 A.M.

Sam McCannell's second-floor office at the Midtown Station was even more undernourished and chaotic than Chris Spell's. The muted, unwashed beige walls were lined with uneven rows of cheap pressboard bookshelves, each filled beyond its natural capacity with a disorganized array of journals, outdated magazines, and long forgotten stacks of papers, reports, and notes. Filing was well off McCannell's list of life's priorities and a need for organization existed only in his mind. Still, this disheveled, unappealing place seemed the appropriate lair for a man like McCannell.

Crammed into the tiny office this morning, Mary Boor, Chris Spell, and Joe Mendoza all stared through their exhaustion at the red man. He sat slumped in his cracked and torn leather chair, huddled behind stacks of paper and files heaped randomly across his insignificant, 1950s metal desk. McCannell, in turn, stared unfocused at the black telephone in front of him, one hand holding up his massive head, the other lying in wait for the call he was sure would come. Next to the old desk, wedged between it and the office wall, a uniformed female officer stood motionless, also waiting in silence. She stared down at a miniature, silver-gray tape recorder that lay on a pile of papers on the desk. It was connected to a jack at the base of McCannell's telephone by a thin, black cable. In her hand, the officer held a portable transceiver, its microphone at the ready. Her head was wrapped across the top by a thick plastic band that ended in padded earphones. Within the closeness of the room there was an unnatural silence, except for the occasional quiet rush of tired breathing.

The Lieutenant glanced at each face in turn, once again assessing the plan they had discussed, endlessly fretting about what had happened last night and that morning. If McCannell was right, their man would make the telephone call they all expected, and he would make it soon. Yes, it would be soon now — *if* McCannell was right.

What kept the Lieutenant in a barely controlled panic was the alternative to their plan. If Sam was wrong – if there was no phone call – he was sure they would find Sandy's abandoned body as they had found the others. McCannell had made a few, significant misses with this guy. He was having more trouble than usual with this freak and Sam's mistakes had Spell very concerned. What if he was wrong on this? What if this guy didn't call? If the red man was wrong and they had wasted precious hours waiting for a call that never came, well...

Mendoza sat on the floor with his back propped against one of the rickety, overfilled bookshelves. He had pulled his knees up tight against his chest and thrown his head back against a stack of magazines stuffed randomly onto the shelf behind. His eyes were tightly closed. Spell could see the thick moisture that had gathered on Mendoza's upper lip and forehead. He looked like he would explode at any moment. He had been taken to the edge of his usual macho control by what had happened. Like Sandy, he, too, had been victimized and was in bad shape.

Spell stared at him for a moment longer, considering whether or not to send him home, debating whether or not to take him off their morbid watch. In the end, the Lieutenant decided it was impossible. The only way to keep some control over Mendoza was to keep him in the mix — hard as that might prove to be in the end.

Spell glanced at McCannell. He looked like he had fallen asleep with his head in his hand. The red man's eyes were also closed, his eyelids fluttering from time to time, and his face was unusually flushed. Still, this was McCannell's way, the Lieutenant mused. With this man, appearances were always deceiving. Spell knew that his friend was awake and waiting. It was just that his mind had gone off somewhere, probably in search of Sandy — possibly in search of where he had made his mistakes in assessing his adversary.

To the Lieutenant, only Mary Boor seemed to be fully there, present in the office with him. She sat on an old wooden chair across from McCannell's desk, snuggled so tightly against its cold metal façade that her knees and legs appeared immobile. She stared straight ahead, looking directly into McCannell's face. Her expression was wide and quizzical. Spell knew and understood that expression. Her mind was racing, worrying, flirting endlessly with possibilities and options. When everything had turned to shit, as it had this morning, the Lieutenant valued her presence beyond all the others. He knew that Boor would always be the one with her feet on the ground and her head on the problem. She would hold together, no matter how ugly things became. He smiled at her in a needful way, but she didn't see him. She continued to stare straight ahead, caught somewhere in her private thoughts.

When the telephone finally rang, its alert knifed through the silent room with incredible effect. The officer with the headphones immediately raised the transceiver's microphone to her lips and whispered, "Call in... start the trace." From across the tiny office, Mendoza started violently from the shock of the sound, his knees trembling and his eyes now open wide and staring wildly at the ringing telephone. The Lieutenant looked quickly at McCannell and then at Mary Boor. The red man's eyes were now open and his head began to nod up and down. He was looking at Mary, giving her a silent signal.

Mary shuffled uneasily in her chair, trying to extricate her long legs from their imprisonment against McCannell's desk. She reached toward the telephone receiver. They had agreed it would be her who would first take the call. That would allow more time for the trace — a few important seconds that just might make the difference.

She let the telephone ring a second time, and a third. Between the shrill rings that had riveted everyone's attention, she glanced from McCannell to Spell, searching for any last minute change in the plan. There was none.

On the fourth ring, she answered.

"Dr. McCannell's office," she said in a calm, metered tone. She stared at McCannell, waiting to see his reaction. He gave her a tight, reassuring smile.

Mary listened intently for a reply, her eyes now captured by the hypnotic rotation of the tape in the recorder next to the telephone. For several seconds she waited in absolute silence, unwilling to breathe, waiting for some sign of life on the other end of the line. Finally, she could wait no longer.

"Dr. McCannell's office," she repeated. "May I help you?"

"I'm surprised to hear a human voice at this time of the morning," he said in a halting, husky voice.

Mary Boor's face went instantly pale. Although she had never heard his voice before, she instinctively knew that this was the man she so desperately wanted. She glanced quickly at McCannell and nodded her head up and down, indicating it was the call they all expected.

"We try to keep this line manned as often as we can, sir. May I help you with something?" she answered in a stoic, controlled tone.

"I want to speak to Doctor McCannell," he said with abrupt determination. "McCannell..." he emphasized.

"He's not in his office right now, but he's in the building. Would you like to wait while I page him?"

The man on the other end laughed knowingly — an unusual,

forced laugh with a threatening lilt. "Sure, why not?" It wasn't really a question.

"Ok, hang on," Mary said. Rather than put the caller on hold, she carefully laid the handset next to the telephone and quickly placed her forefinger to her lips, indicating to everyone in the room that they should remain completely silent. Spell thought he noticed a slight trembling in her hand. From behind his desk, McCannell's face was drawn into a tight smile. He seemed to be counting the seconds to himself, waiting for just the right moment to pick up the line. When he felt it had arrived, he reached down for the handset and placed it tightly against his ear. The uniformed officer adjusted her headphones and squinted resolutely at the recorder on the desk, making sure that nothing would be missed.

"Sam McCannell," he said in a metered monotone.

"Well, Doctor, that was a trite ploy, that little trick with the secretary."

"Sorry, I didn't understand that" the red man said in tired voice.

"That little gambit with the woman, Doctor. An obvious stall to trace the call, I'd say. It won't do you any good, though. I'm using her cell phone, Doctor."

"Whose cell phone?" McCannell asked in a high-pitched, hurried voice.

"Jesus Christ!" Jamieson spat across the line. "This is a disappointment to me, Doctor McCannell! Here you are, fucking around with cop bullshit, trying to stall around, when I'm trying to hold a meaningful conversation. Now, I know you're not *that* stupid, so why do you think *I'm* that stupid!"

His voice was angry and sharp.

"I don't think you're stupid at all," McCannell replied in a conciliatory tone. "That's not what I think at all…"

For several seconds the line was silent. "All right, Doctor,"

MISSION DISTRICT MURDERS • Michael D. Kelleher

Jamieson finally mumbled. "Let's not get off to a bad start here. We have a lot to talk about…"

"Is Officer Janus alive?" McCannell interrupted. Immediately, he scrunched up his face, realizing his mistake. This was the kind of man who should never be interrupted. The red man had found himself instinctively caught up in the fear they all shared — and that had been a mistake. He took in a deep breath and waited, hoping he had not fucked up too badly.

"Yes, for now…" came the quiet, determined reply. "But how long she remains so depends on whether or not you're going to fuck with me, Doctor. Do you understand that?"

"Yes." McCannell nodded silently at the others, indicating that Sandy was still alive. Mendoza let out an audible gasp and bobbed his head.

"All right, then. I said we have a lot to talk about. I want you to listen to me, to hear what I have to say. Will you do that?"

"Yes."

For several more seconds, the line was quiet. In the background, McCannell thought he heard the whining of a motor and wondered if it could be a ceiling fan. The sound was just like the one he heard most nights in his own kitchen. He closed his eyes and tried to draw up some image of the man on the telephone, to dredge up some mental picture of the room from which he was calling. Nothing came. He looked up at the uniformed woman listening intently to the conversation. Silently, with his eyes, he asked if she was capturing all she had heard. She nodded up and down.

"What do I call you?" the red man said weakly into the mouthpiece. "Give me a name, please. It would make it easier for me."

From the other side of the desk, Mary Boor gave a hint of a smile. She knew what was on McCannell's mind. He was struggling

198

to put some control into the chaos, working toward building a bridge to the man on the other end of the line.

"You can call me Jamie, Doctor. That's not my name, but I like it."

"Ok, Jamie," McCannell said in a soft, easy tone. "That's fine with me. You can call me Sam, if you like."

"No, I *don't* like," came the harsh, immediate reply. "We don't know each other that well, yet, do we?"

"No," McCannell said, with obvious repentance in his voice.

"All right, Doctor. I want you to meet with me. I want you to talk to me. Now, we can fuck around here and get it all wrong. If you do that, she dies. You can play cops with your friends, fuck around and try to fuck this up if you want to. But if you do, she dies. You know that I'm not playing here. You know what I can do and you know I've danced around you with those other women. So, the bottom line is simple: fuck around... and she dies. Do you believe that, Doctor?"

"Yes, I do," McCannell replied in a serious tone. "I understand that you're very capable of doing what you say you will. I don't want you to hurt Officer Janus. I'll cooperate. I want to meet with you, Jamie."

Chris looked at McCannell and then at Mary. Silently, they exchanged an understanding of what had just occurred. McCannell had made up his mind. He was going to meet with this man, and he was going to do it alone.

"Good, Doctor, good," Jamieson announced. "I want to be perfectly clear on this. Your pretty friend here is wired with an explosive device. The device has a timing mechanism. I'm going to tell you where and when we will meet. I'm going to tell you what to do. If anything interrupts or delays our meeting, this little lady will be nothing more than splattered body parts on my living room wall.

Do you understand that, Doctor?"

"Yes," the red man answered. "I understand."

"Good," he said in a whispered voice. "Good…"

For several seconds the connection was quiet, the silence only broken by the light hum on the other end of the line. Once again, McCannell tried to summon up some image of that sound. It was too regular for a fan — too even. It sounded more mechanical. Hadn't the caller said "living room?"

"All right, Doctor," Jamieson began. "You will be alone at the park bench in Androni Park at exactly six this morning. You will be *alone*. Now, I imagine that you know the bench I mean, don't you? You've been there, or at least know of it, right? You've seen her on that bench, haven't you?"

"Yes. I know the place you mean, Jamie." McCannell was flooded with the photographic images of Jamieson's victim, Joanne Callin, sprawled horribly on the park bench.

"Good. You be there at six… alone. You know the area and you know that I'm very familiar with it. I will drive to that bench and you will get in my car. If you're not alone… if there is any fucking around… your young friend dies a horrible death. You understand?"

"Yes, but how will I know you? How will I know your car?" the red man asked quickly.

"Don't fuck with me!" Jamieson shouted. "That was a stupid question, Doctor. Just be there. Remember, any fucking around and you'll never be able to gather her parts into one place!"

Instantly, the line went dead with an angered slam.

The uniformed woman made a slicing motion across her neck with her right hand, indicating that the connection was gone. She put the microphone to her lips and pushed the transmit button. "Did you get anything on the call?" she hurriedly asked the technician on the other end. Immediately the reply came back: "Cellular phone.

Nothing."

McCannell let the receiver fall from his hand and crash onto the top of his desk. Mary Boor reached for it and placed it gently back in the cradle. She moved her hand to the left and tapped McCannell's arm in a reassuring way. "You were great, Sam," she whispered. "You were really good."

Spell nodded his agreement and stared at McCannell. The red man looked terrible. He was pale and sweaty, obviously pushed to the edge by his conversation. From across the small office, Mendoza cleared his throat and shook his head up and down, mimicking Spell's movements. "Yeah, Sam, thanks. Thanks..." his voice trailed off and he hung his head on his chest, his hands cradled together so tightly that his fingers looked pained and bloodless.

"Jesus..." McCannell mumbled as he stared at his wristwatch. "We only have about an hour, Chris."

January 21
Midtown Station — Communications Center
5:50 A.M.

Chris Spell turned away from the Communications Officer sitting at his console and moved close to Mary Boor — close enough to speak only in a whisper. "I hope I didn't screw up with this surveillance thing, Mar. I hope I didn't make a mistake sending Joe along in the helicopter." His voice was pleading and uncertain, his expression strained.

Mary reached out and stroked his upper arm with her right hand. "Me too, Chris," she answered in a soft voice. "I don't have a problem with Joe going along on the helicopter, though. I think he needed to do *something*. The waiting was really getting to him. The air surveillance is a risk, but you had to do something in the way of backup. I'm not sure about the transmitter, though. You may get by with that one, you may not, depending on how sharp this guy is. What you definitely *won't* get away with is cutting Marley out of this plan. When he hears about it, he'll shit all over you, Chris."

"Fuck him!" the Lieutenant growled, more loudly than he expected. The Communications Officer whirled around in his chair and stared at Spell, a stern, angered look on his face.

"Sorry," Spell quickly announced in the officer's general direction. "I wasn't talking to you…" The Comm Officer turned back to his station and shook his head from side to side, obviously thinking the worse of the Lieutenant.

"Sorry, Mar…" Spell whispered, looking unusually sheepish and still staring at the back of the young man's head.

"Listen, Chris," she interrupted in a scolding tone, "you did the best you could. Let it go now. We need to focus on what's happening *now*, not get hung up on what we did an hour ago."

The Lieutenant hunched up his shoulders and glowered at the floor. "Yeah, I know you're right… but I can't help it. I'm worried as hell. If we had done it Sam's way, he would have just wandered out there on his own, without any backup at all. I couldn't let him do that, could I? I mean, that would have been wrong for sure. I had to give him some kind of backup."

"Yeah…" Mary answered without looking at him. To the Lieutenant, though, she didn't sound as certain as usual.

"Listen, Chris, Sam was convinced he could handle this without any backup. Either that, or he was afraid this guy would pick up on *anything* we tried and that would put Sandy in even more jeopardy. That was Sam's way of looking at this situation; that was *his* decision. I know it was a tough call, Chris. Either way, it was a tough one. Now, we just have to see it through the best way we can."

Spell rubbed his eyes with the back of his right hand and nodded his agreement. "Ok, well, it's done now, Mar," he said in a stronger tone. "All we've got is the location transmitter and the aerial surveillance. If we lose those, we lose Sam. If this freak uncovers either of them, we lose Sam. If we lose Sam, we lose Sandy. I couldn't deal with that, Mar. I couldn't deal with that…"

"A lot could happen here, Chris. It doesn't have to be *all* bad," she whispered as quietly as she could.

The Lieutenant let out a groaning sigh and turned away. He stood stiffly behind the Communications Officer, staring at the blinking lights and displays on the console and watching the back of the young man's head as his hands moved quickly across a row of dials, making last minute adjustments of some kind. There was nothing he could do now but wait. The location transmitter, which had been hastily stitched inside one of the cuffs of McCannell's pants, was working just as it should, sending evidence of the red man's location in Androni Park. That was good. The helicopter was in place, hovering near the park bench, but not too close to the rendezvous point. It was manned with a pilot, a surveillance specialist, Joe Mendoza, and all the equipment that would be needed to track McCannell's movements. That was good.

Still, there was nothing else to do but wait, and that was bad. It was making the Lieutenant crazier by the minute. All the other possible options, all of Spell's best suggestions, had either been discarded by the team because they were too dangerous or the red man had flat-out refused them. In fact, McCannell had wanted *nothing* in the way of backup — not even the tiny transmitter or the surveillance team. In the end, McCannell had only compromised with Spell because time was running out and the Lieutenant had threatened to abort the meeting in Androni Park. Neither man was happy with the compromise.

Now there was nothing Chris Spell could do but wait.

Androni Park, 6:00 A.M.

Sam McCannell sat alone on the weathered park bench where Joanne Callin's mutilated body had been found less than two weeks earlier. He was wrapped in a thick, tan overcoat to protect his stout frame against the swirling fog and angry southerly wind that had beaten across the entire city throughout the night. Still, despite the warmth of his coat, McCannell was cold and shivering, mostly from exhaustion and anxiety. Behind him, the stand of towering, spindly eucalyptus trees, which had once hidden Herbert Jamieson's vehicle from view, now groaned and creaked with each blustery breeze.

He sat motionless, unthinking, staring straight ahead to Androni Parkway, feeling nothing but the persistent chill in his fingers, arms, and legs. McCannell had moved beyond his uncontrolled fear of an hour earlier. Now, he was caught in a numbing cocoon of resignation; he was unwillingly suspended between caring and not caring, adrift between fear and commitment. Now, he cared only that *something* happen, and that it happen soon. Like Chris Spell, he was worn out from the waiting, the worry, and the uncertainty.

From somewhere in the grayness overhead, the eerie groaning of the eucalyptus trees was intermittently broken by the distant, choppy whine of an SFPD helicopter. McCannell tried to picture the men in the helicopter hovering above him. He wondered what they were feeling, what they were seeing from up there. Most of all, he worried about Mendoza and whether or not he'd be able to deal with those things about to take place.

For a moment, McCannell stared up at the swirling ceiling of fog above the tree line. Its thickness killed their aerial reconnaissance plan. In fact, it was dangerous for everyone involved, just as the red man had said it would be. The SFPD was far too close for comfort; they would be much too obvious for the man McCannell was going to meet. The red man scowled at the noise of the chopper overhead and grumbled to himself. This was not the way he wanted things to go down. This was Spell's way.

As the helicopter drifted away once again, the surging breeze suddenly calmed and the rhythmic moaning of the eucalyptus trees faded to an easy, soothing rustle of leaves wagging against each other. It was then that he heard the husky rattle of an automobile moving slowly up Androni Parkway in his direction. Instantly, McCannell sat upright and turned his head to the left, searching through the fog for the source of the sound. Rolling toward him, at a painfully slow pace, was a green and white sedan boldly marked "Tudor Cabs" on the hood and doors. The vehicle crept steadily toward the edge of the Parkway, moving parallel to the bench where McCannell sat, and pulled to a stop. Inside, the hatless driver bent forward and to his right, straining to look out the closed passenger's window in the direction of the park bench. It was obvious the driver was looking for someone.

For a few seconds, McCannell sat perfectly still, staring back at the driver and considering the situation. There was no way of knowing if this was the man he was supposed to meet or just an intermediary of some sort. Either way, the red man decided, he needed to find out.

McCannell pushed himself up from the park bench and started in the direction of the cab. By the time he arrived at the edge of the Parkway, the driver had reached across the passenger's side of the vehicle and rolled the window partially down. McCannell stepped up to the passenger's door and bent down to look at the man behind the wheel. He was young, no more than twenty-five, frail, and obviously confused about the situation in which he found himself. It was clear that this was not the man McCannell had arranged to meet.

"Are you Dr. McCannell?" the young man squeaked.

"Yes," McCannell answered in a quizzical, halting tone.

The driver grabbed a white envelope that lay on the seat next to him and pushed it in McCannell's direction. The red man reached through the passenger's window and took it, rolling it over in his hand at the same time. On the face of the envelope, in careful block printing, was his name. McCannell instantly recognized the printing.

"I'm supposed to give this envelope to you and wait," the driver said, his eyes wide with anticipation and his voice thick with uncertainty. "I've been paid already," he added, as if to convince his waiting fare that everything was all right.

McCannell nodded and stepped back from the vehicle door. He pushed his right forefinger into the fold of the envelope and quickly ripped it open. Inside, he retrieved a letter-sized piece of paper with the familiar, neatly constructed block printing on it:

DOCTOR MCCANNELL:

DESPITE OUR CONVERSATION ABOUT MEETING ALONE AND WITHOUT TRICKS, I WILL ASSUME YOU HAVE ARRANGED SOME SURPRISES FOR ME. I DON'T HOLD THAT AGAINST YOU. I WOULD DO THE SAME THING IN YOUR PLACE. TO MAKE SURE WE ARE NOT INTERRUPTED OR DELAYED, YOU WILL DO THE FOLLOWING: TELL THIS DRIVER TO TAKE YOU TO THE BUSH PARKING GARAGE. WHEN YOU ARRIVE, INSTRUCT HIM TO DRIVE YOU TO THE THIRD FLOOR, SOUTHEAST CORNER OF THE GARAGE. WHEN YOU ARE THERE, YOU WILL GET OUT OF THE CAB AND WAIT AT THE STAIRWELL IN THE SOUTHEAST CORNER. YOU WILL TELL THE DRIVER TO CONTINUE ON TO PIER 41 AND WAIT THERE. YOU WILL NOT SPEAK TO THE DRIVER OTHER THAN TO GIVE HIM THESE INSTRUCTIONS.

DOCTOR MCCANNELL, IT IS IMPORTANT THAT YOU FOLLOW THESE INSTRUCTIONS PRECISELY.

YOU KNOW WHAT THE ALTERNATIVE IS, DON'T YOU?

JAMIE

McCannell read the message a second time, making sure he hadn't missed anything. When he had finished, he pulled open the passenger's door and slid in.

"Driver, take me to the Bush Garage — the third floor," he announced in a solemn tone.

The young man stared at McCannell, his mouth hung slightly

open. It was obvious that he was becoming more confused by the minute. For several seconds, he made no movement. He just stared at his fare, his thin, pale lips dangling.

"Did you hear me?" McCannell asked impatiently.

"Ah, yeah," the driver finally responded. "Where'd you say?"

"The Bush Garage. Take me to the third floor of the Bush Garage," McCannell snapped.

Like a scolded adolescent, the driver whipped his head around to face the road and released the emergency break at the same time. The cab moved quickly forward, slicing its way through the fog on Androni Parkway, heading for Folsom Street and the Financial District of the city.

Hovering overhead, flirting with the wandering thickets of gray mist, the helicopter tried to keep in visual contact with the green and white cab. But, in the end, it was no use. By the time the Tudor Cab had reached the outskirts of the Financial District, the men in the helicopter had lost their prey among the burgeoning stream of automobiles headed downtown to begin the workday. Now, McCannell was on his own — except for the location transmitter sewn into the cuff of his pants.

Inside the Midtown Station Communications Center, Chris Spell received word by radio that the helicopter crew had lost their target. The team was circling over the southern edge of the Mission District, trying to spot the green and white sedan they had first lost in the fog over Androni Park. The Lieutenant knew it was useless and ordered them back to the ground.

Spell checked with the Comm Officer to be sure the tracking device was still sending a signal. It was.

"Where are they heading?" the Lieutenant asked the young man at the console. "Can you tell me that?"

"Sure. It looks like their heading downtown, Lieutenant...

toward the Financial District."

"Can we keep the signal? I mean, will we be able to track that signal long enough to fix their position and get some backup into the area?" Spell asked in a concerned tone.

"That depends," the Comm Officer replied. "If the target stays in the open, we should be fine. If he goes into a tunnel, or underground, or some kind of building with concrete or metal walls, well, we'll probably lose them. It all depends, Sir."

Spell nodded his head and turned away to face Mary Boor. She wore a worried, dark expression that he couldn't ignore.

"What's wrong, Mar?" he asked.

"Why in the hell is he taking Sam downtown, Chris? That's way off his usual haunt. And what's the deal with the cab?"

January 21
Bush Garage
6:35 A.M.

The Bush Garage is an enormous, nondescript gray concrete structure comprised of eight stories of vehicle parking, five below ground and three above, which covers an entire city block on the periphery of the Financial District of San Francisco. For those commuters who have come to rely on the vicissitudes of driving into the City – and who can afford the daily parking fee of twenty-four dollars – this impersonal sanctuary epitomizes convenience and implies financial success. It offers a location only three short blocks from Montgomery Street, the undisputed Wall Street of the West. Each morning, starting very early, the Bush Garage is the final destination for nearly four thousand vehicular gladiators, who each view a parking place inside its thick, featureless walls as an absolute necessity in the complex cocktail of perceived financial success. To compete successfully in the horror of this daily commute ritual, one must begin well before civilized business hours. Those arriving at the Bush Garage after seven in the morning forgo any possibility of a reasonably convenient start to the work day, and are relegated to a municipal rail and bus system that can best be described as primordial.

However, none of these issues were of concern to Sam McCannell this morning. Not even the ungodly hour.

The red man sat mute, next to the Tudor Cab driver as he navigated the green and white sedan ever closer to the Bush Garage, weaving easily through the clustered, chaotic traffic and racing effortlessly down a confusing series of one-way streets with the obvious skill of his trade. From time to time, the young man with the perpetually confused expression and jerky head movements would glance coyly in McCannell's direction, looking like he wanted to begin some kind of meaningful conversation, apparently searching for an explanation for this bizarre, prepaid fare he had managed to snag as his first of the morning. When he wasn't scanning the thick city traffic or mumbling adolescent obscenities at the faceless drivers ahead of him, the young man would surreptitiously check the taxi's meter, silently calculating and recalculating his unexpected profit. The burly man who had flagged him down on Mission Street a half-hour earlier had been a strange fellow, but obviously not a frugal one. The man with no name had given the driver five, twenty-dollar bills along with the envelope that his fare had opened earlier. He had specified a precise location in Androni Park – a certain park bench – in vivid detail, as if he had sat in that isolated place often. The large, casually dressed stranger had assured the driver that he would make a handsome profit for the morning run, and as the young man neared the Financial District, that promise seemed to be coming true.

As the Tudor Cab approached the east entrance to the Bush Garage, the meter clicked past twenty-two dollars — a standard fare from Androni Park to downtown. The driver smiled through the gritty windshield at the line of cars waiting to snake their way into the bowels of the garage. Yes, it would be quite a profitable morning. At least seventy-five dollars, he calculated. Much more than he usually made in an entire day's tips. No, it didn't really matter that the fat, red-haired man next to him obviously wasn't in the mood for conversation. Hell, he could have it anyway he wanted for that kind of a tip.

The cab crawled impatiently along the curbside lane, following a block-long line of late-model, shiny commuter vehicles, most of which were festooned with middle-aged men appropriately attired in dark suits and tastefully obvious power ties. Once again, the driver glanced at his passenger, careful not to make eye contact. The chubby, wind-blown man next to him seemed out of place for the Financial District. He was wrapped in an enormous overcoat, which was more appropriate for a wintry football game than strolling along Montgomery Street like a peacock on parade. It was certainly nothing like the chic, stylish foggers donned by most of the other commuters exiting the garage for their destinations. This man had no tie, and from what the driver could see, no jacket underneath his overcoat.

The young man glanced slyly at McCannell's shoes, searching for the required black wingtips — a certain hallmark sported by all successful, middle-aged men on Montgomery Street. No, there were no wingtips. In fact, the driver was sure he had seen only an old pair of unstylish brown loafers on the fat man's feet. Worse yet, they were set off with rough, white sport socks. This was all very wrong for the Financial District. This was a strange fare, indeed, the young man deducted.

The driver passed the next few minutes waiting in the parking line, thinking about his passenger, assessing, trying to come to some conclusion about this oddly-attired, pudgy man who was important enough to warrant a hundred-dollar fare but so obviously inappropriate for his destination. In the end, the young man could only conclude that his passenger was a chef. Like the driver himself, the logic of the argument was absurdly simple — once it came to mind. His fare certainly had the right kind of body and, after all, his dress wouldn't matter, if he *was* a chef. No one actually ever *sees* a chef, he thought. *He* had never seen a real chef, anyway. Nonetheless, he was sure that this is what a chef *should* look like. He had seen pictures of chefs before, somewhere.

Without thinking, the driver chuckled lightly to himself, trying to picture McCannell standing behind an enormous, spattering grill in one of the many famous cold weather restaurants in the Financial

District. Yes, this man was definitely a chef. All that was missing was the white coat and high hat. Those were probably waiting for him at the restaurant.

For the first time since he had given the young man directions to the Bush Garage, McCannell turned to face his driver.

"Something funny, my friend?" the red man asked in a scolding, offbeat tone.

"No, sir, not really," the driver replied softly and with a shadowy look of guilt. "I was just thinking about what you do for a living. I do that with all my fares. It's kind of my specialty, you know." The driver's lips were flapping like palm leaves in the wind. An obvious grin of delight replaced the guilty look on his face, now that he realized his passenger had finally demonstrated some sign of life.

"Well, I like to do it," the driver continued his explanation, hurrying his words to make sure he had not offended his fare. "It helps me pass the time. So, when I figure out what my passenger does for a living, well, it makes me laugh and it's fun!" Once again, the driver stared at his passenger, but this time with bright, inquisitive eyes.

The red man cracked the barest of smiles, briefly savoring the irony of the situation in which he now found himself. He quickly remembered that he had been instructed to say nothing; he knew that silence was important. Still, he just couldn't resist the lure that had been set by his youthful companion. It was a moment filled with too much irony to ignore.

"And what have you determined my profession to be?" McCannell asked in a flirting tone.

"Oh, that's obvious now, sir. You're a chef!" he announced triumphantly. "I'd guess you're a pretty important one, too, judging by the way your friend arranged for you to be brought down here. I bet you're a really good chef."

McCannell broke into a roaring, tearful laughter that seemed to momentarily wash away the painful knot in his stomach and the unrelenting tautness in his chest. As the cab negotiated the final turn into the garage and was swallowed up into its concrete darkness, the red man alternatively wiped the tears from the corner of each eye and tried to wind down the pleasurable heaving in his chest.

"Well, am I right, sir? Am I right?" the young man prodded impatiently.

McCannell stared at the driver and saw his obvious youth and simplicity. It was a wonderful, immeasurable moment — a fleeting few seconds during which the red man wished he could *be* that young man with a heavy tip in his pocket and a sure sense of what he had just accomplished. There was no way McCannell could do anything but move downstream with the unstoppable illogic of his new friend.

"Yep, you're right," he chirped at the driver, trying his best to plaster a facade of awe and fascination across his fleshy face. "That's amazing. You're really an amazing young man," he confirmed. "Now, please get me to the third floor, ok? I'm running late and that just won't do, you know. My customers will be waiting for me and it just won't do to be late."

"You bet!" the driver announced, a broad, child-like grin smattered across his face. "In a flash..." The young man snapped his head forward and leaned toward the windshield, obviously giving his full attention to the last few turns as the cab worked its way upward to the third floor of the garage. After a series of dizzying, left-hand turns that sent McCannell's stomach riding a momentary wave of nausea, the sedan screeched to a stop on the polished concrete driveway next to a narrow, poorly lit stairwell.

"Ok!" the driver said in a victorious tone. "We're here!" He whirled around in McCannell's direction, a genuinely pleased look on his face. The red man began to fumble around in his overcoat pocket, instinctively searching for some paper token of appreciation for the young man's efforts. The driver recognized the familiar, shuffling movements and, for the briefest moment, considered whether or not to improve his take. No, that just wouldn't do. After all, this was an important man — a chef.

"Sir, I've been paid and tipped already," the driver said, indicating with a wave of his hand that McCannell should stop his search.

The red man smiled and pulled an empty hand from his pocket. "Good, thanks," he said as he pushed open the passenger's door.

McCannell wrestled his frame from the cab and launched the door closed behind him with a snap. In a moment, with the mandatory squealing of worn tires and the roaring flourish of an overworked engine, the Tudor Cab with its savant driver pulled away from where McCannell stood and disappeared into the corkscrew-driving ramp that led back to the street.

"Jesus..." McCannell mumbled to himself. "I forgot to tell him about Pier 41..."

It was 6:45 A.M.

Beneath Sam McCannell's feet, the five-foot thick concrete floor vibrated rhythmically to the unremitting stream of cars entering the garage from three stories below. As the endless line of vehicles filed into the entrance on Bush Street, each eventually worked its way to the nearest vacant parking space, disgorging its frustrated and anxious occupants to make their way on foot to Montgomery Street. With five floors of parking underground and three above, the area of the garage where McCannell stood waiting was always the last to be assaulted by morning commuters. Its relatively poor proximity to Montgomery Street, which added the equivalent of another long city block to a commuter's walk, made these parking spaces suitable only for the unfortunate late arrivals in the morning chaos.

There, in the farthest corner of the third floor, McCannell waited, the gnawing rumbling at his feet, the air inside the garage foul and metallic from the exhaust of hundreds of moving cars below. His eyes nervously darting back and forth along the open floor in front of him, the red man felt a numbing coldness in his legs and hands — a more penetrating sense of iciness than should be expected on even such a foggy, windy morning. No, this was not the usual unwelcome bite of an early city morning that he felt. This was the unsettling numbing of a soul-gripping fear that he thought he had left behind at the Midtown Station an hour earlier.

Now, here, he was afraid, and the trembling that began at the soles of his feet was much more than the harmonic rattling of the concrete floor. This was a trembling that arose on its own, from deep inside his soul; it attacked the joints in his knees and assaulted the core of his stomach in a way that nothing but uncontrolled fear could. The red man felt a stinging tautness in his jaw and neck; he sensed the irresistible spasms of anxiety as they danced unfettered around his eyes and mouth. He knew the painful tension of strained muscles across the backs of his hands and recognized the excruciating grip of spontaneous tightness that caused the normally plump, relaxed fingers inside his pockets to roll up into contorted, unnatural fists.

McCannell tried to take back the control that he knew had slipped away since he left Androni Park. He thought about Chris Spell and Mary Boor, the helicopter that should be somewhere above, the location device in the cuff of his pants. All that he had asked from his friends had been done — even more. He would have the best of backup, or at least the best that he was willing to allow. The choices had been his and now he must deal with them. For all these reasons, and for Sandy, he was more frightened than he had ever been before.

McCannell forced his mind back to safer, more familiar territory, trying to summon up his best vision of the man he was about to meet, working through the worn, unemotional checklist of a profiler. The red man scurried through each of the things he knew about this man, or thought he knew. Now, there was a name — Jamie. That was a start. It was a point of commonality that he would use when the appropriate time came. That was good. But he would need much more. He searched for something meaningful, for something that would make him feel better about the situation.

A series of slide-like images raced through McCannell's mind — a disjointed, multi-framed cacophony of scenarios of men with dark hair, or red, or gray, or blonde; images of a well-dressed man, or one who was shabby and unkempt. Many of the men in his mind were large, some were lean and fit, others burly and imposing. Still, none of them seemed familiar. None seemed a man like himself. In the end, no image he could conjure up was the right one — or perhaps they all were. McCannell realized that he knew almost nothing of importance about the man he was about to meet. He was only sure that what he *really* knew about Jamie was trite and insignificant.

Suddenly, the red man came full face with his fear — an unfathomable terror born of almost complete uncertainty about what he thought he knew about Jamie. All his efforts at profiling this man, all his work toward understanding the man who had brutally murdered at least four women in his city, were now useless. Worse, all the psychological games that McCannell had played, with all those adversaries over all those years, now seemed to amount to nothing more than useless mind-fuck. Nothing he had done in all those years had prepared him for this moment. That was all just one big jaw-flapping, ego-driven, mind-fuck. Now, the red man had to deal with the reality of the sick business of serial murder. Now, his enormous skills at playing the game of profiling came to nothing and his only abiding interest was his own survival.

In this moment, standing alone and huddled against the descending stairway of the Bush Garage, Sam McCannell experienced only one sensation of which he could be sure — only a single meaning that he held fast. He didn't want to die in this place, and the only way he could be sure of survival was to run away. Anything less than that was inconceivable and foolhardy. His best – his only – option was to flee the meeting, to work his way back to a safe place, to hide behind the grandiose, predictable, and immutable guesswork that had been his life and trade.

The mind-fuck game of profiling was one thing, but meeting a murderer like this was another.

McCannell spun on his heels to peer down the descending stairway, assessing how simple and easy it would be to just disappear to the floor below and into the safety of the rushing crowds on Bush Street. He moved to the top of the stairs, fully turning his back to the parking area, and cautiously slid his right foot forward onto the first descending step. In that moment, with his mind and heart committed to the only safe course he could imagine, the red man's decision was made for him, from behind.

January 21
Bush Garage
6:50 A.M.

The voice from behind him was deep and melodic. It was surprisingly strong and discernable, even in the vacant hollow of the stairwell, even over the harsh rumbling of the vehicles from the floors below.

It had a haunting, familiar quality.

"Dr. McCannell?" Jamieson asked in a polite and even tone.

The red man started perceptibly, his spine instinctively straightened and stretched by the unexpected sound from behind him. He stepped back from the top of the dim stairwell and turned rapidly in the direction of the voice. The man he saw was large in stature and thickly framed. He was dressed in new, dark blue overalls, which covered a neatly pressed, white, collared shirt. Across the chest of the overalls, located just above a narrow pocket on the left side, the words "Bush Garage" had been embroidered in vivid yellow stitching. Herbert Jamieson looked like any one of the dozen or so garage employees McCannell had seen scurrying around the structure on the lower floors.

"Christ…" McCannell mumbled, his eyes wide and staring. In every scenario he had imagined, the red man had pictured his adversary inside a vehicle, but never on foot. In each vision, this man had squealed to a stop next to his prey, thrown open the passenger's door of his car, and forced McCannell inside the car at gunpoint, or using some other weapon. Nowhere in his imagination had McCannell pictured the man he had set out to meet as standing just a few inches from him, dressed as a maintenance worker, with a wry, sardonic smile plastered across his face. The shock of seeing his adversary there, directly in front of him, sent the psychologist into an instant panic.

Instinctively, McCannell took a step backward to distance himself from the man in the blue overalls. As he did, his right foot slipped on the shiny, concrete landing and he felt himself beginning to slide uncontrollably backward into the abyss of the steep stairwell. Instantly, a burly hand snapped forward and grabbed McCannell's overcoat, pulling him against gravity and putting him back on balance.

"You need to be more careful, Dr. McCannell. There's no point in breaking your back *here*, is there?" Jamieson said in a slow, solemn tone. His large, square face beamed at the chubby man, now dangling helplessly at the end of his arm. As soon as McCannell was steady, the hand was withdrawn with the same quick, direct motion.

McCannell nodded his head up and down but said nothing. For a few seconds, he stared into the face of the man in front of him. Jamieson's features were geometric and sharply defined; his head was unusually large and finished with a neatly trimmed crop of once blonde hair that had turned a musty gray at the sides. There was nothing about this man that was small — nothing at all diminutive. He was stout, firm, and square — obviously a man who valued strength and had worked hard to preserve his own, even though he appeared to be in his early forties and had begun to show the inevitable evidence of middle age. It was clear that the flabby and mostly sedentary psychologist was poorly matched with the man he now confronted.

Realizing his plight, McCannell's hands hung limp at his side, his fingers trembling noticeably. For several seconds, he continued to stare at the man in the blue overalls, his eyes spacious and unyielding, his gaze transfixed. There was nothing else he could do.

"I'm Jamie," the dark, melodic voice announced. "At least, you can call me that for now." The big man nodded his head slightly, as if to add emphasis to the introduction, but did not extend his hand or make any other movement. Rather, he just stared back at the psychologist, carefully studying his features with narrow, cold blue eyes.

McCannell shuffled his feet from side to side, as if to test the solidarity of the floor, while searching desperately for something to say. "Thank you," he mumbled without thinking, instantly realizing how trite and useless it must have sounded to the man in front of him. Quickly, he dropped his gaze away from Jamieson's and began to absently study the floor in front of him.

Without speaking, Jamieson pushed a large brown paper bag in the red man's direction, stopping its forward movement just before it touched McCannell's chest. McCannell snapped his head up quickly, unsure of what had been thrust toward him and fearing the worst. He hadn't noticed that Jamieson had been carrying a bundle in his left hand.

"What's this?" McCannell snapped at him in a shaky voice, gesturing with his head at the paper bag below his chin.

"I want you to strip down to your underwear and put these on," Jamieson ordered, now pushing the bundle lightly against McCannell's chest. "I want you to leave your clothes here, on the stairwell, Dr. McCannell." His voice was stern and even deeper than before. There was no room for negotiation.

"Why?" the red man asked. "What's the point..."

"Don't argue, Dr. McCannell! You're in no position to argue. Please, just do what I ask and do it quickly," Jamieson interrupted.

McCannell's eyes moved from the paper bag to Jamieson's face. This man was not joking. He had left no room for discussion; his expression made his determination obvious. To make the point, Jamieson pushed the bundle hard into McCannell's chest and quickly pulled his hand away, letting the package roll against McCannell's overcoat. The red man instinctively grabbed the paper bag and held it tightly in his hands.

"Go ahead, Dr. McCannell. Do it now!" came the husky voice.

McCannell delicately opened the paper bag and looked inside. It contained a white shirt and blue overalls, just like those that Jamieson wore. He quickly stepped to the corner of the stairwell and slid into a small alcove that separated the descending stairs from the main floor of the garage. McCannell set the bag down next to his left leg and began to remove his clothes, starting with his heavy overcoat. As he removed each piece of clothing, he carefully laid it in front of him. All the while, Jamieson watched intently but did not inspect or touch any of the discarded clothing. Finally, when McCannell stood in front of his adversary in only his shorts and white sport socks, Jamieson gave an approving shake of his head.

"All right, Dr. McCannell, that's fine. Now put those on, please," he said, gesturing toward the bundle on the floor.

McCannell withdrew the shirt from the bag, slipped it on, and quickly buttoned it. He then retrieved the blue overalls. For several seconds, he struggled to maneuver his chubby frame into the overalls, obviously having a difficult time with the fit. Finally, he managed to don the garment, which pulled tight against his full frame and looked ridiculously small on him.

"Well, my apologies, Doctor. I see that I should have gotten a larger size," Jamieson chuckled as he watched the smaller, stout man pull and tug at the ill-fitting garment.

His hostage was not smiling.

"I have no shoes," McCannell complained, pointing at his socked feet with an exceptionally red blush to his face. "Can I have my shoes back, please?"

Jamieson bent down and gathered up the shoes that McCannell had dropped in front of him. Carefully, he examined each one, inside and out, painstakingly covering each millimeter of the items. Finally, he tossed them on the floor, back in front of McCannell.

"Yeah, you can put those back on. They look fine to me," he said in an assured tone.

As McCannell slipped back into his aging loafers, Jamieson gathered up the red man's discarded shirt and pants, crumpled them into a tight ball, and stuffed them into the paper bag. He then retrieved the overcoat and began to inspect it from top to bottom, feeling the seams and lining carefully, and examining the pockets by pulling the lining inside out. When he had finished, he laid the overcoat on top of the paper bag and pushed the pile into the corner of the stairwell with his left foot.

"Ok, Dr. McCannell, here's what we're going to do," Jamieson began. "We will leave your clothes here. You and I are going to walk down the stairwell, down to the first floor, down to the Bush Street entrance. From there, we're going to walk a few blocks to my car. Then I will take you to your friend. Do you understand me?"

"Yes," McCannell answered, his voice still unusually high and uncertain.

"All right, you first," Jamieson said, pointing down the stairwell. "You keep pace with me, now. Don't move ahead too far. Please don't talk to anyone. Just walk down the stairway and head toward the Bush Street exit. We're just two garage employees going on a break, got it?"

McCannell nodded and remained silent. He turned away from Jamieson and moved down the stairwell, making sure he did not rush his steps. Behind him, he could hear the heavy footfall of his companion, always close, always watching. Jamieson, too, said nothing as the two men descended the three flights of stairs and arrived at the first floor of the garage.

As McCannell emerged from the stairwell, he turned to his right and headed across the floor of the garage, moving toward the Bush Street entrance. To his left, the long line of cars continued to move slowly into the garage, filling the air with thick fumes and a constant, low rumbling. As he walked, the red man tried to glance to his left, hoping to see a familiar vehicle or a comforting face. Perhaps the backup units knew where he was? Maybe Mendoza had worked it out from the helicopter. Maybe they knew his location and were already at the site?

He needed something… anything.

Despite his care, Jamieson must have noticed McCannell's head movements and quickly moved alongside his prisoner, walking close to him on his left and blocking his view of the incoming traffic. When the pair reached the Bush Street entrance, the interior of the garage became suddenly lighter, now filled with the whitish gray of the foggy morning, and the air became breathable once again. McCannell sucked in a huge breath and tried to relax the muscles in his chest and stomach.

At the entrance to the garage, the red man paused for a second, uncertain of which direction to take. Jamieson gently pushed on his arm and waved his hand in an easterly direction, toward Montgomery Street.

"We're going this way," Jamieson announced, maneuvering his large frame so that it was very close to McCannell's and nudging him gently down the Bush Street hill toward the Financial District.

For the next block and a half, neither man spoke. They walked, side-by-side, past the end of the Bush Garage and down the hill. Along the way, they were swallowed up by the stream of briskly walking commuters and workers heading toward Montgomery Street. When they were more than a block past the garage, Jamieson finally spoke.

"Doctor, did you have any electronic devices hidden in your

clothing?" His voice was nonchalant and unhurried.

McCannell stopped dead in his tracks, his mind reeling with possibilities. What should his answer be? Either way, he sensed terrible danger. If he lied, this man may know that and lash out. If he told the truth, he might be angered and uncontrollable. For several seconds, McCannell stood frozen in place.

Jamieson again prodded his captive by the arm, urging him to keep walking at the required pace while he spoke. "Doctor, please answer my question truthfully. Whatever happens between us, we need to keep it honest." His voice was still slow, but determined.

McCannell dropped his head as he walked. For a few seconds, he considered what Jamieson had asked. He thought about the man next to him. The conclusion he reached was simple and inevitable: this man was intelligent and determined. He also seemed reasonable — at least for the moment. For the first time since he had arrived at the garage, McCannell's fear seemed to drain away. McCannell decided that the truth was his best choice.

"There was a device sewn into the cuff of my pants, Jamie. It was there to let the officers know my location. It's back at the garage now. There are no other ones," he said softly without looking at the man next to him.

"Well, that's all right," Jamieson replied in a comforting, easy tone. "I would have thought less of you if you didn't try something like that. I just want to be sure that we're not interrupted for a while. I'm sure you understand."

McCannell nodded up and down, and kept walking.

For the next several minutes, the unlikely pair walked in silence, pacing each other and moving along the crowded sidewalk, unnoticed by the hurrying crowds. When they finally reached Montgomery Street, Jamieson again nudged McCannell by the arm and indicated that they should now head across Market Street, for the first time moving against the hoards of walking commuters going north to the Financial District. When they reached Mission Street, a long block past Market, Jamieson guided his charge into an open-air parking lot.

"All right, Dr. McCannell, we're here," Jamieson announced, motioning with his arm in the direction of an older, dark sedan that lay directly ahead. He moved to the passenger's side of the vehicle and pulled the door open. It gave out a squeaking, grinding noise of a hinge long overused and ignored. McCannell noticed that the car had been unlocked and that the vehicle looked worn and quite old, much like his own loafers. He took a few seconds too long in deciding to enter the unwelcome destination.

"Please get in," Jamieson prodded, holding the door fully open like a chauffeur. "We're just a few minutes away, Doctor."

McCannell reluctantly slid past the open door and tucked himself uncomfortably into the front seat. At his feet was a collection of disorganized newspapers, Styrofoam cups, and other, less identifiable debris. Jamieson slammed the car door behind McCannell, again accompanied by a grinding groan of metal on metal, and stepped quickly to the driver's side. He slid easily behind the wheel and started the engine. Like the passenger's door, it exuded an unnatural, unhealthy groan before it came to life.

In a moment, the disheveled sedan was working its way out of the crowded parking lot and moving easily up Mission Street, lost in the perpetual traffic of the boulevard, heading in the direction of Bernal Heights and Jamie's lair.

As Jamieson's vehicle crept away from the downtown area on Mission Street, Chris Spell yelped his unyielding frustration at the Communications Officer.

"For God's sake, where is the signal coming from!" he demanded.

"It's weak and intermittent, Lieutenant. Our target must be in some kind of structure that's interfering with the transmission. My best guess is the area near Bush and Montgomery." The officer was red in the face and obviously angry at the Lieutenant's tone. Still, he held his tongue and continued to play with the knobs and dials on the panel in front of him.

Spell raced across the room to a desk in the corner of the Communications Center. There, on the wall, was a street map of the City — a very large, detailed map that covered most of the dingy wall. He moved close to its multi-colored face, squinting especially hard at the area marked "Financial District" and studying its details.

"Mar, what do you think?" he said over his shoulder after a minute of staring at the map. "What's down there? Where do you think he took Sam?" His voice was forced and worried.

Mary Boor moved next to him, also leaning close to the map and searching her memory of the downtown area. "Well, if the cab went into some kind of structure that's breaking up the signal, I'd guess it's a parking garage, Chris. It would be a good place to lose us *and* the signal."

Spell continued to stare at the map for a few seconds. Finally, he looked to his left, directly at his friend, with a worried expression.

"Yeah, that makes sense, Mar. Fuck! This guy *is* good..."

Spell turned back to the map to examine it one more time. For a moment, they both scanned the streets in the Financial District, trying to summon up their memories of the area, trying to picture the possibilities.

"I'd guess the Bush Garage, Chris," Mary said in a low, firm tone. "It would be in the right location and it's a huge, concrete structure. That would account for the signal breakup."

"Yeah, I agree, Mar," he said, putting his arm on her shoulder and forcing a weak smile in her direction.

Spell stepped quickly back to the Communications Officer and instructed him to send two, plain-clothes backup units to the Bush Garage. Within moments, four officers were wandering the floors of the garage, looking for any sign of Sam McCannell. One of the detectives – a lean, dark man in his late thirties, not unlike Joe Mendoza in appearance – was assigned to the stairwell area in the center of the Bush garage. At 7:15 A.M., just as Herbert Jamieson's car turned left off Mission Street onto Courtland Avenue, the young detective reached down to inspect the abandoned overcoat and paper bag that he discovered in an alcove on the third floor.

January 21
Midtown Station — Communications Center
7:20 A.M.

Chris Spell turned abruptly away from the Communications Officer and dropped his head to his chest. "We're fucked..." he mumbled, his face bloodless and drawn. "We've lost him..."

Mary moved quickly next to him and laid her hand on his forearm. She quietly led him to the corner of the room, to the desk underneath the large city map, and nudged him into a waiting chair.

"All right, Chris," she said in a serious tone. "There's nothing we can do now but wait. Sam is on his own. We all are."

Bernal Heights District

Sam McCannell felt a light, insistent push at his back as he climbed the peeling, uneven stairs to the unkempt Victorian flat on Courtland Avenue. It was not a reassuring nudge.

"Go ahead, Doctor," Jamieson said in a stern voice from behind. "The door is open."

He reached for the battered brass doorknob and felt it spin uselessly in his hand. It had obviously not worked properly in some time. Glancing across the face of the battered door, McCannell raised his hand to the wooden frame and gave it a tentative push. He started as it rolled opened with a light squeal, revealing an unlit, cluttered hallway with a series of doors to each side. Jamieson slid across the familiar threshold behind him, again giving McCannell a gentle poke on the back to move him further down the hallway. From behind the two men, the aging door closed with a rattle, further draining the interior of the flat of its little ambient light.

"Where's Sandy?" McCannell asked in a soft, unsteady voice.

"Is she here?" His eyes darted up and down the hallway, searching each door. None were open.

Jamieson pushed his large frame around the red man and moved toward a six-paneled door immediately on their left. Quickly, he reached down and twisted the knob, throwing the door open with a flourish. "In here," he said abruptly. "She's in here..." He stood aside, still standing in the hallway, and motioned with his head toward the interior of the room.

McCannell stepped delicately past his abductor and into the living room. Like the rest of the flat, it was dark and cluttered, arrayed with a chaotic combination of old, battered furniture and random stacks of paper debris. For a moment, he squinted in the dimness, trying to adjust to the low light and searching across the room for something familiar.

There, in the corner, propped against the wall, was Sandy Janus. Her head was bent down on her chest and several strands of thick rope were wrapped tightly around her upper arms and torso. Her clothes were dirtied and torn; her legs spread unnaturally far apart. She looked especially diminutive and alone. McCannell moved carefully in her direction, avoiding the clutter strewn on the floor, trying to focus on her chest and looking intently for evidence that she was breathing.

"Is she alive, Jamie?" he asked in a worried tone as he approached her.

"Yes," came the monotone reply.

"You said she was wired with a timed explosive. I don't see it. Is she?"

"No, Doctor, she is not."

McCannell turned his head quickly to face Jamieson. The large man had moved silently into the dingy room and was now standing a few feet behind McCannell, his bulk positioned ominously between his two captives and the living room door. Their eyes met and, for a brief moment, were locked in silence.

"You lied to me about the explosives, Jamie. I thought you wanted our meeting to be based on honesty," the psychologist said in a scolding voice.

A dark scowl instantly assailed Jamieson's face, sending a bolt of panic rampaging through McCannell's chest. Perhaps he had gone too far. Maybe he should not have challenged his captor on the point.

However, in a few seconds, Jamieson's scowl was replaced with a knowing, easy grin.

"Well, Doctor, I suppose we've both lied to each other. We'll have to talk about that. That's one of the things I want to talk about. But, for now, you might want to check on your friend over there." His huge right hand jiggled in Sandy's direction, flapping back and forth impatiently. McCannell turned back to the far end of the room and stepped quickly to where his colleague was propped against the wall.

The red man dropped to a squatting position and reached out his left hand, gently caressing Sandy on the shoulder. She was breathing heavily and seemed to be semiconscious. His eyes examined the bruising on the side of her face. It looked painful but not dangerous. As he rubbed her shoulder, the small woman lifted her head and seemed to look squarely at him, although her eyes appeared unfocused and hazy.

"Oh, God... Sam?" she muttered in a shaky voice.

"Yeah, Sandy, it's me. Are you doing all right?"

"I'm scared as hell, Sam. I'm scared...."

He squeezed harder on the top of her delicate shoulder. "I know. It's all right now, Sandy. Jamie has no plans to hurt you," he said in a voice loud enough to be heard across the room.

"Who's Jamie?" she asked, still not completely aware of her surroundings.

"He's the man…"

"I'm Jamie," the big man interrupted from behind McCannell. "You're here at my invitation, Officer Janus, as is Doctor McCannell."

Sandy shook her head from side to side, trying to jolt herself back to full awareness. After several seconds, she snapped her head up and stared in the direction of the deep voice from behind her colleague.

"I'm not here at *your* invitation, you sick fuck! Get these goddamn ropes off me! Let us out of here *now!*"

McCannell squeezed her shoulder exceptionally hard, letting her know that she should keep quiet. Instinctively, he whipped around to face their captor, trying to assess the impact of her taunt, expecting the worst. Rather than angry, Jamieson once again had that immutable grin plastered across his broad face. He stared back at the roped woman on the floor, ignoring McCannell altogether.

"Doctor McCannell assured you that I won't hurt you, Officer. Don't you believe him?" Jamieson snapped. His face was crinkled and mocking.

"Sandy, why don't you…" the red man interjected, trying even harder to calm her.

"Fuck you!" Sandy shouted across the room. "Who the fuck do you think you are!" she screamed.

A broad smile passed across Jamieson's face. He glanced down at McCannell, who stared back at him with obvious fright.

"Doctor, stay out of this conversation!" he ordered. "*You're* the reason this happened — all of it. Now, for the moment… for once in your miserable, pompous, self-righteous life… shut the fuck up!" Jamieson screamed.

The red man instantly flushed and began to shake. His mouth hung open, silent and stunned.

"Listen to me, Sandy," Jamieson continued in an even, controlled tone. "I'm going to let your friend here untie those ropes. I think you'll be more comfortable that way."

The big man reached with his left hand underneath his blue overalls. For a few seconds, he rummaged around inside the garment. When he withdrew his hand, it held a shiny, black semi-automatic pistol, which he brandished in her direction. "When the Doctor unties you, please move to the couch there and sit down. Don't move from there. Will you do that?" he asked politely.

Sandy stared up at her captor, her eyes transfixed on the weapon. She nodded up and down, agreeing to his terms, but with a scowl etched on her face.

McCannell tucked his left hand behind her small frame and slid her forward, balancing her torso against his arm to reach behind her. For several seconds he fumbled with the tight knots, trying to work them loose. Eventually, he managed to free one of the thick strands and was finally able to remove all her bindings. Throughout the process, she stared intently at Jamieson, watching him as he slid across the room and cleared a stack of discarded newspapers from the beaten, dirty couch. She noticed that he never took his eyes off McCannell.

He never – not even for a moment – took his eyes off the red man.

As the last strand of rope fell away from Sandy's arms and torso, she puffed out her chest and took in an enormous breath. Slowly, painfully, she wiggled her upper arms back and forth, working to restore the lost circulation. Then she slid her legs repeatedly along the unpolished wooden floor, finally bending them at the knees in unison, trying to relieve the pain that had assailed them for so long.

"Thanks," she mumbled, still staring at Jamieson.

"All right, Officer Janus. Please come over to the couch and sit down now," he ordered, waving the handgun in her direction.

She put an arm on McCannell's shoulder and struggled to get to her feet but immediately slid back hard on the floor. It was obvious that she was still too shaken and stiff to make headway on her own. McCannell jumped to his feet and tried to grab her underneath her right arm to help her up.

"No!" Jamieson shouted, seeing his male captive now standing. "You stay where you are, Doctor. Just help her up and stay exactly where you are!"

Carefully, slowly, McCannell dragged Sandy to her feet by holding her underneath her right arm. When he saw that she was erect and somewhat steady, he immediately sat back down on the floor.

"Sandy, are you ok?" he whispered up at her.

She nodded and began to take small, unsteady steps toward the couch. With several pained, jerky forward movements, she finally reached the end of the couch. When she arrived, Sandy put out her right hand to steady herself against its large, tattered, overstuffed arm. From there, she stiffly turned her torso to the right and collapsed into the cushions with a loud sigh of pain and relief. She sat motionless, her legs dangling from the couch, her body in a half-sitting, half-prone position.

Jamieson yanked on an old wooden chair with his right foot and dragged it close to the couch, positioning it between where Sandy sat and the door to the room. He quietly backed his frame into the chair and sat down. For several seconds, he surveyed his two captives, moving his eyes, in turn, from one to the other. Officer Janus was clearly in pain and exhausted; it was obvious that she was no immediate threat. McCannell sat with his legs outstretched, his upper body propped against the wall, in the same location where Sandy had been kept bound for the past few hours. His face alternated between ashen and flushed. He was deeply afraid and unable to hide it.

"All right," Jamieson began in that familiar, melodic voice. "This is good. I see that Officer Janus is much more comfortable now. So, before we begin, I would like to ask you both something. Will you two agree not to do anything stupid? Will you both do that? If you do, you will both live."

"Yes," McCannell replied instantly. "We won't pull any heroics here, Jamie."

Sandy said nothing. She just continued to stare at her captor with an expression that seemed blank and distant.

"I didn't hear your answer, Sandy," Jamieson said, looking intently at the woman on the couch. "Your friend here was quick to agree, but I haven't heard *your* answer yet."

A brief smile crossed Sandy's lips and, for a few seconds, she said nothing.

"I think you'll kill us anyway," she finally answered, a sorrowful but determined expression on her face. "That's what you do, isn't it? Kill people?"

Jamieson nodded his head from side to side, slowly. "Not unless I have to, Officer Janus. That's not my *first* choice. I would prefer not to kill *you*, especially. You remind me of..."

"Yeah, Marion, I know..." she interrupted. "Whoever that was..."

"Is..." he corrected. "Whoever that *is*..."

Now, his face was sorrowful, his expression dark and distant.

"All right, Jamie," Sandy offered in a whisper. "I won't do anything stupid, I promise." She stared back at the large man, searching for some reassurance that a bargain had been struck.

"Neither will I," Jamieson replied. "Neither will I..."

Secrets and Lies

"Is there something I can get for you, Officer Janus? Are you thirsty?" Jamieson asked in a polite tone, his expression soft and apparently genuinely concerned.

"Water, please. I could use some water," she replied with a light shake of her head. She pushed herself even deeper into the cushions of the couch, still trying to work the last of the stiffness from her legs. The side of her face and head throbbed from his blow hours earlier.

"All right, I'll get water" he said, lifting himself easily from the chair. Jamieson reached toward the living room door and pulled it toward him. Moving directly across the hallway, he pushed open the bathroom door. Inside, the small, dank room was also cluttered with random stacks of newspaper. In a few seconds, he returned to the living room with a tall, narrow glass of water and offered it to her. Sandy pushed herself to an upright, sitting position on the couch and extended her hand toward him, accepting the glass with a noticeable tremor in her right hand. She drained it completely, without taking a breath. Jamieson sat back in the chair, his eyes, at first, transfixed on McCannell, then on her.

"We have some important matters to discuss," Jamieson announced to no one in particular, stretching out his long, burly legs in front of him. "Let's start with you, Doctor," he continued, whirling his large head around to stare directly at McCannell in a cold, threatening way.

The red man pulled his legs up to his chest and shuffled his torso more firmly against the wall. He glanced quickly from Jamieson to Sandy and back again, a quizzical, frightened look on his face.

"Doctor, do you recognize the name Marion Jamieson?" the big man said in a solemn tone.

McCannell's face instantly turned a bright red and his eyes dropped to the floor beyond where he sat. It took several seconds for him to answer.

"Yes, I remember her," he finally replied in a hoarse whisper.

"Well, she's my wife… my ex-wife, actually," Jamieson said with a stern expression. "My name is Herbert William Jamieson."

"Oh, Christ…" McCannell moaned. He shot a quick, panicked look at Sandy on the couch. She had a concerned, confused expression on her face, and wide, fearful eyes. She stared back at McCannell, silently asking what was going on. He quickly dropped his head and roamed the floor in front of him with his eyes, unwilling to meet her stare. Suddenly, his plump body began to shake uncontrollably and he yanked his knees even closer to his chest, as if to protect himself from some unseen force.

"You see, Sandy, there are some things that your friend here hasn't bothered to tell you," Jamieson announced in a loud voice, now looking directly at her. "For one thing, I'm sure Dr. McCannell has made quite a production out of defining and re-defining me and my crimes with you and the other officers on the task force. He makes his life and trade that way. He is the contemporary guru of the criminal mind. In fact, he probably gave you and your friends quite a profile of me, didn't he?"

Jamieson paused, waiting for her answer. She looked intently back at him, but said nothing.

"Well, Officer Janus, didn't he spend a lot of time telling you all about me – all about the kind of monster who will kill women – women who looked just like you? Didn't he?" Jamieson's face was growing red and full, his voice strained and boisterous. He stared at her, unmoving, silently demanding some kind of reply.

"Oh, no…" McCannell mumbled from the corner of the room.

"Please don't…"

"Shut up!" Jamieson screamed at him, never taking his eyes off her.

Shocked at his outburst, Sandy began to nod up and down in a slow, rhythmic way. "Yeah, Sam worked out a profile on you." she said softly.

"Yes, I'm sure he did," Jamieson said. He was calmer now, less flushed. "I'm sure he took great pains to create a good profile. Now, Officer, please be honest and tell me how accurate it was. From what you've learned, was he accurate about me?"

She nodded again. "I guess so, in some ways…" She thought for a moment. "It's not a science, Jamie. What he does it not a science…"

"What he does is pure bullshit and lies!" Jamieson yelled, his body stiff and leaning toward her on the couch. "His *life* is bullshit, secrets, and lies!" He sucked in a huge breath and pushed his upper body hard against the back of the chair, raising his head to face the ceiling and momentarily closing his eyes. After a few seconds, he dropped his head, opened his eyes, and looked directly at Sandy. His expression was easier now, but very determined.

"I have no regard for this man," he spat, waving the gun in his hand in McCannell's general direction. "I have no regard for him because he is a liar and an arrogant ass. He would have you believe that I killed those women for reasons that aren't true. The truth is that I killed those women because I want to destroy your friend in the corner there. I don't want him dead. No. That's not what I want. I want him destroyed. I want the one thing that he really values. I want to be inside *his* fucking head! I want you and everyone to *know* this man for what he really is. That's why you're here, Officer Janus. That's why all this has happened."

He sat back in the chair and lowered the gun to his lap.

Sandy shook her head from side to side — a long, sorrowful series of small movements. "Are you telling me that you killed four innocent women because you hate Sam McCannell and want to see him ruined? Is that what you're telling me? If that's the truth – the real truth – you are truly a sick fuck!" she shouted back at him, her mouth twisted and raging.

Jamieson grinned at her and waited before answering. "I like you, Sandy. You have balls that won't quit. That's very appealing in a woman. No, it isn't that simple. I'm only telling you this so you'll understand the meaning of what's about to happen."

He turned in the chair and reached toward the top of a small, three-legged table near the door. His large hand retrieved a neatly folded piece of paper. "It's all here," he said, unfolding the paper and holding it in his right hand. For a moment, he studied it in the dim light of the living room, checking its content for a final time. Then he stood up from the chair and walked toward McCannell. For a few seconds, he stood over the cowering psychologist, a look of cold determination on his face. He let the paper fall from his hand and drift to the floor next to the red man.

"Pick up the paper, Doctor," Jamieson ordered as he returned to his seat. "Pick it up and read it carefully. When you have finished reading it, just lift your head and indicate that you're done. Don't say anything at all."

McCannell grabbed the paper and pulled it close to his face. He tried to focus on the typewritten page through the trembling in his hands and the dampness in his eyes. The document was titled, "Statement of Samuel McCannell."

For the next several minutes, the red man studied the page in front of him, examining each line carefully, taking in each word. As he silently read, Sandy sat stiffly on the couch, her eyes transfixed on her colleague. She had never seen him in this condition. His body shook visibly, particularly his arms, legs, and hands. Tears were rolling down his flushed, sagging cheeks. He looked terrified and weak. Finally, after what seemed much too long a time for such a short page of information, McCannell raised his head and stared blankly at Jamieson.

"I have only one question for you, Doctor. It's important that you answer it honestly. If you do not answer it honestly – if I believe you have lied to me in any way – I will kill you where you sit." With that, Jamieson pointed the gun directly at the red man's head, his finger ready on the trigger.

From the couch, Sandy gasped and pulled her legs up from the floor. She could not take her eyes off McCannell, who was now sobbing openly.

"My question is this, Doctor. Is there anything in that document that is untrue? Is there any word in that document that is not the absolute truth?"

McCannell dropped his head and tried to suck back his sobbing. "No," he said weakly between gasps. "It's all accurate... It's all true."

Jamieson let out a satisfied rush of air and briefly closed his eyes. His left hand relaxed onto his lap, the gun no longer pointed at his captive. Across the room, McCannell struggled to control his sobbing and his breathing slowly became more regular. On the couch, Sandy looked from one man to the other in astonishment, her mouth open, her chest heaving with fear and confusion.

"What's going on here?" she whispered at McCannell. "What is this all..."

"You'll know very soon, Officer Janus," Jamieson interrupted. He slowly swung his gaze back to the red man. Without moving his head or eyes, Jamieson reached inside his blue overalls and retrieved a tiny cellular telephone. With a quick motion, he tossed the device toward McCannell. It bounced off the red man's left leg and landed gently on the floor next to him.

"Doctor, I want you to pick up the telephone and dial the number I will give you. The woman who answers will be Jane Riordan. You know who she is. She is expecting your call. When she answers, you will say who you are and tell her that you have a statement to read. You will add nothing to the statement. You will take nothing away and you will not change a word of the statement. When you've finished reading the statement, you will hang up the telephone. If you don't follow these instructions precisely, I will blow your head off you where you sit. Do you understand me, Doctor?"

"Oh, no..." McCannell whimpered. "I can't do that. Please..."

Jamieson raised the gun to chest level and pointed it directly at McCannell's head. "The choice is yours, Doctor. The number is 555-1345. If you don't start dialing within five seconds, I'll kill you." His voice was low and even.

From the couch, Sandy shuffled and stiffened. She waited for the blast that would end McCannell's life.

"Sandy, please stay out of this," Jamieson ordered, sensing her involuntarily movements. "Don't be the cause of his death," he sternly warned.

She sat back as quietly as she could, staring at the gun in her captor's hand.

With shaking, unsteady fingers, McCannell began to dial. As he did, he struggled to control his breathing and subdue the persistent rattling in his throat.

The line rang once... twice...

"Jane Riordan," she said with obvious excitement in her voice.

McCannell fumbled with the paper in his left hand, the telephone in his right. He took an audible breath.

"This is Sam McCannell," he said in a halting, shaky voice.

"I recognize your voice," she said quickly and quietly.

"I have a statement to read to you."

"Yes, I know," she said. "The recorder is on…"

McCannell's eyes grew large and even more terrified. He shot a glance at Jamieson sitting in his chair. The man in the blue overalls was waving the gun in his left hand, indicating that his captive should get on with it. McCannell pulled the paper closer to his eyes and carefully read each word to Riordan.

Statement of Samuel McCannell

In 1995, Herbert William Jamieson was employed as a paramedic with the San Francisco Fire Department. At that time, he was married to Marion Wellings Jamieson. I was employed by the San Francisco Police Department as a psychologist on staff. As part of my responsibilities, I provided free counseling to members of the SFPD and the SFFD, as well as their families, on a limited basis. I was compensated for these services by the SFPD and I provided counseling when requested and as I saw fit. I was free to involve myself in certain cases if I chose and free to refer individuals to other personnel if I so decided. All case files were closed to protect the identities of the people who used my services.

In September of that year, Marion Jamieson came to me to discuss her concerns about her husband, William Jamieson. She asked me to meet with her husband because he was unwilling to bring his problems directly to me. According to Mrs. Jamieson, her husband was concerned that any indications of a psychological problem would end his career and leave him destitute. For some time, Mr. and Mrs. Jamieson had experienced significant marital problems. According to Marion Jamieson, these were due mostly to Mr. Jamieson's psychological state, which resulted in bizarre and unhealthy sexual demands on his wife. Among the symptoms described to me by Mrs. Jamieson was Mr. Jamieson's intermittent fugue states, which he could not control, and because of which he was afraid to seek medical attention. Mrs. Jamieson made it clear to me that she loved her husband, but that she could no longer deal with the relationship unless he received immediate help.

I never attempted to contact William Jamieson to arrange for any medical or psychological attention, despite his wife's repeated requests. In fact, I had a sexual encounter with Marion Jamieson, which was not sought by her. This happened in my office at the SFPD in October 1995. When I forced myself on Marion Jamieson, I knew that the basis of the problems with Herbert Jamieson were sexual; these had been described to me by her. Despite this knowledge – or because of it – I forced myself on Marion Jamieson, and then threatened to end her husband's career if she ever discussed what had occurred.

Later, I advised Marion Jamieson to divorce her husband and bring charges against him based on the sexual problems that existed in the marriage, all of which were due to her husband's psychological disorder. I also gave Marion Jamieson approximately four thousand dollars of my own money to pay for her legal expenses.

In dealing with Marion Jamieson and her pleas for help for her husband, I violated her trust as well as my professional oath. Worse yet, I may have indirectly contributed to the murders subsequently committed by Herbert William Jamieson, known in the press as the "Mission District Monster."

Everything in this statement is true.

At the other end of the line, Jane Riordan gasped loudly and started to speak. McCannell never heard her. She was instantly cut off by his finger on the disconnect button. On the couch, Sandy sat staring at her colleague, her eyes wet and dark. The red man let the phone drop from his hand and slide to the floor. He rolled onto his side and curled himself into a tight ball, sobbing loudly, his chest heaving uncontrollably.

For several minutes, only his sobbing broke the silence of the dingy room. Finally, it was Sandy who spoke.

"Oh, all of this was about revenge," she whimpered, staring sorrowfully at Jamieson. He sat slumped in the chair, his eyes nearly closed. For several seconds he said nothing.

"I don't know, Sandy," he finally mumbled in a barely audible voice. "In part, yes. But I don't know. All I know is that this was the only way to stop the killing..." His voice trailed off to a series of jerky sighs.

"You didn't have to kill them," she said in a pleading tone. "You didn't have to mutilate them. *None of this* had to happen." She dropped her head and tried hard to hold back the tears.

Jamieson pushed himself away from the chair and stood over her. His expression had become much softer, almost pained. "She couldn't love me after him," he said, waving his right hand in McCannell's direction. "He made it so that she couldn't love me anymore, Sandy. I strangled them so they couldn't tell on me. I took their hands so they couldn't swear against me. I used them to bring him to me. Sometimes it made sense, what I did. Most of the time, I hated what I did — I hated what I'd become. All I wanted was someone to help me. That's all Marion wanted." Jamieson's voice was shaky and uncertain. Suddenly, he seemed small and insignificant, pleading his case to her like an errant, evil child. Then, just as quickly, his face became firm and full, his eyes once again small and focused.

"I need to finish what I started, Officer Janus. I need to do that now." He turned away from where she sat, stepped to the living room door, and pulled it open. For a few seconds, he paused at the threshold and spoke without looking at the woman on the couch. "I'll be right back, Sandy. Please don't move from there."

Jamieson disappeared through the door and turned to his left. She could hear him moving quickly up the hallway and opening the door to the adjoining room. In a moment, he returned with an old black telephone in his right hand. As he stepped into the room, he pulled on the long cord, dragging the instrument to the couch and setting it on the cushion next to her. She looked carefully at the telephone. Yes! Unlike the cellular telephone lying next to McCannell, any call from this device could be traced — if the line could be kept open long enough.

"Officer Janus," he began, "the address here is 16300 Courtland. I want you to call someone you trust to come and get you. I don't want you to be here when the fire starts."

"Fire?" she repeated in a worried tone. "What fire?"

"You see these papers all over the house?" he asked, not waiting for an answer. "I've been saving them for today." With his left hand he reached toward her and laid the handgun next to the telephone.

"I want you to call someone you trust to come and get you. You can take the gun and do what you want with it so you feel safe. I want you to make the call now, please."

Instinctively, Sandy's right hand fell across the handgun and gripped it tightly. She stared up at him, stunned and uncertain of the meaning of what had happened. As she dragged the gun across her lap and locked her finger on the trigger, Jamieson backed away and slumped into the old wooden chair again. He closed his eyes.

"Do you want me to shoot you?" she asked indignantly. "Is that how this game is supposed to end — with *me* killing *you?*" Her voice was high and strained, the gun now pointed at his chest.

"That's your choice, Sandy. Whatever you do, I suggest you do it quickly. I can already smell the smoke, can't you?"

Sandy sniffed the air. It was true! There was a faint odor of smoke from somewhere beyond the living room. Her eyes widened and she felt a hot flush cross her face. Quickly, she placed the gun on her lap, pulled the receiver off its hook, and dialed the Midtown Station.

"Badge number 60613. Give me the Comm Center — emergency!" she shouted at the woman who answered. The call was immediately transferred.

"Comm Center, Officer Foyle," he said in a routine tone.

"Give me Mendoza or Boor or Spell. This is Janus!" she yelped. "Do it now!"

The young man swiveled around in his chair to face the two officers behind him. "I have Officer Janus here," he said excitedly. "She wants you," he continued, ignoring the Lieutenant and nodding at Mary Boor.

"Trace that call!" Spell ordered in a sharp voice. "Do *not* lose it!"

Mary jumped to the station next to Officer Foyle and pulled the handset to her ear. "Sandy, are you all right?" she asked.

"I'm fine, Mary. Sam is in trouble. Please don't waste any time asking questions. Get officers, paramedics, and the SFFD to 16300 Courtland right now! This place is on fire!"

"Yeah, doing it now…" Boor said. "Tell me what's…"

The line went dead.

Mary Boor gave the instructions to Foyle, grabbed the Lieutenant's arm, and headed for the door. "We've got them both, Chris. They're both going to be all right! Let's go!"

At the Comm Center door, Spell paused for a moment and turned to face the Communications Officer. "Make sure that Mendoza knows where we are!" he shouted. "Give him the address!"

"Jamie, we all need to get out of here now," she pleaded with him. "I'm not going to shoot you, I just want us all to get out of here alive!" She laid the gun back down on the cushion and looked up at him.

"I won't be joining you, Sandy," he said in an even tone. "I'll get this piece of shit out of here, if that's what you want." He waved his right arm in McCannell's direction with a disdainful, angry motion.

"Of course I want him out of here!" she screamed at her captor "I want us all out of here!"

Jamieson flung himself from the chair and stepped over to where McCannell lay, still sobbing and in a fetal position. He quickly bent down and grabbed the red man under the arms, roughly swinging him to his feet and supporting his weight.

"Please get the door," he ordered as he moved across the room.

Sandy jumped from the couch, the adrenaline of the moment making her movements quick, painless, and precise. She pulled on the door and stood looking at the man in the blue overalls with his charge.

"Let's go!" he said in a loud voice. "I'll be right behind you."

The smoke from the next room was already thick in the hallway. Sandy could hear the crackling of fire from nearby. It was obvious there were only moments left before the entire place would be an inescapable inferno. No time to argue.

She stepped into the hallway, turned to her right, and made for the front door of the flat. In a few steps she was there and threw the old door open, allowing the gathering haze of smoke to rush outward, into the cold, foggy morning. The inrushing fresh air gave the fire beyond the living room more life and she saw a sheet of flames shoot from the doorway into the hall. In the outline of the blackening, smoke-filled hallway, she saw Jamieson dragging McCannell toward her.

When he reached the landing, Jamieson pushed past her and maneuvered McCannell down the steps, letting his limp body roll onto the sidewalk. He was still shuddering and sobbing, unable to move or speak. Sandy positioned herself next to the red man and tried to prop him up to a sitting position. He just rolled onto his right side and into a tight ball on the cold concrete.

Jamieson looked down at her with a friendly, determined smile. "He's fucked up in the head, Officer Janus. You really should get him some help…"

With that, Jamieson bounded up the stairs and disappeared into the flat. From the safety of the sidewalk, Sandy could see intense flames beyond the closed windows. She heard the random explosions of shattering glass from somewhere deep inside Jamieson's home. Smoke was rolling and billowing out the open door and from everywhere along the front and sides of the structure.

One Month Later
Bayview District

They sat huddled around Mary's low, plain coffee table, each with the remnants of a glass of Valpolicella in hand, each staring out across the blackness of the waters beyond her living room. It had been an unusually quiet night for these friends, but not a somber one. Winter would soon be gone, replaced by a chilly, foggy spring and an even more uncomfortable, unpredictable summer. There was nothing about the climate in this City that made sense. Like so much of this place, even the weather seemed random, unyielding, and chaotic.

Sitting on the couch, Joe Mendoza slung his arm around Sandy and gently pulled her head against his neck. She sighed deeply and tried to keep the wineglass balanced in her hand as she snuggled closer.

"What did they call it?" she asked in a whisper. "What's wrong with Sam?"

"They told me it was a catatonic disorder," Mary answered. "I guess he doesn't know what's going on around him. They told me it could last for days, weeks, or the rest of his life. He just couldn't deal with what happened, I guess."

"God, that's awful," Sandy mumbled, her mind struggling to remember him as he was the first time she met him, not as she had last seen him. She drove her head further into Mendoza's neck and laid her free hand on his thigh.

Chris Spell turned away from the view beyond the living room window and carefully set his glass on the end of the coffee table. "I guess you never really know about people, even when you think you do," he complained in a low, sorrowful tone.

The room fell silent for several long moments. Outside, a finger of wispy gray fog snaked across the face of the wide window and momentarily stole their view of the bay.

"What are you going to do with yourself now, Chris?" Mendoza asked. "I think it was a mistake for you to give it all up."

"No, it wasn't a mistake. I should have done it a year ago. I feel good about it, Joe. I can spend more time with my friends now." He reached across the table toward Mary Boor, who was sitting at the end of the couch. She lifted her hand and took his. "I need to do some catching up. There are days when I feel old and days when things are all right. I guess I'm just ready for something new. And I could sure use some old fashioned loving," he finished with a grin.

Mary gave his hand a hard squeeze and let out a deep laugh. Chris moved to the couch and sat on its fat arm, close to her.

Several more minutes of silence passed among them.

"What do you think happened to him?" Mendoza finally asked in a slow monotone, his eyes drifting closed to shut out the fog. "What in the hell could have happened to Jamieson?" His voice trailed off to a low grunt of dissatisfaction.

"Well, there wasn't a body in the flat," Mary answered in an analytical tone. "I guess that means he's out there somewhere. I suppose he slipped out in the confusion. Maybe he put one of his paramedic's uniforms on and just walked away with the other guys who responded to the scene."

"Yeah, you're right," Mendoza said in an angry tone, his eyes suddenly wide and focused. "He's out there and he's gonna start up all over again. He's gonna start killing again. Just wait… you'll see."

"No, that's not going to happen, Joe," Sandy interrupted in a soothing, sure tone. "That's *not* what's going to happen. He's finished with all that… if he's still alive."

Mendoza's back stiffened and he wiggled uncomfortably against her. "Why do you think that?"

For several seconds she did not answer. Her eyes followed the dying, translucent wisps of fog beyond the window, searching for the reassuring twinkling of the row houses on the hills across the bay. Yes, they were there, as they had always been. That was good — that was certain. She let out a light breath and closed her eyes.

"He told me it was finished, Joe. He told me that and I believe him."

Also by Michael D. Kelleher:

In the late sixties, a serial killer calling himself the Zodiac terrorized the San Francisco Bay Area, committing brutal, random attacks, and bragging about them in letters to the San Francisco *Chronicle*.

In Santa Rosa, fifty miles to the north, investigators Manny Bruin and Mick Millian were asked to tail potential suspect Byron Avion, an odd, portly man admittedly obsessed with the Zodiac. He had other eccentricities as well, not the least of which was his large collection of cardboard boxes, carefully stacked and tied shut with white nylon rope.

But peculiar habits do not a criminal make — that is, not until the bodies of young female hitchhikers began appearing in ditches, tied up with white nylon rope. That and a dozen other connections convinced Bruin and Millian that Avion was the Highway 101 Murderer, a Zodiac-style killer who prowled the Santa Rosa area.

Despite the connections, a decade-long investigation was unable to connect Avion to the crimes, or connect Zodiac to the northern murders. Bruin and Millian eventually became so frustrated that they dubbed Avion "Suspect Zero," and hoped for something to break the case open. When that break finally came, it re-wrote the book on homicide investigations and forever changed the direction of each man's life.

Available everywhere fine books are sold.

Dead End Street® highly recommends these titles:

Suzanne Rosewell is the youngest female partner in the history of her prestigious Wall Street law firm. She's a strong, driven woman with the

will to succeed. Then she meets Elias Garner, an enigmatic black Jazz musician who carries an ancient golden trumpet and represents the even more furtive "Chairman" (whom we learn heads the most powerful corporation on earth).

Elias explains that God has always placed among us thirty-six righteous people — each of whom "knows the divine will" and all of who must be accounted for if humanity is to redeem itself. Five are missing and Suzanne is asked to set aside her career to search for them. If she is unsuccessful, it appears that the world cannot exist beyond the sunrise.

A painful break-up/break-down chases marketing wiz Sandy Lowiltry from her Silicon Valley home. She comes to rest on the Oregon Coast, where she seeks solace in the opera-themed sanctuary of the Hotel Bel Canto and the arms of a handsome eccentric who spends his days combing the beach for sea glass.

Sandy soon learns what the tourist ladies already know — it's easy to fall for Frosted Glass Man. Besides great sex and alarmingly intricate campsite cuisine, Frosty offers do-it-yourself mythologies that would melt even the coldest heart. But will it be enough to quiet the whisper of ambition, the voice inside Sandy's head that chides her for settling? Will she really leave behind Silicon Valley for love in such a strange package?

Available everywhere fine books are sold.

ANOTHER FINE OFFERING FROM

DEAD END STREET®